TALES FROM THE ANNEXE

Other Books by Audrey Driscoll

The Herbert West Series

Book 1. The Friendship of Mortals
Book 2. Islands of the Gulf Volume 1, The Journey
Book 3. Islands of the Gulf Volume 2, The Treasure
Book 4. Hunting the Phoenix

She Who Comes Forth

TALES FROM THE ANNEXE

seven stories from
the Herbert West Series
and seven other tales

AUDREY DRISCOLL

CONTENTS

Foreword   7

Seven Stories from the Herbert West Series

The Nexus   11
Fox and Glove   27
From the Annexe   55
A Visit to Luxor   71
One of the Fourteen   93
The Night Journey of Francis Dexter   119
The Final Deadline of A.G. Halsey   135

Seven Speculative Tales

Welcome to the Witch House   155
The Deliverer of Delusions   167
The Ice Cream Truck from Hell   179
The Colour of Magic   205
A Howling in the Woods   233
The Glamour   251
The Blue Rose   269

Afterword   287

FOREWORD

In my novel *The Friendship of Mortals*, Herbert West has a hidden annexe to the private laboratory in his cellar. That's where he works on the most secret of his secret projects. The first seven stories in this collection are sort of like that—spinoffs from or supplements to the four novels of the Herbert West Series. One of them is also a bridge to *She Who Comes Forth*, the novel that follows the series. The last story in this set, "The Final Deadline of A.G. Halsey," is a prelude to an as yet unwritten sequel.

SEVEN STORIES FROM THE HERBERT WEST SERIES

THE NEXUS

55 Church Street
Arkham, Mass.
May 11, 1915

Mrs. Willamina Devlin
1600 W. Linden Avenue
Chicago, Illinois

My Dear Willa,

Greetings in the name of Nodens, Lord of the Great Abyss!

You are probably surprised to be reading a letter from your old professor, Augustus Quarrington, twenty years after you were his student at Miskatonic University. I am equally surprised to be writing to you, in fact, but it is necessary for me to communicate a matter of the first importance to one who is wise, broad-minded, capable of action, and is besides one of the Initiated in the secrets of the Inner Temple. That individual, dear lady, is you.

So—to answer the question you are doubtless asking now: What does the venerable Professor Q. want from me? I shall proceed to do so, but my answer will be lengthy. Get yourself a cup of tea, my dear—no, an entire pot of tea, and perhaps something stronger—and find a comfortable chair.

I had my 101st birthday in January, and I have an idea I will not see another one. I have had my share of years, and I am ready for the next world. This letter is, in a way, my Last Will and Testament for matters of a spiritual sort. Preserve it and re-read it once a year, and if you perceive certain things I shall presently describe, do not hesitate to take appropriate action.

I must tell you a story, one that began many years ago. As a young man (do not worry—I am not about to launch into a tedious autobiography encompassing an entire century), I (like you) was drawn to the world of occult wisdom after reading certain books, even while pursuing studies in my chosen field of Philosophy. Eventually, I became an initiate of the Church of Starry Wisdom in Providence, because it appeared to offer an avenue to the knowledge of the Ultimate Things. I did not realize what price was required for that knowledge, until I had progressed sufficiently in the hierarchy of the Starry Wisdom as to become privy to its central secrets. One of these was that of the Shining Trapezohedron and the thing summoned thereby. I need say no more of this, except that this summoning required the ultimate sacrifice.

I was not a participant, nor was I involved in selecting the victim. The deed was done when I was away from the city. No trace was found, and I knew none would ever be. "Missing" was the official conclusion. Call me a coward, but once I realized the truth, the only thing I could do was to remove myself from the scene. I was glad indeed when I heard, years later, that the Providence sect was disbanded. But it was only one of many.

I left Providence and wandered the world for a time, in a state of discontent and anxiety. After many years, I allowed myself to be drawn to Miskatonic University in Arkham.

Emerging from my fog of disillusion, I resolved to oppose the minions of him who is known by many epithets, one of which is "Haunter of the Dark." Another is "the Crawling Chaos." I was not alone in this effort. Collectively, our Fellowship took as its protecting entity Nodens, Lord of the Great Abyss.

In 1870, not long before I settled in Arkham and while I was still a rolling stone, I rolled to Egypt, ancient land of marvels and secrets. Truly, one could spend a lifetime there and discover only a fraction of the wisdom that land contains.

After exploring Alexandria and the Nile Delta, and a brief sojourn in Cairo, I sought the wonders of Upper Egypt— ancient Thebes and the Western Necropolis, beneath the peak of el-Qurn. While in Cairo, I had received a message summoning me to a Congress of scholars in Luxor. The scholars included archaeologists, paleographers, geologists, botanists, chemists, artists, poets—and one philosopher! We were all transported to that town among the ruins of the ancient civilization.

Transported, I say. The organizers of the Congress had arranged for a river boat large enough to accommodate us all. The vessel's saloon served as conference chamber as well as dining room. We became acquainted as we were propelled upstream by efficient engines. I found it heartening that even scholars of warring nations laid aside any nationalistic differences and concentrated on the exchange of ideas and the search for knowledge.

During our upstream journey, I took special note of two individuals in our group. One of them was very young—a Russian who could not have been twenty. At first, I assumed he had accompanied an older relative, but no—young Liadov was a scholar in his own right, a linguist and paleographer. His father owned a shipping company, and the family was in some way related to the musical Liadovs. He made a most favourable impression on me; he listened more than spoke, and when he spoke to me, it was to ask about my ideas regarding invisible forces. At his request, I sent him several of my books on my return to America. Although I have not seen him since, I believe he carries one of the threads of the tapestry whose weaving I have made my life's work. (Bear with me, please; I recall your dislike of the laboured metaphor.)

The other individual—this one is directly connected to the point of this letter. (Yes, my dear, I am approaching the point. It is in sight, if only on the horizon.) His name was Lawrence Dexter, an Englishman in his twenties, from one of the great universities. He was studying anything and everything to do with Egypt, he said. Perhaps so, but I thought his motive was not a thirst for knowledge, but mere curiosity, an itch to ferret out secrets for the thrill of it. Not the best motivator for scholarship, in my experience. Such individuals lack the perseverance to slog through the dull and tedious—but necessary!—aspects of learning. He was also very good-looking, displaying his classical profile, blond locks and expressive grey eyes with a deliberation that was both amusing and annoying. I suspected he was what some call a "ladies' man," and eventually I was proven right. More about that later.

With our ship secured at Luxor, a number of feluccas were arranged to take us across to the West Bank and the Valley of the Kings. I had read about the discoveries made among the tombs and temples and was eager to see the place with my own eyes. Disembarking, we clambered about the rocks of the limestone valley, peering into openings that were at once inviting and sinister. The entire valley is said to be as full of caves and tunnels, both natural and man-made, as a Swiss cheese is full of holes. The archaeologists among us speculated about the number of tombs the place contained; the consensus was dozens, most of them unexplored. I thought I could feel their influence—a kind of tension in the air, a rippling of the atmosphere produced by undiscovered secrets. It was intoxicating. No wonder so many have devoted their lives to exploring this stony place!

We had an unexpected guide to the Valley. It's possible he had been hired to provide local knowledge, and that his dramatic arrival was part of the arrangement. We were standing about in a number of very European-looking groups, when a man on horseback galloped up to us, halting his mount before any damage was done, apart from startling a few of us. The horse was white; the man who dismounted was dressed in black. Most Egyptians wore *galabeyas* in dull white, grey or faded blue, but this man's was black, as was his turban.

"Welcome to the Necropolis," he said, gesturing widely with his arms. "I will show you this place, if you wish. I know it well."

He exuded a peculiar power, perhaps because of his imposing height, the length of his arms, and the keen glances from under that black turban. Summoning a boy from a group of youths gathered some distance away, he turned the horse over to him and motioned to us to follow. And we did, without visible hesitation.

He certainly knew his way around the valley and the tombs. Over several hours, he showed us around, pointing out tombs that had been excavated, and allowing us to enter a few of them, lighting lanterns which must have been kept within for touring purposes. In the faint, flickering light, the pictures and hieroglyphics appeared to move, an effect at once pleasing and uneasy. Our guide declared there were many more tombs to be discovered. "There is much work to be done here, many secrets to be revealed, by scholars such as you. You will be instruments of progress."

Lawrence Dexter hung on the fellow's every word, and young Liadov observed him intently. "Our guide looks like one of the pharaohs himself," Liadov said to me, as we trudged back toward the river along the narrow, dusty road. "I wonder if he lives in that village someone told us was full of bandits and dealers in forged antiquities."

"Qurna? I've heard its inhabitants are descendants of the old tomb-workers."

Liadov laughed. "Tomb-workers and tomb robbers. Both, I suspect."

"Perhaps so, but they are part of this place, and have been for a very long time. But this man—I don't think he's one of them."

At the boat landing, we were greeted by the sight of a white tent that had not been there when we arrived. Our black-clad guide opened his arms toward it and then to us, in a gesture of welcome. "I hope you will refresh yourselves before your river crossing," he said. "I arranged for tea and delicacies to sustain you after our tour."

Indeed, there was tea, and pastries and dates, and there were servants bustling about, handing out cups. It was pleasant enough, but the longer I observed and thought, the stranger all of this seemed. The servants were strangely subdued, moving like automatons and never speaking, even when addressed by the few Arabic speakers among us. Later, I inquired whether any of the others in the group knew who our guide was, and who had arranged for him to greet us. No one knew.

As we boarded the boats to return to Luxor, the man gave each of us a metal token. "A reminder of this day, in the hope you will return," he said, handing me a disc engraved with the alchemical symbol for sulfur, which is called by some the Leviathan Cross. I no longer possess it (for I dissolved it in acid years ago), but I recall its appearance quite clearly. The symbol, although powerful, has no connection to Egypt, either ancient or modern. As far as I know, no one else was given this symbol; others' tokens bore symbols associated with Egypt—the *ankh*, the feather of *Ma'at*, the *wedjat* eye. I was not in a position to ask the giver for an explanation; nor did I wish to do so.

That ended my Egyptian adventure. I returned to my academic life and fetched up at Miskatonic, where I became immersed in writing and teaching. Eventually I became the quaint eccentric I am today.

Miskatonic drew me, as I have said, because it is the locus of one of the few known copies of the *Necronomicon*, the fabled work of esoteric lore compiled in the Eighth Century by Abdul Alhazred of Sana'a in Yemen. Contrary to commonly held opinion, the *Necronomicon* is not inherently evil. The lore it contains has been used for evil purposes, but with skill and intention, it can be directed toward benign ones. Rather like alchemy, which, as I hope you remember, is a perilous enterprise whose outcomes range from wonder to disaster. Because the *Necronomicon* has been for so long the focus of curiosity, despair and passion, the book has acquired its own power. It summons from afar those who are susceptible to its influences. It summoned me, and one other of whom I must speak presently.

Perforce, I had to establish a relationship with the University Library, since that is where the *Necronomicon* resides. Librarians came and went over the decades, and I made sure to become acquainted with them. I suggested changes to the housing of the volume, and advised its keepers to protect it by restricting access to it.

Willa, do you remember your fascination with Arkham? Of course, it differs in so many ways from your hometown of Chicago, but there was another reason. Arkham is a place of <u>convergence</u>. It was not by accident that a copy of the *Necronomicon* made its way here. The nearby village of Kingsport is an outpost of one who reveres Lord Nodens, who has bestowed upon him the gift of prolonged existence. He dwells in an ancient house that clings to the edge of the highest cliff to the north of Kingsport. I have myself once ventured up to that house, and was invited within. Since then, I have been bound forever to this region.

Fortunately, I soon obtained a professorship in Philosophy at Miskatonic University, having managed to maintain credibility in my old field of study. Miskatonic tolerates eccentricity more than most universities. From my niche in academia I was able to reach out to researchers and <u>others</u>—the curious, the mischievous, the brilliant, the lost, the insane. These others, some of them familiars of the Crawling Chaos and his followers, were the ones I was eager to watch.

I began to study intensively the forces that operate here—the climate, the plants, the creatures of the woods, fields, and waters; and, of course, the town's long and chequered history. Much strangeness has grown here, much evil, and yes—much good as well. I could write entire books—what am I saying? I have done that, but do not fear, this letter is not one of them. I have already digressed from my message. As an excuse, I could say I was setting the background for you, but I must admit you do not need as much as I have provided. You know enough of my work and are sufficiently cognizant of the Inner Secrets to consider what I am about to tell you in its proper context.

I maintained links with the Fellowship of Nodens and continued to fight the secret war against the Church of Starry Wisdom, recruiting to this cause any that had the necessary outlook and abilities.

For this reason, I retained an interest in Lawrence Dexter. As I had predicted, he abandoned Egyptology soon after the Congress of Luxor, seeking the greater excitement (as he no doubt thought) to be found in occultism. Not for wisdom, I suspect, but for "thrills." You may accuse me of unfairness here, saying that I condemn the man from inadequate evidence. It's true I was never close to him, but I observed his activities for decades, and base my assessment on these observations.

For some time, he was associated with the Hermetic Order of the Golden Dawn, but parted ways with them and flitted to the Church of Starry Wisdom. It had representatives in London and a well-established outpost in New York City, which may have explained Dexter's decision to relocate there in the 1880s. And now I ask myself if it's possible that he was influenced by whatever token he accepted from that mysterious pharaoh-resembling guide in Luxor in 1870. Those tokens were invitations, and that guide, I fear, was the Crawling Chaos himself, or at least one of his avatars.

Dexter did not long remain with the Starry Wisdomites. Whether he left them voluntarily or not, I do not know, but eventually he established his own society. A society of one, as far as I could tell. By then he was somewhat notorious, with a veneer of glamour. He travelled about giving lectures and published a number of books and pamphlets. Most of his followers, not surprisingly, were women attracted by his looks and charming manner. For he was charming; I do not deny that.

In 1895, he was murdered. My surveillance of the man indicated that soon after his move to America he became acquainted with the wife of a Boston businessman called Hiram West. Anna Derby West, the wife, became quite besotted with Dexter (or his ideas, but I suspect the former) after meeting him at one of his lectures. They began a liaison about 1885. It must have been episodic, partly because of geographical constraints, but also because the lady's husband was known as "Hiram the Undertaker," an epithet bestowed for reasons besides his family's connection to the funeral trade.

Dexter was shot on the street one night and took several days to die. I'm told his deathbed was attended by the erring Mrs. West. The shooters were never apprehended, as far as I know, and Anna Derby West disappeared from public view about that time.

The interpretation of these events seems obvious: Dexter seduced a gangster's wife and the gangster had him murdered, and then did away with the wife. Perhaps so. But when I first heard about it, I wondered if Dexter's death was brought about for reasons other than his dalliance with Mrs. West, and if, in fact, the seemingly obvious reason was a smoke screen for something less obvious and more sinister.

Willa, you may or may not be aware of what I am about to reveal. If not, I ask that you keep it forever to yourself. (And if you are already privy to this knowledge, you would already know the need for secrecy.) Among those of us who are the custodians of the Inner Secrets, there are those who do more than study ancient manuscripts and preserve ancient rituals. There is a body of individuals charged with the grave responsibility of carrying out missions assigned to them by the Inner Temple. Invariably, these missions are directed—after intense and prolonged study and debate—against those who constitute a threat, not only to us and our cause, but to the greater world. Yes—I speak of the Destroyers, the deliverers of death. They are individuals of integrity who strike gravely and reluctantly in situations of dire need.

In short (and yes, I hear you laughing, Willa!)—in short, I wondered if Lawrence Dexter was the target of such a mission. Why? Because, light-minded though I believed him to be, he may have somehow acquired a crucial bit of knowledge or an artifact of power. He was, after all, at one time a member of the Starry Wisdom sect, and being as fickle as he was, he may have become a dangerous loose end. I am not in any way associated with the Destroyers or those to whom they are answerable. I am only speculating, and it is quite possible I am wrong. But recent events have brought this to mind in a more than casual way.

Almost a decade after the murder of Lawrence Dexter, I stood before a new class of students registered for my "Philosophical Excursions" course. You must remember it; you excelled in it, as I recall. Among the eager young faces looking back at me was one that reminded me of Luxor more than 30 years before—classical features, blond hair, and light-coloured eyes that gazed into mine with a trace of insolence. His name was Herbert West.

Even without his striking appearance, young West would have caught and kept my attention soon enough. He was one of those students who delights in debate, constantly questioning the old professor, demanding proof of his every statement, and proposing alternative theories. His attitude was that of the absolute rationalist, insisting upon an objective explanation for every phenomenon under the sun.

You may imagine what a spectacle Mr. West and I made for the rest of the class, as we thrashed out various points of contention. At times, I had to exercise my professorial authority to curtail our debates and keep to my lecture schedule. In truth, though, however irritating I found him, I was intrigued by Herbert West and wanted to learn more abut him. Although he was nominally the son of Hiram "the Undertaker" West and his wife Anna Derby West, I was certain his father was actually the late Lawrence Dexter. His appearance and birthdate made that conclusion inescapable.

Since such a delicate family matter was, technically, none of my business, I said nothing about it to young Mr. West. What I did was deliberately to include him in that year's group of students for my Profiles and Predictions study. This was, of course, contrary to my usual practice of random selection. I rationalized this breach of my principles by arguing that the tests I administered to my subjects might reveal valuable, indeed, crucial information about Herbert West.

The revelations were indeed crucial, even more so than I reckoned. There is no need to describe the tests I performed on him; they were exactly the same as those I administered to you and all my other subjects. But the results! They were even more spectacular than yours, which caused me to dub you a Nexus. So it was with young West, although he is a creature altogether different from you. Here is an extract from my notes:

He is an unstable element with great potential for good or evil. To avoid the pain of his invisible wounds, he has created for himself a *cold veneer that separates him from others. To discover his excellence, it may be necessary to do him harm, <u>perhaps destroy him</u>.*

There's the nub. It may be necessary to destroy Herbert West. Ever since I wrote these words, I have watched him, especially after he entered the School of Medicine here at Miskatonic. More than once his extracurricular experiments nearly got him expelled. I have observed no softening of his ultra-rationalism, that reduces the value of a human life to zero. He is devoid of empathy and lacks altogether a sense of wonder at the mysteries of the created world. I suspect him to be capable of committing murder, should he deem it necessary for the purpose of furthering his research into the phenomenon of death.

For several years, and especially in this past year, since war broke out in Europe, I have contemplated calling upon the Destroyers to remove Herbert West from the world.

And yet—Herbert West has "great potential for <u>good</u> or evil" and <u>excellence</u> that may be discovered by extraordinary means. I do not want to assume responsibility for destroying one who may, after transforming experiences, become a positive force in the world, an instrument of light. My studies in alchemy have shown me how an element of power can change from destructive to benevolent (or the reverse) in the blink of an eye. And a good alchemist never wastes anything that may be useful in the completion of the Great Work, however worthless it appears at first. What element represents Herbert West? What element may diffuse his potential for evil? Alchemical sulfur is one of the three primes. What was the significance of that token I accepted in 1870 and destroyed on the assumption that it was an invitation to serve the Haunter of the Dark?

With these uncertainties, and knowing that my departure from this world is approaching, I created a bond. Using the *Necronomicon* as a catalyst, I forged a <u>resonant link</u> for West's salvation.

I began haunting the Library again, spending hours in the Reading Room and even getting permission to visit the stacks. Perched in some quiet corner like an owl, I observed the librarians at their work. Earnest souls they are, loving order and precision, especially the cataloguers. Most of the time they keep to their own realm, transcribing and typewriting descriptions of books and applying to their spines gummed labels bearing combinations of letters and numbers obscure except to the initiated.

One among them, a young fellow called Charles Milburn, caught my attention. Discreet inquiries revealed a background of family tragedy and fallen fortunes. This, apparently, had brought him to librarianship and to Miskatonic. In him I sensed something beyond the ordinary. <u>Sensed,</u> I say, for his external appearance was entirely unremarkable.

In the winter of 1910, I learned that Milburn had been appointed by the University Librarian to be the custodian of the *Necronomicon*. This furnished an opportunity. I mentioned the book in a conversation with West. He was, as I've said, interested in death, and whether it may be scientifically reversed. <u>Scientifically,</u> *nota bene*! I steered his attention to Alhazred, pointing out that the man had written much about death and life and the links between the two. I cited specific passages, and directed Herbert West toward Charles Milburn. Then I waited.

My experiment was successful. A friendship developed. I suspected West had recruited Milburn as his assistant in his revivification efforts, but that did not matter. To me, the key was the link between Milburn and West. Eventually, I hoped, Milburn would assume the role of protector and guardian which I had formerly carried out from a distance.

Willa, I imagine by now you are appalled. What has old Quarrington come to? Madness, senility, or both? But as I recall, young Willamina Devlin was an adventurous thinker with a curious mind and a passionate heart, pulling on threads and following them to their sources. I called her a Nexus, because I thought she would draw together a diversity of people, thereby generating powerful conjunctions. And so you have.

Now, finally, to my request, the reason for this exceedingly long missive: I am 101 years old, and can reasonably expect soon to pass from this life. The war in Europe has drawn young Herbert West away from Arkham and therefore removed him from the benevolent influence of his friend Charles Milburn. I had hoped Milburn would prevail upon West to return. I wrote to both of them, but so far to no avail. I do not know what effect exposure to war will have on the thing I have perceived in West—the great potential for evil or excellence. It may be that violence and death on a gargantuan scale will create a creature upon whom the Destroyers must be called. Or perhaps his role as healer rather than combatant will have some sort of tempering effect.

And what do I expect you to do? Only to be <u>aware</u> of Herbert West. Read the Boston papers. Subscribe to the *Arkham Advertiser*. I know you love New England. Perhaps you and young Amelia may travel here from time to time (for I am certain West will return to Arkham). Be aware and follow your heart.

I am now trying to forge another link, one that transcends time and distance. You do not have to <u>do</u> anything more than I have suggested here. Have no fear, either for yourself or your daughter. For I think of you as <u>my</u> daughter, and of Herbert and Charles as my sons (although they know nothing of this). Having no children of my body, I have had to find substitutes among those whose minds have touched mine, with whom the Universe has forged bonds of love and compassion.

Believe this.

I remain, in all sincerity,
Augustus Quarrington.

FOX AND GLOVE

Arkham, May 1912

A pair of shoes descended the stairs. Elegant, dark brown shoes with pointed toes and three straps over the instep, fastened with square metal buttons. Above the shoes, well-turned ankles in pale stockings and a skirt hem of maroon silk. And then a ruffled velvet jacket in a peculiar shade of orange.

It couldn't be Alma. She never wore such colours, which were in any case rather odd choices for a pleasant spring evening. But this stair led to Alma's apartment and nowhere else.

The owner of the shoes had a pale, sharp-featured face under a purple hat adorned with pheasant feathers. Her dark red lips did not smile.

"Good evening," I said, removing my hat. The lady nodded but remained silent. Her heels clicked down the stairs, the sound followed by the slam of the front door.

~o0o~

"I met a lady on your stairs," I said to Alma, during a lull in our conversation over dinner at the Arkham Lobster House. "She was in a hurry. Didn't stop to pass the time of day."

"Hmm." Alma swallowed, laid down knife and fork and took a sip of wine. "Harriet Fox. She wasn't pleased with me."

"Surely not! What about?"

"She thought I could help her with something. She was wrong."

"Help her with what? Is she a friend of yours? I've never heard you mention anyone named Harriet."

Alma picked up her cutlery. "More an acquaintance than a friend. She belonged to my literary group for a couple of months. The one you haven't wanted to join." She smiled and lightly tapped my hand with her knife. "Once she realized how few male members there were, she switched to the Arkham Amateur Players. They're more her style, I guess."

I recalled the woman on the stairs. Dramatic potential there, certainly. "Ah, so you believe Miss Fox—it is 'Miss,' isn't it—is seeking a husband, perhaps?"

"She's a man-hunter, all right." Alma applied more pepper to her potatoes. "I'm not sure if her objective is marriage or mischief."

"Is that why she wanted your help? Finding a likely prospect?"

"Are you planning to volunteer, Charles?" This must have been a rhetorical question, because she didn't wait for an answer. "No, it's something else altogether." She tilted her head. "You know Prof. Geoffrey Dodd, don't you?"

"Prof. Geoffrey Arthur Wyman Dodd, known to our student body as GAWD. I know him more by repute than directly, although I've heard more than I ever wanted to about his views on how the Library should be arranged. Oh, and I've seen him on the stage. Can't remember what play, though."

"He was the founder of the Arkham Amateur Players," said Alma.

"'Was?' Let me guess—your friend Harriet usurped the leadership."

Alma shook her head. "No. Well, not yet. The thing is— Prof. Dodd died this morning."

I paused with my glass halfway to my lips. "Really? He wasn't that old, was he? Fiftyish?"

"Maybe. Harriet was with him."

"Was she hoping you could help her bring him back to life?" That awkward thought was followed by another I kept to myself. *Because I know someone who could.* "Exactly when did he die?"

Alma gave me a curious look. "I don't know. Harriet didn't say. She was more concerned about a missing book."

I raised my eyebrows. "Really? Dodd's lying dead in front of her and she's fussing about a *book*?"

"She said she 'couldn't bear to lose it, now that Geoffrey's gone.' That's what she sobbed into my shoulder, at any rate. The book was a gift from him. Or maybe something inside it was a gift from him. Something like that."

I set down my folded napkin and leaned toward her. "So what *did* she want from you?"

"To help her find this book, of course."

"Ah, yes. We librarians have uncanny powers for sniffing out books, don't we? Is this book in Dodd's house?"

"I suppose so. She thought since I'm a librarian I'd have a special talent for figuring out how someone organizes his books."

"Hmm. Strange notion. In fact, everything about this business is strange, including Miss Fox herself. She gave me a peculiar look when I met her on your stairs. A calculating look." I stirred my coffee. "You know, I do believe I can help her."

Now Alma's eyebrows shot up. "Oh? How would you do that, Charles?"

"I would… investigate," I said, and immediately wished I hadn't but realized it was too late. "I'd have a look at Prof. Dodd's personal library—see how many books there are, and whether they're arranged methodically or chaotically. Then I would make an educated guess."

"I suppose you'd want to talk to Harriet first, wouldn't you?" Alma sat straight, clutching her napkin. Her cheeks were pinker than usual. Wisps of hair from the loose knot on the back of her head framed her face in a golden glow. She looked adorable.

I smiled. "Well, yes, I imagine I would have to talk to her at some point."

"I'll bet you can't do it. Can't find this book, whatever it is." Alma released the napkin and tossed it aside. "I mean a real bet. A wager."

I no longer knew if we were joking. I suspected Alma wasn't. "All right. If I find Harriet's book, you lose. If I give up, you win. What happens then? What are the stakes?"

"It'll be a surprise." Alma smiled a little cat smile. "I'll give you a big surprise if I win and… hmm, I guess maybe a different surprise if I lose." She held out her hand. "Shake on it?"

We shook. "Surprises all around," I said. "Well, I guess I'd better get busy."

Alma assumed a severe expression. "I wouldn't take anything for granted, if I were you."

~o0o~

He always says no more than six hours for viability. It's been a lot longer than that.

A half-hour later, I knocked on Herbert West's door, glad to see a light in his study.

"*Entrez si vous osez.* Door's not locked."

As I stepped over the threshold, something sharp struck me in the forehead. A paper dart lay at my feet.

"A direct hit!" West raised both arms in a victory gesture and reached for another sheet of paper. "What brings you here, Charles?" He began to fold another dart.

I picked up the one that had hit me and rubbed the sore spot on my forehead. *If he's making paper darts, he's bored, and if he's bored, he might be intrigued enough to do it.* "I have a subject for you."

West raised an eyebrow. "*You* found a subject? A dead dog? You know I've given up on animals."

"No, no! A human subject. But we have to hurry. He died this morning, Alma said. I'm not sure exactly when, though."

"All right, Charles. What's all this about? Sit down and start at the beginning."

"A man died this morning. A lady is desperate to retrieve a book from his library, but has no idea how to find it. I told Alma I could help her, so we have to—"

West laughed and slapped his hands on the arms of his chair. "Ah, the things we do for love! Sadly, though, I don't select my experimental subjects in order to please your lady friend."

"It's more than that. It's a perfect opportunity to test your theory."

"And what theory might that be?" West gave me an ironically intent gaze.

"That revivification can be useful to the general public, even when it doesn't result in a full return to life. Remember, you told me so yourself when you first asked me to help you. It can reveal information that would otherwise be lost."

"In this case, the whereabouts of a *book*. Forgive me, Charles, but that isn't a matter of great importance to me. Even if it pleases Alma." West let fly another dart. It hit me in the chest.

"But it's an opportunity to practice your techniques. What harm could that do? And you don't seem all that busy right now." I picked up the dart and waved my hand at the dozen or more on the floor under the mantel clock.

West blushed. Or maybe it was annoyance that pinked his cheeks. "How would you know whether I'm busy or not?"

I unfolded the dart, revealing lines of West's handwriting. His scribble, rather. Here and there, a word revealed itself. 'Duration,' 'proof,' 'will show.' And 'revivification'—several times. I looked up. "What is this, anyway?"

West rose from his chair and snatched the paper from my hand. "An immodest proposal. Nothing you need to know about."

"You're asking for permission to do research on revivification? Officially?"

West crumpled the page and dropped it into the fireplace. He gathered up the paper darts and tossed them in as well, along with a lit match. "As you can see, I'm not. Idea reconsidered and rejected. *Finis*."

"All right, then, let's get started."

He stared at me. "Didn't you hear me? I'm not interested."

"Keep this in mind, then—next time you need me to help you with something you consider important, like revivification, I might just have urgent business elsewhere." I turned and headed for the door.

"What's the name of the deceased?"

I stopped but didn't turn around. "Geoffrey Dodd, Professor of English Literature at Miskatonic University."

"Otherwise known as the cardiac case that came into the Emergency Room at ten this morning and expired a few hours later."

I whirled around. "How do you know that?"

"I was there. I spend a good deal of my time at the hospital, as you know quite well. If you'd named the fellow at the start, it would have put a different complexion on the matter. All right, let me think. He died just after two p.m. Eight hours ago, give or take. It's worth a try, but there's a considerable risk. You know I'm under surveillance by Dean Halsey and his minions until I graduate. I don't want to risk my future career for this little whimsy of yours."

He'd been tidying the papers on his desk but stopped and looked at me. "Wait—Alma Halsey. She's the one who put you up to this. How do I know she isn't working with her father to set a trap for me?"

"How can you think that? For one thing, it isn't something Alma would do. And anyway, she actually made me a bet I wouldn't be able to find the book. But of course she doesn't know I could ask Dodd himself about it."

West eyed me speculatively. "A bet! Well, well, Charles, I didn't realize there was something more at stake here.

Something significant, I imagine. No—don't tell me. I'd rather use my imagination. All right, let's get going."

~o0o~

A brisk walk brought us to a rear door of St. Mary's Hospital, with which I had grown familiar since becoming West's accomplice in revivification of corpses. We hurried along the dim corridor to the morgue. West closed the door and switched on the light.

A casual glance at the labels on the corpse chambers revealed no one named Dodd. West checked the record book.

"Hmm. That was fast! He's gone. 'Transferred to mortuary,' it says. You know what that means."

I realized what he was getting at. "Oh, your mortuary. I mean your family's."

"Of course. 'Go west with West's.' Well, that's where we must go too. Let's hope Dodd hasn't been embalmed already. I'll just get my gear from the lab."

We dashed to the dank little room West called his lab. It was a grudging concession by the university authorities to his expressed need for a place to pursue 'special research projects.' Little did they know how special.

West packed the essentials for revivification into a canvas satchel. "You realize, of course, that I can't take any of this stuff." He waved a hand at the specialized apparatus for supporting the fluid reservoir, pumps, and pressure regulators. "Which means the chance of total failure is excellent."

"Well, but we're used to that, aren't we?"

"Indeed," said West, with a glare. "I hope you're prepared for whatever Miss Halsey will demand when you lose your bet with her."

The Arkham location of West's Funeral Homes was on the opposite side of downtown from the Miskatonic campus and the hospital. It must have been close to midnight by the time we arrived at the back of the building. A group of hearses stood in the parking area, darker shadows in the shadow of the antiquated brick structure.

West hesitated. I assumed he was searching his pockets for a key, but then I wondered if he in fact had one. His family owned the business, but he wasn't an employee or company official.

"Now, Charles," West said, directing me toward a nearby tree, a weeping willow. "Stay right here and don't make a sound until I tell you it's all right. And hold onto this." He handed me the satchel and approached the double doors used by the hearses. Next to them was a smaller door with a light overhead. West pressed a button next to this door and a bell clanged inside.

Accustomed to absolute secrecy while on these enterprises, I panicked. "What are you—?"

West gestured me silent. "Wait."

The door opened, revealing a burly figure silhouetted against the brighter light inside. "I thought it would be you, Mr. Herbert," said a voice, so velvety-soft it barely registered on my eardrums. "Just visiting?"

Distracted by my jolt of panic, I failed to hear West's reply. Then I was taken up with keeping my feet still and my breathing quiet.

"…the usual places on Water Street," said West. "No, the other one. I'll wait for you here. If he doesn't show up, just bring it back. …drinks on me." I heard a rustle of paper and clink of coins.

They went inside and after a minute the other man came back out. He stood under the light by the door and lit a cigarette, which gave me an opportunity to get a look at him. He was taller than West but shorter than I, solidly built and bald-headed. His high forehead, made higher by the lack of hair, was equipped with eyebrows like caterpillars above small, deep-set eyes. His nose looked like it had experienced considerable abuse. Full lips clenched the cigarette above a prominent chin.

He covered his pate with a flat cap and sauntered to an automobile parked near the hearses. I heard the engine crank up, and a few seconds later, the vehicle's lights came on. I pressed myself against the tree, expecting to be illuminated and discovered, but the car backed out and turned onto the street.

The door of the mortuary opened again. West waved me over. "Come on, Charles!" A note of anxiety sharpened his voice. "Hurry up!"

West led the way down the hall and into a room that reminded me of the hospital's morgue. "Dodd's in number 8," he said, dragging over a gurney. "Let's get him into the work room, pronto."

"Who was that fellow?" I asked, as we extracted Dodd's corpse and transferred it to the wheeled contraption.

"Jeremiah, the night watchman, otherwise known as the innkeeper of the dead. He knows me; in fact, he sometimes runs errands for me, which is what he's doing now. A false errand, of course, but I made it worthwhile to him. He'll be back in a couple of hours, so we have no time to waste."

"How do you know he won't tell anyone you were here?"

West grinned. "Because he's not supposed to run errands while he's on the job. *Quid pro quo.*"

We wheeled Dodd into the work room and set up the familiar revivification equipment—pump, rubber tubing, pressure meter, and the flask of violet-coloured fluid.

Unwrapped, laid out, and awaiting the procedure, Dodd looked like a man of marble—pale almost to whiteness, with sinister blue and purple mottles. His face, which I had seen enlivened by enthusiasm as he rendered some character in a play, or reddened with annoyance while he argued about the arrangement of books in the Miskatonic University Library, was now like a fist clenched in a final resolve. I began to doubt our chances of success.

With each of us doing our parts, the revivifying fluid was quickly administered. While we waited for it to do its work, West went over to a desk nearby and opened a thick binder. He leafed through it and wrote something on one of the pages. "There, that should do it," he muttered. "Now, let's see how Dodd's doing. It would be awkward if we were still conversing with him when Jeremiah came back."

An anxious half-hour passed before Geoffrey Dodd showed the first signs of renewed life—fluttering eyelids, laboured breaths, and a faint pink flush on the waxy cheeks.

"He won't last long," said West, after a cursory examination. "If you want to get anything from him, you'd better do it now."

I leaned over Dodd. "Geoffrey Dodd, can you hear me? My name is Charles Milburn. Prof. Dodd, what do you remember?"

West rolled his eyes and silently mouthed the question as he pressed the bell of the stethoscope to Dodd's chest. He made a winding up hand motion, the meaning of which was perfectly clear. *Just get on with it, Charles.*

Dodd's eyes rolled and opened, disclosing black pupils and not much more. His lips worked under his grey moustache and parted to show a pale tongue. "Who asks?" His voice was like the faint buzzing of a winter bee.

"I have a message for you from Miss Harriet Fox. Harriet."

"Aah, my little vixen. My foxy one." He exhaled the words on a gasping breath. "Yellow, yellow, light's too yellow. Everything's yellow…" He twitched his fingers in a feeble attempt to wave something away. "Yellow fog and blue lights, blue haloes. So strange…"

West perked up. "Ask him about that. How long has he been seeing it?"

I shook my head. Dodd's voice was so faint and wheezy, I thought the fading back to death must be starting already. "There is no fog," I said, turning back to him.

Dodd was buzzing again. "White bells, white as her hands. White gloves… So pure, so white, but even they looked yellow." His lips trembled into a smile. "She brought me flowers for my heart."

"Geoffrey," I said, "please listen to me. You told Harriet about a book she has to find. She's having trouble finding it. She needs a clue."

He laughed. Or tried to. "I forgot, forgot to say… 'bitter weeds and rue.'"

"Is that the title?" I asked. *It can't be that easy.*

"'Plucked in the garden, all the summer through,'" whispered Dodd. "Title? You know better than that, young man."

West stood a few feet away, arms folded and a smirk on his face. *All set to say he told me so.*

I bent closer to Dodd's face, my palm on his breastbone. "Professor—Geoffrey, tell me, please, what book is it?"

"Dead paper," said Dodd. "Dead. But a nice little edition. Eighteen ninety-six, cover bright blue, gold lettering. She'll love it, even before she looks inside. Oh, little vixen, you let me count the ways." He smiled again. "So heavy." His right hand twitched and grasped mine. "'I shall but love thee better after death.' You know that. Aah."

His hand relaxed. Geoffrey Dodd was dead. Again.

"All done?" said West, coming over. "Found your book, have you?"

"You know damned well I haven't," I said, astonished at my impulse, quickly quashed, to punch him in the nose. "I tried, but I guess that's that." I stepped away from Dodd.

"Too bad you didn't ask him about those colours. It sounded interesting."

To you, maybe. "Look, Herbert, thanks for humoring me."

He laughed. "You'd better quit the scene before Jeremiah shows up. Meanwhile, I'll put Prof. Dodd back to bed."

~oOo~

Slouching homeward along the quiet streets, I thought about Dodd's final utterances. They were different from his fragmented complaints about yellow fog. They reminded me of something.

I broke into a run, or as close to one as I could manage. Lines from some play? Or poetry? Love poems by... someone. Shakespeare? No. Keats? Shelley? Wordsworth? I had no talent for remembering this stuff.

But Alma might know. Didn't she belong to a literary circle? I dismissed the question of whether it was right to ask her for help, given our wager, and made my way back to the house where she lived.

The main door was locked for the night. Not like last October, when our affair began. That had also been right after I had helped West with a revivification.

I muttered a curse. Then I had an idea. Scrabbling around near the sidewalk, I gathered a few pebbles. I knew (of course I knew!) which window was her bedroom's. The first three pebbles fell short. The fourth one tapped the glass. So did the fifth, with a "ting" that to my ears sounded loud enough to wake the neighbourhood. The curtains parted and the sash went up, revealing Alma's blond head. I waved my arms like a demented windmill and heard a soft laugh as she vanished. I hurried back to the door and followed her up the stairs. Alma was still laughing as I gathered her in my arms.

My memory hadn't failed altogether, or maybe Alma's presence sparked something. As we emerged from a deep kiss, words spilled from my mouth. "How shall I love thee? Let me count the ways..."

"Close, and maybe better," Alma murmured into my neck. "Do you think Robert said that to her as he undid her corset?"

I pulled away. "Who's Robert? I thought his name was Geoffrey."

"Are you still thinking about Dodd? Or Harriet? Even while you're quoting Elizabeth Barrett Browning to me?"

"No, not really. Elizabeth Barrett Browning—that's who wrote the poem? I never would have guessed."

"You philistine, Charles. It's from her *Sonnets from the Portuguese*. That title was supposed to hide the fact that they were love poems written by her. Is that why you woke me up? To check a quotation? What have you been up to since dinner?"

"Talking with West."

"Don't tell me *he* was reading poetry to you. Or were you telling him about Harriet and Prof. Dodd?"

"Well, Herbert does have a logical mind, you know. And it turns out he was at the hospital when Dodd died."

"But surely Dodd didn't tell Herbert West what book he sent Harriet to look for." Alma backed away from me, rubbing her arms.

"No, of course not." I embraced her again. "You're cold. I know a way to warm you up."

She pushed me away. "Not now. Not yet. We have a bet, remember? And I have a feeling you're grasping at straws."

"I'm not, actually. Which reminds me—do you know where Miss Fox lives?"

"You're going to call on her in the middle of the night? I have no idea where she lives. It's your job to find the answers. And speaking of jobs, you and I are due at ours in just about six hours. I'd rather be awake and alert then. So I advise you to go home and get some rest."

~o0o~

I actually considered Alma's advice to go home and sleep. After all, the real urgency had been to revivify Dodd before he was beyond reach. I could resume—or, to be honest, begin—the search for the mysterious book the following day. After work. After the day's doings had diminished my enthusiasm, which meant I probably wouldn't do it at all. I would have to admit my failure to Alma, and even though that meant she would win our bet, I suspected it wouldn't raise her opinion of me.

No—it had to be now or never.

Dodd's house—that was the place. Why? I didn't know why, but that's where I directed my steps after my dismissal by Alma. I knew where it was because I'd gone there once to evaluate some books Dodd wanted to donate to the M.U. Library. It was only a few blocks away from Alma's, on Garrison Street, where the mansions of the wealthy gave way to the quaint but decrepit haunts of students and artists.

The house stood silent in the pre-dawn darkness. A dead man's house. I looked over the gate and down the front walk to the steps which would know its owner's feet no more. Despite his brief and unnatural return to life at the hands of my friend, Geoffrey Dodd was dead. Hopelessness enveloped me. I didn't know Harriet Fox, nor she me. Why should I care about her stupid book?

Because it was the dead man's final wish that she find it. And you dragged him back from death to ask him about it. That's why.

A light moved inside the house, faint and fleeting. My first thought was that Dodd's ghost was roaming the husk of his life, saying farewell to his books. A ghost wouldn't need a light, though, surely? I crept down the walk, up the steps, and peered through the glass in the door. All was dark within. The light must have been a product of my weariness. But no—there it was again, descending the stairs from the second floor. A flashlight illuminated the steps, and also a pair of shoes with pointed toes and three straps fastened with square buttons.

Harriet Fox, in Prof. Dodd's house. If I wanted to ask her some questions and offer my assistance, here was my chance. I rapped on the door.

Her arm must have jerked, sending the beam of light into an erratic sideways movement. Heels tapped out disturbed urgency as she approached the door. She opened it a crack and looked me up and down.

"Who are you, and what are you doing here?"

"My name is Charles Milburn. I'm a... colleague of Prof. Dodd's. And I might ask the same questions of you."

"Are you a reporter?"

I smiled. "No, I'm a librarian."

"Oh! Can you—?" She opened the door wider, but kept her hand over the flashlight, muffling its light to a dim orange. "But first—why are you here at all? It's hardly the time to call on a colleague."

"Especially one who's dead."

"Indeed." Her voice was solemn, her expression serious, but I did not detect the grief of the recently bereaved.

"You must have a key to the house, since you're Prof. Dodd's... secretary? Or his housekeeper?"

As I expected, she stiffened and thrust out her chin. "Neither, Mr. Milburn. I am... a friend." She pursed her lips slightly on the final word and smiled a secretive, closed-lipped smile.

"May I ask you a few questions, Miss—?"

"So you *are* a reporter."

"No, I really am a librarian. At Miskatonic University Library. That's how I became acquainted with Prof. Dodd."

She uncovered the flashlight, letting it shine between us. A few moths fluttered around it and she batted at them with her free hand. "So what are you doing here?"

"Looking for a book," I said, watching her face.

She inhaled sharply. "Oh, you too—I mean, isn't that interesting. Especially at this hour of the night."

I shrugged. "I thought it likely that by tomorrow a posse of relatives and other worthies would descend on the place and complicate matters. I imagine you had a similar idea."

She clutched her flashlight tightly enough to make the light tremble. "Come inside," she said. "We can talk more comfortably there."

She turned and preceded me into the foyer. Her light briefly illuminated a ghostly bouquet of white flowers on a small table. Some had shed their tubular petals, which lay limp and flaccid on the dark wood.

I followed the trail of her perfume into the house. It reminded me of violets, but with some darker element. A light shone from a room at the end of the hall. It was at the back of the house, I realized; with the curtains closed, our presence would remain invisible from the street.

A desk and worktable indicated this was Geoffrey Dodd's study. It was, of course, full of books, but a stack of newspapers and a number of pipes in an ashtray overflowing with cigarette butts and dottle suggested this was where he spent his leisure time.

Miss Fox went to a cabinet in one corner and picked up a decanter. "Would you care for some sherry?"

"Thank you," I said. "Although it seems an outlandish time for a drink."

She smiled and filled a couple of glasses. "No time was outlandish for Geoffrey. I'm sure he wouldn't mind."

For the first time, I got a good look at her. She was a little shorter than Alma, her figure curvaceous. Her hair, a dark auburn, was gathered off her face into a chignon. Pale olive skin contrasted strongly with the dark red lipstick. The maroon silk dress must have been the one she was wearing the first time I saw her, on the evening of the previous day.

As she handed me a glass, I noticed that her eyes were the same colour as the liquid it contained. She gestured toward a pair of armchairs. "Let's make ourselves comfortable."

"How did you meet Prof. Dodd?" I asked, when we were settled.

"Through the Arkham Amateur Players. I joined just as Geoffrey was casting for *A Midsummer Night's Dream*. He chose me for the part of Helena and I accepted. There was a bit of resentment from the other members, since I was so new, but Geoffrey overruled them. He was a brilliant actor and director. We became friends."

No nuanced hesitation here, I noted with amusement. "And that was... when?"

"Oh, a year ago, perhaps. No—last fall. Less than a year. How strange." She gazed into her glass as though seeking something.

"Did you... were you with him when he died?"

She looked away from me, to the other side of the room, where ranks of book spines made a brownish haze punctuated with gleams of gilt and the occasional bit of brighter colour. "It was such a shock. We had just finished breakfast when he complained of pain and collapsed. I really didn't expect it so soon." She bit her lip. "I mean—Geoffrey wasn't even sixty and such a dynamic man. So full of life. I couldn't conceive of him dying. But then, he was full of surprises too."

"He wasn't ill recently?"

"Not really, no. Mr. Milburn, you must be anxious to find your book."

"And you are anxious to help me?"

A small smile. "I wouldn't be much help. I have no idea how his books are arranged."

"What—he never gave you a tour of his personal library?"

"Of course not. Geoffrey was a teacher and a trickster. He thought his students learned best if they had to solve riddles."

"I can believe that. What sorts of riddles?"

"Oh, things like, 'a translation that isn't, to conceal the meeting of minds and hearts.' But it's all like this." She waved a hand. "A forest of books. You can't read most of the spines, and they all look alike, and how would I know if something's a translation?" She covered her face with her hands and rolled her head from side to side. "I'm so *tired*."

"Where have you searched already?"

She raised her head and gazed at me, lips slightly parted. "You're clever, aren't you? I suppose librarians have to be. All right, I *am* looking for a book. He told me he'd put a special gift for me inside a book in his collection. But I had to find it myself, using that clue. And now I can't ask him for another one."

I sat and thought. Dodd had apparently wanted her to have a particular book. I was quite sure I knew what book it was and what it looked like, which she obviously did not. But how to find it?

"Well, let's start right here." I scanned the shelves for a bright blue book with gold lettering. Of course, the spine might be a different colour, but I brushed that thought away.

My search yielded nothing more than the realization that the books in this room were those Dodd would have used in writing academic treatises, along with a few shelves of rarities and first editions. My hopes rose when I found these, but they were all older than the volume I sought.

At first, Harriet Fox watched me search, but at some point she excused herself and left the room, returning just as I gave up.

"Let's have a look at the other rooms," she said. "Almost every room in the house is stuffed with books."

"All right. We'll have to use your flashlight again, though, unless we want to advertise our presence."

She handed me the flashlight and I switched it on as I left the study. The light caught a small brass plaque above the door of the room across the hall. Engraved on the plaque was the symbol for Mercury. I directed the beam to the corresponding spot above the study door. Jupiter. Next door, Saturn.

"Did Prof. Dodd have an interest in astrology or astronomy?" I asked.

"Not as far as I know."

"Well he labelled his book rooms after the planets, or maybe the gods of the ancient world." I pointed to the symbols. Suddenly, I had an idea. "Let's find Venus."

I was wrong. The Venus Room was small and packed to the rafters, not with books written by women, but with the erotica of three thousand years. I darted from one smallish blue book to another, only to be disappointed. I rubbed my eyes and rested my forehead on the edge of a shelf.

The scent of dark violets told me she was near. "No luck?" I shook my head.

"You're not about to give up though?" She had an open book in her hand, of naughty Japanese prints. I looked from a titillating scene to her face, which wore a look of expectation, and felt a little dizzy.

"Well, are there other rooms?" I said. "A Diana room, perhaps? Or Minerva? But they aren't planets."

"Is the Moon a planet?" she asked.

"Sort of. It depends if you're an astronomer or an astrologer, I guess. Why?"

"Because, that last day—only yesterday—he said to me, 'I know you'll find it, even if you have to go to the Moon.' At the time I thought it was just Geoffrey being Geoffrey. But now I wonder if it was a clue."

"Let's go to the Moon!" Weariness gone, I dashed up to the second floor. Two rooms bore the symbols of Neptune and Uranus. The first contained books on seafaring, the second, magic and alchemy. I was tempted to linger in that one, but denied myself. At the end of the hall, a door revealed a set of narrow steps, with another door at the top. Above it was a small plaque with a crescent engraved upon it—the sign of Luna, the mutable Moon.

In the confined stairway, Harriet's perfume enveloped me in an embrace of musky violets. Hinges squealed as I opened the door. There was no electric light up here, but the flashlight's beam revealed an oil lamp on a small table and next to it, a box of matches.

The glow from the lamp awoke the shelves of books, bringing out colours and metallic lettering. Running my eyes along the spines, I saw book after book by women—Sappho, the Brontë sisters, Austen, Eliot, Mary Shelley, Mrs. Lovechild, Madame de Staël. Among them, a spine of cornflower blue, lettered in gold. Here it was at last. I made myself leave it untouched and turned to my companion.

"I've found the book I was looking for. Do you want to have a look for yours?"

She decided to start with the shelf I had been examining. Methodically, she removed each book in turn, opened it, flipped to the back, ruffled its pages, and returned it to its place. She never looked closely at a title page, or any other page, for that matter.

Sonnets from the Portuguese was about three-quarters of the way along the shelf, so I observed her actions for several minutes. Her expression did not change as her slender fingers grasped the blue book and executed the open, flip, ruffle procedure. Then her eyes widened, her lips twitched, and she emitted a small sound of excitement as she removed an envelope from within the book.

She thrust the slim volume carelessly into the gap it had left on the shelf and opened the envelope. A satisfied smile took over her face, making it briefly beautiful.

"I gather you've found your book?" I said, stepping close to her.

She folded the papers and stuffed them back into the envelope. "Yes, I have. Many thanks for your help, Mr. Milburn."

"You're welcome, Miss Fox."

"How did you know my name?"

"I'm clever, remember? Actually, I'm a friend of Alma Halsey." And as she turned to leave, "Don't forget your book."

"Oh, of course." She snatched it from the shelf. "But what about you? Didn't you say you found the book you were looking for?"

"Oh, I did, and the experience was quite amusing, but I think I'll let it rest in peace."

~o0o~

I was worse than useless at work that day, but managed to avoid Alma, although I caught her looking at me speculatively once or twice. I left early, pleading a headache which was quite real.

A sharp rap at my door woke me from a sound sleep, which I realized had taken place on my sofa.

West eyed me with amusement. "To liken your appearance to an unmade bed would be to insult such beds, Charles. Isn't that the rig-out you were wearing when we worked on Dodd? What have you been up to?"

"I had a late night," I mumbled, pushing my fingers through my hair. "And then an early morning."

"Settling your bet with Alma? What were the stakes?"

"I'd rather not say. What're you doing here, anyway?"

"Talking with you." West laughed. "Actually, I have some news about the late Prof. Dodd I thought you might find interesting. How about if you freshen up, as the ladies say, while I make us some coffee?"

I had to agree with this excellent idea.

"So what about Dodd?" I asked, half an hour later, relishing the aroma of the fresh brew wafting from the cup in my hand.

"According to shop talk I overheard at the hospital, Dodd had an unstable heart. He'd been on a regimen of drugs and prescribed—and proscribed—behaviour for years. His dramatic pursuits were thought to be either a symptom or a cause of his condition. Apparently, he'd been advised to exercise caution and not overstimulate. The man who looked after his case opined that a recent connection with a much younger woman may have destabilized him." West smiled and swirled the coffee in his cup.

"This amuses you? Dodd's condition?"

"No. Well, a little, but that's not the point. The point is that I could have enlightened these gentlemen considerably, if I'd chosen to. In fact, I might have caused trouble for our senior heart specialist, except I didn't think it was worth it to spill the beans about revivification simply for a bit of theatrics."

"What are you getting at, West?"

He set the cup down with a decisive click. "Merely that Dodd died of an overdose of digitalis."

"Digitalis," I said, wiggling my fingers. "Derived from Latin for—"

"It's a commonly used drug for heart failure, derived from the plant known as foxglove. Good for regulating an irregular heartbeat, but it's tricky stuff. Too much is worse than too little. It seems Dodd got too much, either by exceeding the prescribed dose or ingesting more of it in some way."

"How do you know that?"

West rolled his eyes. "How do you suppose? You heard what he said when we managed to revivify him."

I shall but love thee better after death, I remembered.

West jumped to his feet and adopted his lecturing manner. "If you recall, Dodd said everything looked yellow. *Yellow.* And he saw foggy blue haloes around lights. Those hallucinations are symptoms of digitalis poisoning. I have no doubt whatever that's what killed him."

"Wouldn't there be some sort of evidence—a post-mortem?"

"Too late. Dodd's corpse is dust and ashes."

Judging by the satisfied expression on West's face, mine must have shown my astonishment.

"The work order specified that Dodd's body be cremated immediately after his death. Those instructions were marked 'by request of the family,' and carried out promptly." He laughed. "Luckily, Dodd had no family. Not here in Arkham, anyway."

"So how could they request anything? Oh, I get it—*you* wrote the instructions."

West applauded. "Very good, Charles. Goodbye, evidence, including that caused by a certain procedure performed *post mortem*. That was the logical way to deal with it, so don't imagine I'm going to run to the police to tell them about revivification."

"But this case is exactly what you need to convince the Dean and College of its value! You could cite it in that proposal you were writing."

"That proposal is also dust and ashes. If I had solid physical evidence to back up the claim, it might be worth a shot.

But I don't. And Dean Halsey is so prejudiced against me it would take more than a single case, even if it were ironclad. And," he added, with one of his calculated stares, "don't you so much as breathe a whisper into Alma's dainty ear about Dodd's revivification, or any other. Both our lives will become very unpleasant if you do."

After West left, I sat and let my mind run over the events of the past couple of days. Less than a year after Harriet Fox joined the Arkham Amateur Players, Geoffrey Dodd died suddenly. All right, he had a weak heart, but even so... Indecently soon after his death, Harriet was determined to find a book she clearly cared little about, except for the envelope inside it, an envelope that contained what must have been a generous gift from her lover. I thought of the bouquet of white foxgloves on the table in the foyer when I entered Dodd's house, and its absence when Harriet and I said our goodbyes as dawn broke outside. She had the book under her arm and extended her hand to me. Her cold hand, with its slender, agile fingers. Her dark red mouth curved in a smile — of relief? Of triumph? Her peculiar, violet-scented perfume enveloped me one last time as she administered a kiss to my lips before slipping out the door.

~oOo~

The following evening, I gave Alma an edited but entertaining version of my ultimately fruitless wanderings in the late Prof. Dodd's house, and conceded the bet. We celebrated her victory in a way that was a pleasant surprise to us both. So pleasant that I refrained from telling her about my final sighting of Harriet

Fox. Final because she soon left Arkham, never to be seen there again.

In the busy main hall of the Miskatonic University Library, I caught a glimpse of her orange jacket amid a jostle of students. I hid behind a pillar and watched her approach the Returns window. She handed a book to the clerk and immediately left the Library. I went to the sorting area and asked to see the book she had returned. I don't know what I expected—Prof. Dodd's copy of *Sonnets from the Portuguese,* perhaps? Instead, the clerk pointed out a volume bound in dull grey buckram. *The Preparation, Utility, and Administration of Digitalis purpurea, or Foxglove, in Failure of the Heart.*

FROM THE ANNEXE
an untold tale

If I had purple ink, I would use it here, although by rights this should be written in my own blood.

This is my account of something beyond friendship between myself and Herbert West, physician and necromancer. After I lost Alma and the secret glory, I created this for myself, from memories and longings I discovered after it was too late. I knew it to be self-indulgent, foolish, even pathetic. But I did it because I had to. And because I knew him so well, I wrote him as he was, not as I wished him to be.

~oOo~

I had begun to suspect something about him. The thing that made me almost certain happened at one of the dinner parties he held for his professional colleagues. Looking back, I'm surprised it didn't at the same time reveal me to myself.

I can see it again, vividly—all of us gathered in his parlour, Billington playing the piano, West and Nichols singing some duet with such enthusiasm that when they finished, we all cheered and applauded. Except Williams, who was gazing at my friend with a fixed and hungry stare that had only one possible meaning—even to me, naïve as I was.

And then the look he gave Williams—I expected the man to fall dead on the spot from the sheer icy intensity of it.

What did any of this have to do with me? Nothing, then. So what if I suspected—no, knew—that he was attracted to men rather than women? I was not so naïve as to be unaware of this phenomenon. I had read my Plato. I knew what sort of love was discussed in "Phaedrus."

I thought of the many times I had observed him during our experiments, while we waited for signs of returning life. I watched his face, self-absorbed or animated, his moods like changeable weather reflected in his eyes. I told myself I was observing him for the sake of gathering knowledge about one who was to me remarkable. I was like a scientist watching the growth and flowering of a rare orchid he has been privileged to discover. But something far less scientific motivated me, even then.

I entertained doubts. Surely this could not be. It was Alma I felt this way about. She's been away too long, I thought. No one can substitute for her. I've tried to find that person, these five years since she left, without success. What had I been looking for? In truth, I had to admit that no vivacious, blue-eyed blond had measured up to some elusive image of perfection. I had assumed that image was Alma's. But I was wrong.

~o0o~

It began, or did not, but could have, in the winter of 1920, when, to his distress, he found and then lost his mother. After her funeral, I invited him to my rooms. In his eyes I could see the orphan he had become, and I did not think it would be good for him to be alone. We sat in uncomfortable silence, nursing our drinks. Well, I nursed mine, but he put away several, and eventually they had an effect.

He stood and began to pace. I said nothing, knowing this was his habit when he had something on his mind. He stopped in front of me and said, "All my life, I've known exactly what I am, even when I've not been entirely happy about it. I made myself, more than most people do. When I met obstacles, such as my father and my brothers, or the rules of the Medical School, or the rules of death, for that matter, I always managed to find a way around or over or through them. But this—I don't think I can get around it, or away from it. This might destroy me. I can feel a change already."

"I don't understand. What sort of change?"

"Insanity, Charles. It's in my blood. She was my mother; there's no doubt about that. You heard her raving, back there in the lab. And don't forget my father's legacy. I'm the son of a murderer and a madwoman. You know the results of the first. Now this other thing, just when I could see my way clear." He covered his face with his hands.

This was the man who had once said to me, "Nothing can shock me any more." Now something had. I laid a hand on his shoulder, feeling awkward.

"Herbert," I said, "surely it isn't so black as you imagine. Don't forget, I'm the son of a suicide, but I don't think it has affected me in any lasting way. I don't expect to be driven to do what he did."

"That's not the same." He turned and looked at me with an expression of despair. "Suicide could actually be a rational choice, in some situations. And your father, from what you tell me, was a perfectly ordinary, competent individual until his bank failed. This is... insidious. And inescapable."

"But nothing about you has changed since you made this discovery," I said. "You're the same person you were before."

"The person I was before was living in a state of blessed ignorance, with a clear road before him. Now it's full of hidden pits."

I reminded him of his work, his love of it, his fitness for it. I advised him to forget about his parents' troubles and to live as he had lived before. If madness was indeed his fate, I said, it would claim him soon enough, whether he worried about it or not.

"In that case, the kindest thing you could do would be to shoot me. The very thought of becoming one of those dribbling idiots in Sefton fills me with horror. But thank you, Doctor Milburn, for your advice. I shall surely consider it. There's a practicality about it that appeals to me. And now I should go home."

Twice he started for the door, and both times came back. All at once, he said, "At a time like this, I wish you were... It would be good to have someone who..."

He came closer to me. "Charles," he said, "I don't know what you might think of desires that are... abnormal."

I had no idea at first what he was talking about, but that word, 'abnormal,' told me he had not let go of the idea of his flawed heredity. He stood silent before me. The dim light from the lamp in the corner cast shadows beneath his cheekbones and in the caves of his eyes. He had disarranged his hair by running his fingers through it as he spoke, and it fell over his forehead.

In that moment, I experienced a welter of emotions—compassion, confusion, and yes, desire. The thing I had discovered in myself a short time before had returned, with a vengeance. Something unthinkable until now was about to become real. I removed my spectacles, welcoming the blurring of my vision. It was like camouflage, hiding me from myself as I entered an unexplored region.

He was now so near me that I caught a faint narcissus scent of the stuff he used on his hair. Slowly, he raised his hand. His fingers brushed my cheek, the hair at my temple, the line of my jaw. His eyes were rapt, his lips slightly parted. He made as if to snatch his hand back, but I caught it in both of mine and held it to my heart. I heard a sweet, constant note, as though a harp string had been plucked, and reverberated in the silent room.

"Charles," he whispered, "I can feel your heart beating. So fast... You know what I am, don't you?"

"Yes," I said. "But it's all right, Herbert. I want this, I think. I want... you."

For the first time, I saw his beautiful face transformed by passion. He closed his eyes. "Kiss me, Charles."

So I did.

Always, in my dealings with him, he had been the leader. He had given the orders and I had followed them. Now he gave himself to me like a flower. His lips were warm, and tasted of whiskey.

After a long moment, he drew back. "Madness and degeneracy—can you feel it?"

"I don't know what degeneracy is supposed to feel like. As for madness, I suppose you could call it that, but whatever it is, I want to feel it. And so do you, I think."

He sighed. "Wanting has nothing to do with it."

In the darkness of my bedroom, without the acute details supplied by vision, everything became easier. I was fumbling with the buttons of his vest, when he murmured, "So you're not altogether reluctant to do this now? In our experimental days you always jibbed at undressing the subjects." He laughed. I felt his warm breath on my cheek, his fingers loosening my collar.

"You're not a subject, though," I said breathlessly.

"No? I suspect for you this is something in the nature of an experiment."

"Well, yes, in a way," I admitted. "So you must have patience."

I heard a smile in his voice as he replied. "Nine years, Charles. Isn't that patience enough?"

"But I don't know what to do," I said. "That's what I meant."

"Do whatever you like. Do whatever gives you pleasure. I don't think you could do anything to cause me harm."

I had reached the limits of choice. Swept along by a swiftly flowing river to the brink of a precipice, I had only a few moments left in which to change my mind. If I ended this now, it would be forever. This demanded nothing less than my complete surrender. I gave up. I gave in. I let myself be taken over the brink. I no longer cared what might happen. Whether I would be killed on the rocks below, or drowned in deep waters, or dissolved in air, was all one to me. There was only one thought in my mind: *Now he's got me. Now I am his forever.*

I woke in the dusk of dawn, grasping for a departing dream of a warm, salty sea near a country of flowers. He was a silhouette before the window, tying his necktie. Panicked lest he leave before I had pulled myself together, I seized my bathrobe and groped for the role of genial host.

"You're going now?"

He turned to me the face of one addressed on the street by a stranger.

"Yes. Don't bother showing me out."

The door opened and closed, and I heard his steps on the stairs.

I hurried to a window that overlooked the street and watched him walking swiftly along the sidewalk. He looked his ordinary, public self. No one who saw him could possibly have guessed, I thought, chilled by the speed of the transition.

~oOo~

Days went by, and I saw nothing of him. After the second week I went to his house, feeling apprehensive and foolish. Andre showed me to his study with a formality that served only to intensify my awkwardness. He looked up from his desk when I entered and greeted me amicably. For a few minutes we chatted of nothing in particular. Just as I was about to ask a few carefully formulated questions, Andre reappeared, this time with offers of refreshment. I gave up, accepted the suggestion of coffee and prepared for more trivial talk until it arrived. Once the fellow had finally gone, his employer gave me a look of sardonic amusement and said, "All right, Charles, what's really on your mind? You look as though you have a bag of snakes with you."

I thought he knew very well what I wanted to say, but was not about to help me with it. I took a breath and said, "Well, Herbert, I've been thinking I must have done something to offend you the last time I saw you. It's been more than two weeks and—"

"Seventeen days, precisely." He smiled, and I, remembering the occasion all too easily, began to blush. "So what gives you the idea," he continued, "that you offended me?"

I shifted in my chair as my scalp prickled and my cheeks flamed. "Well, nothing, really. It's just that we're… Things are different now, so I thought—"

He stared at me, his eyes suddenly cold "No. Things aren't different."

"But they are! How can you ignore what happened between us? Everything has changed."

"For you, perhaps." He smiled with compressed lips. "Look, Charles, for me, these entanglements are strictly peripheral. Don't expect anything. You'll see me when you see me. Feel free to seek other companions, if you want. Oh, and if you decide to get married, let me know, and I'll stand up with you, as your oldest friend. Now, drink up and go home. I have to finish this tonight."

So the rules for this would be the same as for our earlier collaboration and friendship. When he wanted my company, he would seek me out. Otherwise I was to leave him alone. I could take him on those terms, or not at all. They were the only terms he would offer.

~oOo~

If my affair with Alma had been a steadily flowing river, this one was a series of storms. Was it even an affair, or an aberration? I did not ask him, because I thought it would be presumptuous, or merely disingenuous. I could not be certain he would tell me the truth. Always he reserved that for himself alone.

In my cynical moments, I thought this was another of his experiments—after all, if he could by chemistry and force of will bring a corpse back to life, why not try, by that same will and with himself as the instrument, to achieve a different kind of transformation? But in truth, I think his deliberate revelation to me of his secret was a truce with his sexual self, the culmination of a war that began long ago. I knew he feared betrayal more than anything, and in me he had someone who would never betray him. The death of Robert Leavitt had shown him that.

There were a few happy surprises, as when he appeared on my doorstep late one evening. Sleepy and irritable, I had just awakened from an accidental armchair nap. Giving no reason for his unexpected arrival, he paced around my sitting room, carrying on at length about Medical School business discussed at the meeting he had just left. The gist seemed to be that the "antediluvian fossils" among his colleagues were conspiring to persecute him in some bureaucratic way. Finally, I had enough. As he passed before me on yet another circuit of the room, I took a chance and grasped his arm.

"Herbert," I said, "shut up." The startled look he gave me was sufficient reward for the annoyance I had endured.

"What—?"

I concluded this was to be a rhetorical question, and instead of replying, embraced him. I led him into my bedroom and propelled him toward the bed. He yielded to me, laughing, his fair hair falling back against the pillows. I loosened his necktie and opened his collar. With my lips I felt the strong pulse of life in his throat.

"Charles," he said, still laughing, "I didn't think you could be like this."

"Neither did I." I unfastened the remaining buttons of his shirt.

"I've corrupted you completely, then."

"So it seems."

I had to become accustomed to his hot and cold intervals. There were times when I resolved to take his mocking advice and seek other companions. But the other times made that impossible.

~o0o~

At a banquet to celebrate some momentous event at Miskatonic University, a quirk of place-cards put me nearly but not quite opposite him. I found it damnably difficult to attend to the conversation with those nearest me, for I was acutely aware of him, six feet away, chatting easily with the fellow next to him about some detail of university politics. After his initial nod of greeting, he had not so much as glanced my way.

I knew better than to stare at his face, so I watched his hands instead. I thought of what those hands had done with shining knives and hollow needles, with poisons and secret substances. I thought also of the things those hands had done to me. With my mind full of these images, I looked up for an instant and met his eyes. At that moment I felt completely naked, and knew I was starting to blush. To cover my confusion, I took an ill-considered gulp of wine and nearly choked. At least the subsequent coughing fit accounted for my red face.

He did not look at me again, except for a single, flaming glance, in which I saw a gleam of amusement. He knew what I was thinking, I'm sure he did. That glance was quite deliberate. But later, when we were alone, he said, "You must be more discreet, Charles."

In the entrance hall to his apartment was a large mirror. After we had hung up our coats, he took my arm and turned me to face the glass.

"What do you see?" he asked. "Tell me."

Formally attired as we were, our reflections made a pleasing tableau of black and white against the darkly glowing panelling of the hall. "I see two young professional men," I said. "They have obviously been out at some ceremonial occasion, to judge by their dress. The taller one is a specimen of the homely but sincere Yankee. The other... is by far the better looking."

He laughed. "Well, all right. I should have been more specific." He moved closer to me, put a hand on my shoulder and tilted his head. "What are these two fine fellows? To each other, I mean. What do you see now?"

"I see two friends." I had no idea what this was about. "Quite close friends, I would say."

"Close. Yes. And now?" He turned to face me and drew me toward him, so we stood sideways to the mirror, our bodies close against each other, our hands clasped by our sides.

Slowly, I said, "I see a pair of lovers, Herbert. Is that what you meant?"

He ignored my question. "Some would say they saw a pair of perverts, degenerates, criminals, even. The world does not want to share our happiness, should we be so careless as to reveal it."

~o0o~

Happiness? At close quarters, I perceived cracks in his façade, which until then had seemed flawless and impermeable.

His nightmares, for example.

"No! Let go!" Uttered in in the strangled way typical of those lost in dreams, followed by, "Finished." Followed by a sound like a laugh. And moments later, in a breathless rush of words, "Death to life and life to death, and back again and back again."

"What causes these nightmares, anyway?" In the muddled moments after one of these episodes he was susceptible to questions.

"If I knew, I could probably do something about them, but I'm used to them. I've had them most of my life. They're a little worse than usual now, but I'll survive."

I looked at him doubtfully. "How can you expect to survive, as you put it, with only two or three hours of continuous sleep a night? I think you should get some help with this."

"'Help.' I suppose you mean I should go and see one of those so-called psychoanalysts. You know I have no use for those fellows. As a matter of fact, you're the nearest thing to a remedy I've found so far. So don't fuss."

I suggested the usual domestic cures for night terrors, such as chamomile tea, warm milk, or a sprig of valerian under his pillow. "Do you think I haven't tried all that stuff?" he demanded. "Or at least the ones that aren't utter nonsense. Valerian, indeed! No, what I usually do is get up and find something to do in the lab. The night passes, eventually."

Many nights passed, including not a few when he made it clear he wanted to be alone, or at least not in my company. He did not hesitate to lacerate intimate moments with cutting remarks. In an uncongenial mood, he could assume and wear remoteness better than anyone I have ever known. "Thank you for gracing the evening, Charles. Forgive me, but would you mind showing yourself out? I'm going up now. Good night." And he would drain his glass, set it down and turn away without a backward glance.

~o0o~

Often, the only way I could share his company was in the night streets of Arkham. Insomnia and nightmares drove him out, and I went with him. By starlight, by moonlight, in wind, rain, even snow, we walked, methodically tracing the grid of streets. No convivial strolls, these, but silent marches without a destination, the only sound that of our footsteps, on cobbles, on concrete, on gravel. He spoke in terse expectorations of words, nothing like his usual eloquent phrasings. Anything I said was uniformly ignored.

I asked no questions. I knew he would not tell me the truth. Or perhaps I was afraid he would. He knew, of course, that I shared his guilt for the death of Robert Leavitt. I think he believed this ensured my loyalty. That was why he wasn't overly concerned about my hearing the words he spoke in the clutch of nightmare. And of course, he was right. It took only a little imagination on my part to hypothesize that Leavitt was not his only victim. But this did not drive me away from him; quite the opposite.

He revealed himself to me in stages, never seeking to persuade or to convince, merely saying, in effect, "This is what I am." Even when he showed himself to be a criminal, a murderer, the bond held firm. Behind his gated portals, behind the sculptured perfection of his face was—what? I knew so much about him, but I did not know him at all.

But by this time, I knew I had a unique role—to protect him from the world, and the world from him.

Until the fall of 1922, until Eleonora Desanges and a strange wanderer on the Aylesbury Pike, I was as happy as I have ever been. But something in me knew, even in the middle of happiness, that I was on a small, bright island in a dark ocean.

I found evidence that he had resumed secret and unorthodox experiments in the annexe to his hidden laboratory. I heard someone groaning in agony behind its locked door. And I did nothing. True, I heard the sounds only once. They were not repeated on subsequent visits. I used this to justify my inaction. What might have been different, I ask myself, if I had confronted him with this evidence?

But it was already too late.

~o0o~

I used to play the piano for him sometimes. I wasn't very good at it, but I persisted, for his sake, and for that of the piano, which had been his mother's.

Fumbling my way through a Chopin nocturne, I realized he was standing behind me. He put his hand on my shoulder, and after a moment slid it inside my loosened collar.

"I can feel you playing," he murmured. "Feeling and hearing the music at the same time—not an experience one would have in the concert hall."

It was all I could do not to stop playing then and there, but I made myself hold the final chord for the required number of beats. As I lifted my hands off the keys and stood, he stepped away.

"I'm hungry," he said, and headed for the kitchen.

Food was the last thing on my mind, but I followed him and watched as he chopped vegetables and cracked eggs for a frittata.

"Toast," he said. "Yes, we definitely need toast to sop up the juices." He glanced at me. "If you want to be helpful, perhaps you could slice some bread."

I took the knife he indicated and proceeded to saw at the loaf, wishing my lack of expertise was less evident. By this time, the aroma of coffee had permeated the room. He seemed cheerful, perhaps in response to the cozy domestic scene.

"This is very pleasant, isn't it?" he said, as if he had read my mind. "Think of the two of us, living here together. You would have your own room, of course, and a place to keep all those tomes of yours. And you could abuse my piano whenever it suited you." He gave me a swift look whose piercing quality belied the lightness of his tone. "Would you have liked that, Charles?"

My knife slipped on "have liked," and cut me. I felt the blade slice painlessly into the palm of my left hand. "Yes, I would... have liked it. But I think maybe you—" By this time, blood was welling from the wound. I looked at it, not sure what to do. He came over and took my hand.

"What *have* you done to yourself?" he said, mingled exasperation and amusement in his eyes. Then he picked up the knife and drew it across the palm of his left hand. Seizing mine, he pressed our palms tightly together. Shocked and startled, I nevertheless instinctively interlaced my fingers with his. He gazed into my eyes as our mingled blood dripped onto the floor.

"Now we're brothers," he said, "as well as... whatever else we are. Come along and I'll bandage us up."

In the bathroom, he wrapped a length of gauze around his hand and washed my wound with soap and water. He applied something stinging from a bottle and bandaged it neatly. "There you are," he said, smiling. "Good as new, or nearly." Then he dealt with the cut on his hand just as swiftly. "Now, back to the kitchen. Never keep a frittata waiting."

My hand throbbed, but not painfully. The pain I felt had a different locus. To the question, "Why did he do that?" my mind gave no answer. But my heart said, "He wanted something of you, to keep. Something of your essence. Because he knows it's ending. Because he's preparing to end it."

I did not, then, imagine the horror of that ending.

ENOUGH * END * FINIS

A VISIT TO LUXOR

Who he was, none could tell, but he was of the old native blood and looked like a Pharaoh. The fellahin knelt when they saw him, yet could not say why.

H.P. Lovecraft "Nyarlathotep"

January 23, 1935.

The Doctor and I, we are West of Suez now. We stayed for a few days in Cairo, Egypt and saw the Pyramids and the Great Sphinx. I had a ride on a camel. The camel did not like me, but I did not fall off, and now I have been on a Ship of the Desert as well as many ships on the ocean.

Four days ago, we took a train to this place—Luxor, the Winter Palace Hotel. A very nice hotel; I can't complain about anything. The next day we saw temples and stone statues and pillars. Many big pillars. Luxor Temple and Karnak Temple. Big statues of Pharaoh Ramses the Second. Today I am writing this down, while the Doctor is resting. His ankle is better now, but not enough so he can walk around and see more sights. Tomorrow we are taking a boat to Alexandria, and then we will sail to Marseille.

~oOo~

Now I will write about yesterday, while I remember it all. The Doctor, he says it's important for my memory to write things down so I can think about them later. Ever since he saved my life in the Great War, he has been helping me get better at thinking. I am not good at writing things, but I will try to do it like I am telling a story.

"We are going to the West Bank today," the Doctor said at breakfast. "That's where the tombs are—kings' tombs, nobles' tombs, and the tombs of the workers who built the tombs."

"Are they full of dead bodies?"

"From what I've read, no. The bodies—mummies, of course—have mostly been removed, one way or another."

I did not know why the Doctor wanted to see empty tombs. Dead bodies, even mummies, perhaps he might find those interesting, but if there weren't any, then why? Ever since we left Bellefleur Island, he has been "searching for my true path in life," he says—and that has certainly taken us to some strange places—so maybe looking at tombs is part of that search. He doesn't explain these things to me, of course. "You do not need to burden your brain with subtleties, Andre." That's what he says, but my brain is burdened anyway. Thinking about this kept me busy until we finished breakfast and went out.

We strolled down to the corniche and waited with other tourists for a boat to the West Bank. It took quite a while before the boat had enough passengers to make the boatman happy. Then we zigged and zagged slowly across the Nile River, with the big white sail pushing us along. The river was wide and quiet, but there was a current, so the man sailing the boat had to know what he was doing to get us to the dock on the other side.

We had barely got off the boat when a man came over like he was looking for us. He was dressed like most Egyptian men, in loose clothes that look like extra-long nightshirts, and a turban. "Valley of the Kings, gentlemen?" he said. "Taxi and deluxe tour, this way." He held out his hand to the doctor. "I am Mahmoud, the best guide on the West Bank."

I couldn't figure out whether he really knew us or just thought if he acted that way, the Doctor would hire him. And he did. No one asked me, but I thought it was just as well I had my pistol in my pocket. There was a sign in our hotel warning about robbers and pickpockets.

We got into Mahmoud's taxi, and he drove us past green fields and palm trees. Then we started to go uphill, and there were no plants at all—just rocks and dust. The road narrowed to a path into rocky hills, and Mahmoud stopped the car. A signpost said "This Way to Tombs."

"All right, gentlemen," said Mahmoud, opening the car door. "First the Valley of the Kings, and then the Tombs of the Nobles."

"What is that mountain?" asked the Doctor, looking up past the other tourists, who I figured were heading to the tombs.

I looked up too, at a high hill (well, maybe some people would call it a mountain) behind the Kings' Valley. It was made of layers of loose rocks with solid rocks in between that were probably cliffs. The top came to a point a long way from us. I hoped the Doctor was not thinking of climbing it.

"That is el-Qurn, which means 'the horn,'" said Mahmoud. "You see it is shaped like a pyramid. The tomb-builders thought it was the home of the goddess Meretseger, who protected the tombs from robbers. Of course, the men who built the tombs sometimes robbed them. The goddess punished them for that, but she would forgive and cure the ones who were sorry and prayed to her."

"Is there a path to the top?" asked the Doctor. "I would like to climb it. The view from there must be spectacular."

"Oh yes, there is a path," Mahmoud said. "Many paths, for those who know them, but for travellers such as you, there are two paths."

"There are always two paths," said the Doctor, with a little laugh. "Which would you recommend?"

"The one that starts at the tomb-workers' village by Deir el-Medineh, where the archaeologists are working, is by far the best. I will show you where it is. There is a shrine to Meretseger near the top."

"That is interesting," said the Doctor, and I told my feet to get ready for a hard day.

~o0o~

Well, we did a lot of walking. My feet still feel it, and the Doctor's leg, of course. First, the Kings' Valley, where we went in and out of many tombs. There were no kings in any of them, just people looking at the pictures painted on the walls—of kings and queens and gods with animal heads, standing or sitting very straight holding things in their hands or walking over their enemies. Lots of *hiéroglyphes*—a kind of writing like little pictures—telling who they were and what they did, but I couldn't read it. Then we followed Mahmoud along more dusty roads and found ourselves in a village. Roosters crowed, goats baaed, and children came running over to look at us.

"Are the tombs of the nobles nearby?" I asked. If we were going to climb that mountain (it was starting to look like one now, instead of just a hill), we had better get going soon. The day was getting warmer too.

"They are all around you," said Mahmoud, spreading his arms out. "These people live among the tombs. Inside them, even. Each tomb has its guardian. They will show you. But look out for snakes. They live here too."

That was not something I wanted to hear.

The guardians did show us their tombs, for a fee—not much, but each one held out a hand, and we put money in it. The children followed us and held out their hands too. The Doctor gave each of them a coin.

These tombs were smaller than the ones for the kings, but just as full of pictures. They showed people doing things like fishing and working in fields, or having parties and dancing. They were more interesting than the kings' tombs, but after three or four I was starting to think I had seen enough. And I was tired of watching for snakes. *Assez vu. Allons-y!* But I didn't say it.

We had just come out of a narrow passageway into the sun, when I noticed a couple of men following us. After a while they were gone, but the children gathered around us again, chattering and smiling. They reminded me of my little daughter, so far away. The Doctor and I put more coins in their little hands and they ran off.

An old woman was selling food from her house, and we bought some spicy beans and vegetables rolled up in pieces of thin bread, cups of mint tea, and dates to take with us. While we ate, Mahmoud found someone who sold us a couple of rusty canteens full of water. I hoped it would be enough for our climb and not make us sick.

We followed Mahmoud to another dusty path that went along the lower parts of the hill we were about to climb. After a while we came to a place where people were working, both Egyptians and Europeans. There were tents and piles of dirt and, of course, lots of rocks.

"Those people are archaeologists from France, doing an excavation of the tomb-workers' village." Mahmoud waved at them and they waved back. I took special notice of the place; if we got into some kind of trouble, they might be able to help.

We came to a spot where another path started, this time going uphill. "This is the way to the peak of el-Qurn," said Mahmoud. " It should take you no more than two hours each way. Do you still want to go there?"

Well, I did not, but it was the Doctor's idea, so I waited for him to say.

"Yes, of course. But you aren't coming with us?"

"I am sorry, but no. I have another group I must meet at the ferryboat. Make sure you stay on this path. It is the widest, with signposts that say 'To Summit.' There are many other paths, small ones. Do not turn off on any of them, because they will not take you to where you wish to go. And when you return, Sirs, I will see you in the village by the Tombs of the Nobles." He looked quickly toward the place where the archaeologists were working, and then back at us, and smiled. I wondered what that smile meant.

"All right," said the Doctor. "Well, Andre, let's get going."

"One more thing, Sirs! Meretseger, the goddess of the mountain, is sometimes in the form of a cobra. So be careful!"

"Are there really cobras here?" I wasn't sure if he was trying to be funny with us.

"Yes, sometimes. Most of the time they stay where there are things they can catch and eat—rats or birds. But sometimes people see them on the mountain."

~oOo~

Dust. And grit and pebbles and rolling rocks. Sun glaring back from the grey-white dust, and my feet roasting in their shoes, and my white trouser cuffs turning brown. Why brown, when the dust looked white? That was what I thought while I put one foot in front of the other.

The path wasn't too steep, because it went across the side of the mountain, back and forth, with slopes of sand and gravel above and below. The tricky parts were the stone cliffs, where we had to use our hands to climb. All the climbing made me hot.

After an hour or so we stopped for a rest and a drink of water. I figured I needed to know more about why we had to do all this climbing. The Doctor does not always tell me everything, but it does not hurt to ask. "Is this why we came to Luxor, Doctor? To climb up here?"

He put the top back on his canteen. "Not really, but I thought since we were in Egypt, it was a good opportunity to see this place. The temples and tombs are quite famous. And when I saw el-Qurn, standing like a pyramid over the necropolis, something said to me, 'Go there.'"

I was still thinking about this when he started talking again.

"Do you remember Captain Liadov?"

"Of course! How could I forget him? He was a very good man."

"And a learned one," said the Doctor. "On our voyage with him, he and I had many conversations. It turned out he was acquainted with one of my old professors. He told me they met here in Luxor once, many years ago." He picked up a rock and threw it down the slope, watching as it landed a long way down and slid to a stop. "They came to a congress, a meeting of scholars who wanted to share their knowledge in the pursuit of truths and revelations." He turned back to me and smiled. "Some of these scholars were eccentrics. Lunatics, even. But I wanted to visit the place where they met."

"Up here, on this hill?"

"No, of course not! I don't know exactly where they met, which is why I thought it would be useful to see the whole place at once, from up here. Come along, Andre."

He had not really told me anything. Maybe all he wanted was to see the view from the top. Why not?

We came to what I hoped was the last really steep part, where I had to hold on to sticking-out pieces of rock with my hands while I found places to put my feet. Halfway up, my canteen slipped off my shoulder and fell to the bottom, so I had to climb back down and get it, and then back up again. By that time, the Doctor was way ahead of me and I did not see him until I went around another turn in the path. There he was, standing in front of a place where a doorway and some picture-writing had been carved into the rocks around what looked like a cave.

He was holding his hands up in front of him, like the people in those tomb-pictures, and he was talking, but not to me. Then he bowed down, as though he was going to touch the ground, and I saw it—a cobra, coiled but with its head raised. Only a few feet from him.

"Doctor! Watch out!" I pulled my pistol out of my pocket and fired at the snake. The bullet hit the rock with a cracking sound. Dust flew up.

"Andre! Why the devil did you do that?"

The snake was gone. I went over to the spot where I saw it, but there was nothing.

"There was a cobra! Right there! I thought it was going to spit at you."

"Egyptian cobras don't spit their venom. But it's possible that wasn't a cobra, but the goddess. This place is her shrine."

This couldn't be caused by not enough good air to breathe, like on really high mountains. It was something else. Sometimes the Doctor has these fits of *bizarrerie*, or maybe craziness, when he says and does things that don't make sense. I never know what to say to him then, and now I did not want to waste any time.

"Come on, Doctor, let's keep going. We are not at the top yet, and soon we will have to go back."

When we finally got to the top of the hill, the sun was going down all red behind brown hills far away. To the east, the river reflected light back toward us, but the valley was in the shadow. Yes, it was a beautiful sight, but the Doctor and I did not have time to stand and look at it. I didn't have an electric torch with me. The last thing I wanted was to blunder around up here in the dark.

"How quiet it is!" he said, staring out over the land. "I can feel the power of this place, rising like a mist from all the tombs and temples. And there's something else too, a kind of...

tension between forces, between light and darkness, change and eternity." He moved his arm like he was opening a curtain.

Well, for sure I did not want him to start talking like that again. "Doctor, listen—we'd better get going now, back down. It'll be dark soon, and we don't want to get lost." I was thinking I should have said right from the start that we should come back early the next morning to do this climb, if he wanted it so much. But it was too late for that now.

The Doctor just stood there, feeling whatever it was he felt. I was about to say again that we had to go, when he sighed. "You're right, Andre. Let's go, then."

Going down was harder than climbing up, harder to see and easier to slip. The steep places were specially tricky. We had just climbed down the second one (and I was trying to remember if there was one more), when I heard the Doctor, who was ahead of me again, trip over something and swear.

I rushed to help him get back on his feet. He groaned and nearly fell down again. "I've done something to my ankle— just a sprain, I hope."

He hobbled over to a rock and sat down to feel over the ankle. "Not broken, fortunately, but I don't think I can walk properly. I'll need your help."

He strapped up the ankle with his necktie, and after some testing, we found he could walk slowly, with his arm over my shoulders. It's a good thing, sometimes, that I am a short man.

"You know, Doctor," I said, "those rocks that tripped you weren't on the path when we came up. Either someone put them there after we went by, or we're on the wrong path."

Before he could answer, I heard running feet—thud, thud, thud—and felt hands grab my arms. Four men, one with a rifle. One of them tied my hands behind my back and stuck his hands in my pockets. He pulled out my pistol, showed it to the others and said something that made them laugh. Then they started to hustle us along, but the Doctor almost fell down again. A couple of them grabbed his arms and held him up. It did not help at all that neither one of us could understand their language or talk to them.

We didn't go back down the way we went up. These men knew other ways and other paths. A lot sooner than I expected, we were back in the village by the nobles' tombs, or another one that looked just like it, except now there weren't any chickens or children running around, or people selling food and souvenirs. Dim lights shone through some of the doorways.

Someone pulled aside a piece of leather that hung in a doorway and pushed us inside. The place looked like a tomb, but one that never got shown to tourists. The ceiling was covered in soot. There was a table and a couple of benches. A lamp hung over the table, and on one of the benches sat "the best guide on the West Bank," Mahmoud. He looked like he wanted to be somewhere else.

"Good evening, gentlemen," he said, with a silly smile. "My apologies."

I was about to tell him what I thought about that, when the man with the rifle said something to him, short and sharp. "He wants to know where these came from," Mahmoud said, pointing to a little pile of gold coins on the table.

All I could do was shake my head, but the Doctor said, "Those coins? I have no idea. They are gold? I have never seen them before."

"He says you gave them to the children," said Mahmoud. "When you were here earlier today."

"We gave them coins, certainly," said the Doctor, "but they were ordinary small denominations — copper and bronze. I have more just like them in my pockets. I can show you if you free my hands." I nodded to show it was the same for me.

Mahmoud must have translated, but no one untied us. They searched our pockets again, more carefully than on the mountain path. They took out our wallets and watches, the Doctor's notebook and all the coins they could find. There were no gold ones; anyone could see that.

Everyone started talking at once, including Mahmoud. A couple of times he looked at us, rolled his eyes and spread out his hands like he was saying, "What can I do?" Me, I was wondering what he had already done to get us into this mess.

The arguing got louder, everyone shouting, sometimes pointing at us. Mahmoud seemed to be trying to convince them about something, and even though I couldn't guess what it was, I had a bad feeling. The leader pointed at us again and said something that sounded like an order. Everyone got quiet. Then two of the men grabbed our arms and started to pull us toward the door.

Just then, someone yanked the covering from the doorway and came in. Another man, dressed Egyptian style, but taller than everyone else; he had to duck to get inside.

The men who had been searching us backed away from him, and even the leader looked nervous. The new man said something in a quiet voice. Right away, the ropes around our wrists were untied, and after another couple of orders, our watches and other things were given back. Even my pistol. The villagers' leader pointed to the gold coins and started saying something to the tall man, but he just waved his hand—obviously meaning, "Enough out of you!"

"Gentlemen, this has been a mistake," he said, in perfectly good English, with no more accent than I have. "Please forgive these men for the way they have treated you."

"The mistake appears to concern those gold coins," said the Doctor. "Since they are not ours, they must belong to these people. And we are unharmed, apart from a twisted ankle due to my own clumsiness."

Mahmoud must have translated that, because the villagers' leader looked at the Doctor, nodded and almost smiled.

The tall man did smile. "You are generous. But then, perhaps you can afford to be. I live nearby. I hope you will accept my hospitality for the night." It came to me then that he was not one of the people of the village. They looked ordinary, if you know what I mean. But him—even though he was dressed like them, he wore his clothes like a costume.

He told someone to fetch a donkey so the Doctor would not have to walk. When we got to what I thought was the place where we left the taxi that morning (and how long ago that seemed now!), there was a car sitting there, waiting for us. I know all about cars, and I knew I'd never seen one like this. It had wheels and running boards and other things you see on a car, but it also had wings. Things that looked like wings, anyway. The tall man opened doors and I helped the Doctor climb in. The man with the donkey made a sign with his right hand, stretching out his fingers—at our new friend? at the car? He hopped on his donkey and galloped away.

That car made no noise at all. It took a while before I could tell we were moving; and another strange thing—there were no bumps in the road, even though I remembered thinking how rough it was on the trip in Mahmoud's taxi that morning. And then I realized there were no headlights, just a kind of reddish glow that didn't light up the road—if there was one. I looked behind, but all I could see was blue and purple sparks following us.

A few minutes after we got in the car, we were getting out, in a place paved with flat stones and surrounded by cliffs, just like some of the tombs we had visited in the Valley of the Kings.

"Come this way," our host said. He had a light of some sort in his hand—the same reddish glow the car made. That light was all we could see, so we followed it to a doorway cut in the rock.

Going in felt like being swallowed up. Inside, it was dim and quiet. Two man-size statues stood on either side of a wooden door. Our host went ahead of us and a gold-coloured light grew brighter, until I could see floors made of black and white stone in squares, and rugs, tables and couches. On one table stood a thing made of glass and metal that reminded me of things in the Doctor's laboratory, back in Arkham. The light seemed to come from it. On the walls were pictures and writing just like the ones in the tombs we had visited. I could not see any windows, and the place smelled like dust and stone.

I wanted to leave, but instead I helped the Doctor to one of the couches. On a table nearby, cups of tea and plates of food sent up steam and a good smell that made my stomach rumble.

"Well, Doctor Francis Dexter," said our host, sitting down in an armchair and smiling like someone who is running the show, "once known as Herbert West—this mishap aside, how are you and Mr. Boudreau enjoying your visit to Egypt?"

He knew our names! Even the Doctor's old name! Who was this man? His face reminded me of the statues of Pharaoh Ramses in the Luxor temple—the same kind of nose, and lips that looked like they had secrets behind them. He even had a beard trimmed and shaped to look a bit like the Pharaoh's fake one.

The Doctor looked bothered. "I'm sorry, but we haven't been properly introduced. I must have missed hearing your name in all the confusion back there."

"My name does not matter," said the man. "But to see the son of Lawrence Dexter sitting here in my house, more than sixty years after the Congress of Luxor—that is something."

"You know of Lawrence Dexter?" The Doctor leaned forward.

"Not only *of* him; I knew him. And Quarrington, Liadov, all of them. The Congress met here, in my house. As near as may be to the Royal Necropolis."

"But how did you recognize me?"

"There is a resemblance. But even without it, I would have known you. Precisely how does not matter. What does is this—why did you give gold coins to the children of Qurna?"

"I did not give them gold coins," said the Doctor, "only bronze and copper ones, like these." He put his hand in his pocket and brought out a few coins, their metal dull in the lamplight.

"You saw the pile of gold coins they had there. The children said they got them from you. There is only one way that could have happened." The man looked steadily at the Doctor as he spoke.

"I know nothing about that."

"Do not deny your abilities. But I wonder why you use them for such cheap tricks."

I was so hungry I forgot to be polite and wait until our host invited us to eat. I reached out and took from the plate nearest to me a piece of thin, flat bread and some bits of roasted meat. It was delicious, but as I chewed, it began to taste like electricity, sharp and dangerous. I could not spit it out, so I swallowed quickly, washing it down with tea.

"Why did you climb Ta Dehent?" asked the man. "Or el-Qurn, as it is now called."

"Why not?" said the Doctor. "I wanted to see the view from the top." He was looking at the man, and I guess he did not realize that something strange was happening to me.

"And is that all you saw?" The man stared back at the Doctor; it was like they were fencing with their eyes.

The light got brighter, glaring and hurting me. The painted walls began to spin, the pictures whirling past me. The tall man and the Doctor did not notice. They just sat and kept talking. I could see them through the lights and colours, but when I put my hand out toward the Doctor, I could not touch him. It was like he was far away and I was in two places at once.

The Doctor sat up straight and looked hard at the man. "I saw the Goddess Meretseger. She spoke to me from the small wind that whispered among the stones of her mountain. Is that what you wanted to know?"

Our host nodded. "I suspected something of the sort. I am aware that the land of the dead is not unknown to you. But Meretseger is a dead goddess. Her worship ceased when the royal tombs were abandoned, and the diggers of the present day have not revived it. 'She who loves silence' has been left to silence. And she has never had power in the greater world."

"What of it?" said the Doctor, and I could hear a smile in his voice. "I stood in her place today and I spoke to her. I felt her presence, and I believe she offered me peace and protection."

"Peace! You have much to learn, Doctor Dexter. But tonight you are my guest. Please, eat and drink, as your servant has already." The tall man looked at me and started to laugh.

No, Doctor, don't do it! Don't touch that food! It's poison! But I couldn't make my tongue work to say the words.

"Thank you, but we will not stay." The Doctor's voice was clear and firm. He turned to me. "Andre, let's go." At least he could see me, but did he know I could not move?

The Doctor stood up. It hurt him to do it, I could tell. I wanted to help him, but I was frozen. And between me and him were those rooms and rooms painted with pictures and filled with stabbing light.

The man without a name looked angry—an angry pharaoh. He was even taller now, with a high crown on his head and gold at his throat and wrists. The Doctor, in his dusty, wrinkled linen suit looked small and weak compared to him.

"You do not realize what perils await you, Doctor Dexter. If you accept my protection, you will be safe, and as my servant you will achieve all you desire. If you refuse, you go into the unknown."

"Nevertheless, I choose to leave this place," said the Doctor. "And my friend Mr. Boudreau will go with me. You will release him immediately from the artifice you have worked upon him."

"You dare to command me in my own dwelling?" The pharaoh's eyes blazed with rage. He made circling movements with his hands and chanted words I could not understand.

The Doctor stepped back as though he felt a hot fire, and raised his hands in front of him, like when he was by the shrine on the mountain. "Lady Meretseger!" he cried. "I beg of you — free us from this peril. I refuse his invitation and utterly reject his temptations."

And then I saw it again — a cobra, but huge this time, and with a woman's body, standing behind the Doctor. She raised her arms. The air sang in my ears, a high, steady note, and there was a loud crack, as though a huge sheet of glass broke in two.

I could move again! The flashing lights and whirling pictures were gone. I was in the same room as the Doctor, but now the man without a name was imprisoned in himself. Linen cloths wrapped him round, and his arms were bent over his chest. In his hands were the Crook and Flail, but he could not move. Only his eyes were alive, glowing like hot copper. His voice spoke as though from far away.

"Go, then, Francis Dexter, under the protection of the Lady of Silence. For my purposes, you have shown yourself to be an empty vessel. I think I would have had more success with Herbert West. But remember, she may turn on you in the end and spit you blind for your sins."

"I know that," said the Doctor. "I accept it. Goodbye to you."

"One more thing — I will outlast you, and some day another of your blood will come to me here. Then we shall have a different ending."

The light faded and we found ourselves in total darkness. I reached out my arms, and the Doctor must have done the same, because we bumped each other.

"You don't happen to have a torch, do you, Andre? No, of course not; I would have seen it when those men searched our pockets."

I was busy searching my pockets, and I was lucky. "Just a minute, Doctor." I fumbled with the box of matches I had put in my trousers pocket only that morning at our hotel. "This is better than nothing," I said, and struck one.

It wasn't much better than nothing, because the head fell off and the flame went out before it could get going. I tried another one, and this time we could barely see for a few seconds.

We were in an empty room that looked just like a tomb. The floor was plain stone, not black and white. No furniture, no food, no apparatus, and no Pharaoh, except for a painted one on the wall, staring at us. I saw him only for a second, and I did not want to see any more.

I lit another match. "There's a passage over there," said the Doctor, and we shuffled toward it, holding hands like a couple of scared kids. Match number four lit up the two statues I remembered from when we came in, but the wooden door was gone.

We got out of there so fast it was as though the statues kicked us out, and found ourselves at the foot of a rocky cliff. No doorway, no car, only rocks.

"Let's go, Andre, quickly. I don't know how long the goddess's spell will hold."

Together, we hobble-ran as fast as we could, following narrow stony paths in the dark. The Doctor's ankle must have hurt a lot, but he made himself keep going. Or maybe that goddess was still helping us.

Finally, we came to a road. A car stood there, a regular car, not the strange one that took us to the stranger's house. Someone got out and flashed a pocket torch at us. I reached for my pistol.

Whoever it was put up his hands and shone the light on himself, to show he wasn't armed, or maybe as a greeting. It was Mahmoud the guide. "There you are, gentlemen!"

"Mahmoud! I didn't expect to see you again." I could tell the Doctor was just as surprised as I was.

"I am waiting for you gentlemen, just in case. How did you get away?"

"We declined his offer of hospitality," said the Doctor.

"Good! That's very good!" He looked back and forth at the two of us, as though making sure we were the same people who hired him earlier.

"Who is that man?" asked the Doctor.

"He has many names," said Mahmoud. "Some call him *Alyad Alyumnaa*. That means 'the right-handed one.' Others say he's the Black Pharaoh. He has lived here a very long time and knows everything. Sometimes he goes away, but always he comes back. The people of the village do what he tells them. The tombs are their business, you see. They show them to people like you and sell things they find there or make—antiquities, you know."

"You mean they steal things from the tombs and sell fakes." I forgot to be polite.

"If you say so. But I, Mahmoud, I must work with them if I want to keep my business."

"So that's why you told them which path we took up the mountain," I said. "And they put rocks on it so we would fall over them coming back in the dark, in that place where they jumped us."

"They thought you had much gold. That's all they wanted. But when *he* came and took you away, I did not think I would see you again. You would be called 'lost,' like other travellers who went with him. The police would say you had been killed by robbers. The village men would say you had fallen down a tomb no one knew was there. But everyone would know you went with *him* and did not come back."

"Well, we did come back," said the Doctor. "And now we want only to go to our hotel."

"Of course! There is a boat waiting. I made sure."

"Why? Why are you helping us now, when you helped them rob us before?" I had to ask this and get an answer before I would trust him again.

"You paid me to show you the West Bank. I must finish my job. Mahmoud at your service," he said, bowing and opening the taxi door.

There was a boat waiting, just like he said. Before we climbed aboard, the Doctor handed Mahmoud a handful of coins. "Thank you for waiting for us, Mahmoud."

~o0o~

Later, sitting down to a very late supper at our hotel, the Doctor said,

"It's a good thing you didn't eat or drink any more than you did, and I nothing at all. That must be his way of rendering his victims helpless."

I stopped with a spoon halfway to my mouth. "He is that bad?"

"Yes. Yes, I think he is."

"But who is he?"

"An emissary of an ancient and evil entity, who is spoken of with dread by students of the occult. Refusing his offers was crucial, because once enmeshed with him, one is doomed. We were lucky, Andre. This time."

"And those coins—what about them? Were they really gold?

"It appears so," said the Doctor, busy with his knife and fork and not looking at me.

"But we didn't have any gold coins. I didn't, I know that."

"Neither did I." He took a drink of wine and smiled at me the way he does when he's finished talking about something. But I wasn't ready to give up. I put down my spoon and looked right at him.

"Doctor, did you make those coins turn into gold?"

"Not consciously, Andre. If they did, it was not by any intention of mine. Those children and the other people of the village, they were lucky, that's all."

"And Mahmoud—was he lucky too?"

"Maybe yes, maybe no." He held up his palms. "It's out of my hands. But consider this: that name Mahmoud said—the one that means 'the right-handed one' in Arabic—it may be rendered as 'Dexter.'"

ONE OF THE FOURTEEN

At the Blind Beggar

"…chloroform or ether?"

Someone was speaking. To me. I opened an eye and directed it toward the voice. The day had been more chaotic than usual, and I must have dozed off over my pint of bitter.

"Excuse me," I said to the as yet unknown owner of the inquiring voice. "I didn't hear your question."

"My apologies." The speaker was a man sitting at the next table. "I didn't mean to interrupt your…"

"Nap. I nodded off. Thank you for waking me up before our publican decided I had overindulged."

In the mellow light, the man who had spoken to me appeared a perfectly ordinary, nondescript sort, a little younger than I. His accent, however, was no form of London English, but marked his place of origin as the American continent.

"You asked me something a minute ago—about ether, was it?" How had he identified me as a physician? I had certainly not been using ether today, not that I ever did. The clinic had been full of children and anxious mothers.

"Yes," the fellow said. "I hoped you could tell me something about anaesthetics. Er—may I join you?"

Since we were now engaged in conversation, that was a good idea. "All right. Please do." I drew my glass nearer to make room for his.

In the moments it took him to cover the short distance between us, I collected a few details of his appearance—a thin, pale, anxious face whose proportions were a little odd. Sunken forehead, lumpen nose, weak chin. In this melted candle of a face, a pair of dark eyes displayed a nervous intelligence. I thought I detected a limp in his gait, but could not be sure.

"I'm Edwin Seale," he said, extending a hand.

"Francis Dexter." I felt a distinct reluctance to reciprocate the handshake—I, whose profession demanded a total abnegation of squeamishness. And there was no apparent reason for it. Seale's grasp felt perfectly ordinary, no stronger or weaker than one would expect, nor held longer than was appropriate.

"*Doctor* Dexter, surely?"

There was no point in denying it. "Yes, but I don't think we've met before." I had never seen Edwin Seale at the Antonescu Clinic, but perhaps he worked nearby.

"No, we haven't met," Seale said, his voice softening. "Until now. I've seen you at the Hospital, though. By the way, would you mind if we switched chairs? I hear better on this side." He touched his right ear.

Shifting from a chair into which one has settled to a different if identical one is annoying, but I refrained from objecting.

"Do you work at the Hospital?" I asked, once the chair-shifting business was finished.

"No, I don't work there." A quick smile revealed long, narrow teeth. "People say you're a surgeon."

"Not quite. I occasionally do surgeries. So that's why you asked about anaesthetics?"

"Yes. I was wondering what you thought about ether versus chloroform." He looked at me steadily. "Which is better?"

"It depends." His glass, like mine, was empty. "Look, can I buy you another?"

"Thanks."

En route to the bar, I wondered why Seale had been watching me. I preferred to observe while remaining unobserved. But perhaps he wanted only a companion over a drink or two as the afternoon became evening—especially if the companion would pay for said drinks.

"I don't think you're from around here," I said, returning with fresh pints. "Any more than I am."

"You're right." He took a careful sip, as though he thought I might have doctored the ale.

"American?"

"Canadian."

Of course. His accent was familiar; I had heard it all the time in the hospitals and camps of the Great War.

"I see. Well, back to your question—chloroform or ether? It's not really an either-or. Here in England, ether is always the second choice. Its anaesthetic qualities are fairly good, but it's been superseded by chloroform. The problem with that is it must be administered with extreme skill and attention to avoid overdose and death."

Seale offered a minimal smile. "Of course, it's—it must be awkward when death arrives early to the party."

"Most people find death something more than awkward."

"Sometimes it's unwelcome. Sometimes invited." He took a gulp of ale. "It depends, surely?"

"Weren't we speaking of surgery, though?" I was getting tired of this pointless conversation with an ignorant stranger, but reminded myself that willingness and patience were desirable virtues. "Surgery is intended to repair, to heal," I said. "Death is always unwelcome at that party." Again, I remembered the War. *What a party that was, with Death the happy host, and I the cook and waiter.*

"Repair or reveal?"

What was he getting at? "Reveal? As in…?"

"As in discover. Find the ultimate truth."

"Most surgeries aren't occasions for research, Seale. It's always good to learn better techniques, but the main thing is to help the patient."

Unless the patient is an experimental subject, of course.

Seale droned on while my mind dealt with things best forgotten. "Excuse me; I missed that last bit."

"I was just saying—I'll bet all patients aren't the same. Maybe some are more patient than others?" He smiled again, making me wish he wouldn't. His dark brown eyes regarded me without blinking. "I'm for another," he said. "You?"

I nodded. It seemed he had not, after all, been expecting me to finance his drinks.

Picking up our empty glasses, he made for the bar. His gait, I now saw, was distinctly uneven, not from drink but from a slight limp. Seeing his face full-on as he returned showed me something else. His ears didn't match. Not only was the left lower than the right, they looked quite different. The one on the right side of his head was small and rounded, like a squirrel's, but the left was a large, awkward projection that looked like it had been carelessly fashioned from pastry and grafted into place. The effect was unsettling, giving Seale's countenance a disturbing asymmetry.

A thought came to me. A terrible thought.

"Were you in the War?" I asked, after thanking him for the ale.

"The War." He settled down with a hint of a sigh. "Oh yes, I was in it, and it was in me. Still is." He shook his head.

"Would you like to tell me about it? I'm in no rush." *If I told you my version of the War, I doubt you'd believe it. Or maybe you would?*

A look of gratitude spread over Seale's features. What had I set myself up for? I prepared for a long and possibly tedious evening. But I had to know the truth.

No flood followed, of reminiscences and anecdotes. Seale just sat there, looking puzzled. Against my better judgment, I produced a nudge.

"You were in the Canadian Expeditionary Force? Infantry?"

He drew in a breath and held it for a moment. "I suppose so. Look, I have this." Reaching into a pocket, he drew out a small object and passed it to me.

A Military Cross, the silver shiny with much handling, the ribbon crumpled and grubby. On the reverse, the year 1918 was engraved on the lower arm.

I passed it back. "You were an officer?"

"Mhm, I suppose so." He ran his thumb over the medal and returned it to his pocket.

I tried another angle. "When did you receive this medal?"

Again a silence, longer this time. I drank some ale and waited.

"Pa… Pass…"

"Passchendaele?"

"That was the one. Had to be."

The Battle of Passchendaele had occurred in 1917. I remembered some of its casualties all too well. The date on the medal was 1918. "Are you sure?"

"Aah, they were all the same, the battles. Run out through mud, run back through blood. All the same."

"Can you remember the occasion? That they gave you the medal for?"

"There were lots of occasions. Killing. That's what I got it for."

He seemed to expect a response, staring at me with his hands clasped around his glass.

"That's how it is in wartime, isn't it? How long did you serve?"

"Until they threw me out." He emitted a sound like a small, muffled machine-gun. I assumed it was a laugh. "I was a lot better at it the second time—after I got out of the hospital."

"You were wounded?"

"They didn't put you in hospital for nothing. I just about died, I guess. Don't remember much about it."

"Which hospital were you in, can you remember that?" The answer to this question was disproportionally important to me. *Those ears.*

Seale sat and thought for a long moment, during which I realized it was full dark beyond the windows.

"It was a General Hospital," he said. "Right far away from the front. Now, what was the name of the place? Apples, Stapples, something like that?"

"Étaples." I breathed the word. I wasn't sure I wanted him to recognize it, but his good ear was good enough.

"Yes. Étaples, that was it. The Number One General Hospital." He gave me a keen look from narrowed eyes. "How'd you guess? Were *you* there?"

You've known this was likely to happen sooner or later.

I couldn't lie to him. "Yes. Yes, I was there. Medical Officer. How much do you remember about your time at the Number One? When was it, exactly? During Passchendaele?"

He snorted a laugh. "I don't remember anything exactly. It's all red, and then it turns black. That's all." He licked his lips, slowly.

I had finished my pint and decided something stronger was in order. "I'm for a whiskey," I said, standing up. "You?"

"I don't mind if I do. Many thanks."

Seale had probably experienced a period of amnesia after his hospital stay, I thought. I had seen it in others under similar circumstances. "Do you remember anything from when things turned black?" I asked, after we had raised our glasses in a wordless toast.

"No. But—well, everything was different after that. Easier. As long as the War lasted, anyway." He took the Military Cross out of his pocket again, and rubbed his fingers over it, jabbing the points into his fingertips in a way that must have been painful.

"What did you do after the War? Did you go home to Canada?"

He returned the medal to his pocket. "I tried. But no one knew me. The family—I could tell they'd be just as happy to see the back of me, so I left. Went west." Another harsh laugh. "I know what that means, all right. I mean I took a trip across the country. And back. I just kept moving. Worked at jobs here and there. Couldn't settle."

"What kinds of jobs did you do?"

"Whatever I could find. Nothing lasted long, but some of those jobs were better than others."

"Oh? Which ones were better?"

He took a swallow of whiskey and smiled. "Killing. In abattoirs, slaughterhouses. I was good at it." His eyes took on a glazed, reminiscent look. Perhaps it was only the drink. I realized I had drunk a good deal more than was my habit. It was growing late, I was tired, and I wanted to be quit of Edwin Seale.

But it was too late for that. Hadn't I come to London in a spirit of atonement? I suspected I was in for a long night.

"So you liked killing livestock?"

Seale licked his lips again. "All the deaths. Red and black. But they were only cattle..." He drew in a quick breath and turned toward me.

"Have you seen that book? Vesalius? *Humani corporis fabrica*?"

Miskatonic's Library had a copy of the 1543 edition—all seven volumes—locked up in the vault, of course. I had bought myself a reprint. "I have. My Medical School professors recommended it. The illustrations are quite good, aren't they?"

"Illustrations? They're fine, but just think what that Vesalius fellow did! What he saw. He must have spent a lot of time with dead bodies, getting right inside of them, slicing away. Cutting and looking."

He leaned closer to me and dropped his voice. "Do you think they were all dead?"

I shook off the whiskey fumes. "Well, there's a story that Vesalius dissected a man whose heart was still beating. He went on a pilgrimage to Jerusalem after that—to atone, some said, or perhaps only to escape the Inquisition."

"Pilgrimage. Well, there's an idea." Seale spoke as if to himself.

I decided to take a chance. "Did you try something like that? Vivisection—on those cows, perhaps?"

Seale laughed, as though I had told a joke. "No, that wasn't it. Not cows."

"In Canada, this was?" I tried to follow the trail I thought I had seen, however faint.

"No. Here. London's still the centre of the world, isn't it? A place where a man can find his *niche*." The last word spoken with a peculiar intensity.

"And have you found your niche?"

"I have."

Another moment of silence. I took a final mouthful of whiskey and wondered what came next.

Seale drew in a breath. His sunken forehead wrinkled, and he tapped his fingernails against his glass, which, like mine, was empty. "Doctor Dexter. I want to ask you a favour."

Here it was, whatever it was. I assumed the attentive expression I found helpful with especially anxious patients. "Yes?"

"You really were at that place—Étaples? In the Great War?"

I kept my eyes on his face. "I was."

"I want to show you something."

"Here?" Was the fellow about to display a rash or swelling of some sort?

"No, not here! Not at all. At my digs. Please. It's… it's time."

It's time to deal with this thing, whether I want to or not. Even after twenty years. "All right. Where are your digs?"

"Not far. An easy walk."

"Let's go, then."

In the Fog

The Antonescu Clinic for Foundlings and the Indigent, at which I had volunteered my services since arriving in London more than a year before, proved to be a surprisingly effective venue for penance. Its presiding goddess, the Countess Sylvia Antonescu, was not Romanian—as her name suggested—but an Englishwoman of the most formidable sort. She regarded the clinic as a monument to her dead husband, Count Radu Antonescu. Everything had to be done to her exacting standards, which fortunately resulted in fairly good care for the clinic's patients. Nudging and persuading the Countess Sylvia was a large part of my role as Chief Medical Advisor, even when it involved non-medical problems, such as finding a replacement for the clinic's janitor and handyman, who had disappeared a few days before my encounter with Edwin Seale.

On many an evening, once free of the Clinic and its crises, I took a long way around to my lodgings in Clerkenwell, stopping at a pub for a drink and a meal. I didn't usually drink as much as I had this time, however. My legs felt rubbery and my head threatened to float away, but once outside, breathing lungfuls of the damp autumn air, I felt steadier.

I thought I knew my way around the East End, but in addition to my interior fogginess, an actual mist had rolled over the streets, obscuring my mental map. Seale, however, did not hesitate, but set off with a confident stride, despite his limp. After a misgiving or two, I followed his lead.

I will never know just how far we walked, neither numbers of steps nor the distance a crow might have flown. Seale kept up a distracting flow of words.

"That was it, you see, Doctor. I wasn't fit for much besides killing, either livestock, which was hard work, or people, which was illegal once the War was over. I thought I needed a cure. Hospitals are for curing, aren't they, so that's where I went. To the London Hospital, just over there."

He raised an arm and pointed. Although familiar with the London Hospital, I had no way of knowing whether Seale was really pointing toward it or making a rhetorical gesture.

"So you went to the casualty department?"

"No! I wasn't injured, was I? Not anymore. They would have told me to go away. What I did was, I got a job there."

"But you told me you didn't work at the Hospital."

"I don't *now*. But I did then. Cleaning things—floors, toilets. Taking out garbage. But I was *there*, where people were cured. I was close to the doctors, saw them working. I was in the right place."

Our footsteps conspired a rhythm as we proceeded along the damp pavements, our shoe soles making their distinctive sounds—mine sharp, his dull, with an alternating drag. The fog shrouded us, muffling our words. Small lights gleamed here and there, an errant constellation.

"That helped you, did it? Working in the Hospital?"

He did not reply for several paces. "It helped, but in a different way than I figured. Because I discovered something."

A slight downgrade in topography and a thickening of the fog suggested we were getting closer to the Thames. Blank walls loomed above us, rather than the lighted windows of homes and hearths. Seale nudged my arm.

"In here." He steered me toward a narrow gap between buildings. "Watch your step. Loose bricks."

"What was it you discovered?" Water had accumulated among the broken bricks of the pavement, which gave way to mud as we progressed along the alley.

Seale laughed, a short, hard laugh. "Lots. You'll see when we get there."

Where? I wondered. *And what?*

The Laboratory

Seale stopped by a narrow iron gate set in the wall to our right. He fumbled a bunch of keys from his coat pocket and fitted one into a lock, struggling with it for a few moments before the gate creaked open. "In here," he said again, gesturing with the hand that held the keys.

Why was I going here? I asked myself. This man was neither friend nor patient. I knew almost nothing about him, except that he was peculiar, perhaps disturbed. I was about to enter a dark place full of his secrets. And why had he brought me here? Edwin Seale, I was sure, did not make a habit of inviting strangers into his home, if that's what this place was.

But we have something in common, Edwin Seale and I: an acquaintance — no, an intimacy — with death.

Passing through the gate, we entered a yard cramped between the wall and a narrow, two-story building, probably a warehouse. Seale led the way toward it, walking along a couple of boards laid on the muddy ground.

Duckboards and mud. Leading to blood?

Reaching into a niche next to the door, Seale produced a stub of candle in an old-fashioned candlestick. He lit it with a match and took out his keys again, seeking the correct one. The candlelight fell upon a rusty spade and a pick leaning against the wall. Gobs of wet clay clung to both implements.

"Up here," said Seale, having opened the door. "Come on up." A set of stairs led abruptly to the right. Beyond them, the ground floor was a dank-smelling black void.

"I say, Seale," I said, placing a foot on the lowest step, "what is this place? Do you live here?"

"Indeed I do. Home sweet home. Come along, Doctor. Don't worry, the stairs are solid enough for two."

We clumped up the stairs, twelve of them; I counted. At the top, Seale did more fumbling and key-clinking. I almost offered to hold the candlestick, but figured he must do this all the time, unaided. Finally, we entered his triply-guarded lair. Setting the candle down, he proceeded to light a kerosene lantern.

Its stronger light revealed a room furnished with all the comforts of home—or discomforts, rather. Everything—table, chairs, bed, chests and cupboards—appeared to have been salvaged from refuse heaps, but it was assembled and distributed precisely as if in a cozy bed-sitter. There was even 'wallpaper,' in the form of sheets of newspaper. Months of events, photographs, editorials and advertisements made a jumbled collage of the recent past. On shelves near a balding, seat-sprung armchair, books leaned against one another. A gentleman's room, assembled from refuse.

Rooms, rather. There was another door in the inner wall. Locked, I was sure.

Seale bustled about like any host, lighting a spirit lamp that stood on a packing-case sideboard, and filling a kettle from a bucket. While the water came to a boil, he regaled me with tales of how he had acquired this or that object to furnish his miserable abode.

'Miserable' is no exaggeration; in fact, it's an understatement. Not only because of the shabbiness, the unheated clamminess, the makeshift sparseness of the furnishings. The air was rust-laden and bitter. Despair dripped like a leak from a hostile firmament to stain the newspaper-covered walls. A dust of sorrow lay over everything.

The water boiled. Seale poured it with a hot gurgle into a dented tin teapot.

"How long have you lived here?" I asked.

"Long enough." At home, his face had lost all pub-induced vestiges of wholesomeness, assuming a creased pallor that matched his sad belongings. He picked up the teapot and speared a finger through the handles of a couple of enamelware mugs. "Sit down and I'll tell you."

I wondered again if his hospitality was a prelude to a request for a free medical consultation. Well, why not? If he had come to me at the Antonescu Clinic, I would have been obliged to serve him. For nearly two years I had put myself at the disposal of those in need.

We sat down at the table, one of whose legs had been replaced with a length of lead pipe, more or less the right length. I, as the honoured guest, occupied the only chair, while Seale made do with a wooden crate set on end. He poured out. The tea steamed, emitting its faint fragrance of conviviality.

"The Hospital fired me, six months ago," he said. "Then I got a job at the Kodak factory for a while, but when that ended, I gave up my room and came here to live. I already knew about this place. It's been empty for years."

"Why were you fired from the Hospital?" I brought the mug to my lips, but it was too hot. "I thought you said it was the right place for you."

"It was, at first." He paused, looking into his mug. "Life and death. But those dying ones..."

"I don't understand."

Seale looked up. "Patients that died. I was there. I visited them."

"Visited them?"

"Yes—why not? I was there anyway, mopping the floor or whatever. I'd hear that breathing—you know, rattling. It means they're about to go."

"Stertorous respiration. Usually that's what it means." I watched him closely. "But not always."

Seale made a small dismissive gesture, set down his mug and leaned closer to me. I suppressed an impulse to draw back.

"I'd hear that noise, and I'd know it was time. So I stayed nearby, if it was late at night, with no one else around. Dark and quiet, except for that rattle. Calling me, it seemed. If I watched carefully, I'd see the ghost come out."

"Ghost?" I took a careful sip of tea, relishing its warmth despite an odd metallic taste.

"The soul! What else could it be? You must have seen lots of them, being a doctor. Kind of a white mist, but only for a second or two."

"Not everyone agrees about that, Seale. Some doctors don't believe there's such a thing as a soul. Not as a physical entity, anyway."

"You're right about that." Seale took a gulp of tea. "That's what got me fired." Another gulp. "After I saw them a couple times, I thought I'd try to catch one."

"How did you do that?"

"In a jar, what else?" Seale's voice was husky. "I just held it up to their mouth, where that rattle was coming from. Catch the ghost, clap the lid on. That's all there was to it. No harm done. That's funny, isn't it—how could there be any harm, when the person was dead?"

The offense is called 'offering an indignity to a dead body.' But I didn't say it.

"I see." I set my half-empty mug on the table. The tea was cooling rapidly, a glassy scum floating on its surface. "And what did you do with the ghosts?"

"Brought them here. I told you I had something to show you, didn't I?" He stood up, nudging my shoulder with his hand. "Come on!"

He started toward the door on the far side of the room, looking back to make sure I was following. And sure enough, he got out yet another key. The conglomeration of metal to which it belonged must have been a heavy weight to carry around.

"In here," Seale said, holding open the door with an air of muted triumph. I hesitated. The room was dark.

"Wait a minute," Seale muttered, going back for the lantern. As I had suspected, visitors other than he were rare in this place, and my presence had disturbed his routines.

Carrying the lantern, Seale entered the room. He set the light down and fiddled with something overhead. A match flared, followed by the brilliant illumination of a gas lamp.

The room was smaller than the one Seale used as his living space, with a single uncurtained window high in the wall. A long metal table occupied the centre, with the gas lamp suspended above it. Nearby was a large packing-case, on which stood a second spirit lamp and a retort stand, along with beakers and other items of laboratory glass, as well as a gallon jug half full of a clear liquid. In one corner stood a bucket and mop, and a pile of stained rags. A vaguely chemical odour completed the picture.

Edwin Seale had a laboratory. Superficially, it reminded me of my setup in a remote hut at the military hospital complex near Étaples, France twenty years before. The same air of improvisation within a humble enclosure, but for what purpose?

Intrigued, I examined the contents of a shelf above the packing-case turned lab bench. Seale stood near me, beaming like the proud parent of a prodigy.

A dozen or so glass jars were arrayed on the shelf. Originally, they had perhaps contained jam or pickled vegetables of some sort. Each retained its lid, but two wires about a foot long protruded from each one, through carefully punched holes. One wire of each pair was copper, the other a pale, dull grey, possibly zinc. The ends of the wires inside the jars were twisted together. Paper labels with dates written on them were affixed to the jars. The earliest was 1929 and the latest September 1936, only a few weeks before.

"What are the wires for?"

"If I stick them in my ears, I can hear them talking."

"Really? What do they say?"

"They whisper." He made a sibilant sound through his teeth.

This was beyond bizarre, but I played along. "How did you get those wires in there like that without losing the ghosts? Wouldn't they hop out as soon as you took off the lid, and go on to the afterlife?"

"No. They're still there. I can hear them talking, like I told you. I can't understand them, but maybe someday I will."

I turned away from Seale's soul menagerie. "You captured these souls in the dying breaths of patients at the London Hospital?"

He nodded.

"And that's why you were dismissed from your job there?"

"Correct."

"And now?" I said. "Do you have another job?"

"I worked at the Kodak factory, on the Clerkenwell Road. Where they make film for cameras. Until last month."

"You quit?"

"No, I didn't quit."

I wondered what I could do for this man. Clearly, he was mad, and I thought I knew the reason for his madness. For I knew him. His unevenly placed left ear was my handiwork. Nearly twenty years ago, in the chaos and horror of the Great War, I had handled his body and performed surgery upon it. I had repaired his mortal wounds and attached that ill-matched ear. I had made him whatever he now was.

Perhaps the Countess Sylvia would agree to giving him a place at her Clinic, where I could keep him under my eye. There was that vacant janitor's post...

"So how did you lose that job? The one at the Kodak factory."

His eyes drifted away from mine, to his collection of lab ware.

"It wasn't anything much," he said. "Just borrowing something, like a cup of sugar or a few eggs." He shrugged.

"Well, Seale," I said, facing him and trying to hold his eyes with mine, "I can help you, if you want help finding work. But I must warn you that no one will be sympathetic to pilfering, or to"—I glanced at the jars—"soul collecting."

"I don't do that anymore," said Seale. "I've found a better way." He stepped over to the metal table beneath the suspended lamp and flipped back a folded cloth that lay upon it, exposing a number of knives, a small saw, forceps, pliers, and other tools. They had been laid out like surgical instruments ready for an operation. The knives bore rusty stains. A few pale granules clung to the saw's teeth, and the cloth was stained brownish red.

Seale noticed my interest. "That's why I asked you here, Doctor. You know something about ether, don't you? How to administer it so it works for... as long as it takes? The... patient has to breathe it in, I know that. I've rigged up a thing with a sponge, but—"

The room had grown warmer from the two lamps and our body heat. The chemical odour I had barely noticed before was now stronger, sickly, almost fruity.

111

"Ether?" Suddenly, I recognized the smell. That glass jug. "Seale, how long since you brought that ether here?"

"A couple of months," he said. "Just that half jug. You don't think it's gone bad, do you?" He picked up the jug and started to unscrew the lid.

"No! Don't—!"

The force of the explosion hurled me across the room, along with shards of glass. I landed hard on the floor, slamming my head on the baseboard as the soft, heavy mass of Seale's body slid against me.

I opened my eyes to flames licking the wall behind the lab bench. Struggling to my feet, I nearly fell as I grabbed Seale's arm and dragged him toward the door. I stood grasping my ankles, head swimming and throbbing.

Blood. Too much blood for a few skin lacerations. Seale's neck was gushing blood, probably from a severed artery. I had to get both of us out of there immediately.

Leave him! Get out and leave him to die and burn. You heard what he said, you saw those knives and things, you guessed what he's been up to. He's a monster.

"He's *my* monster. I made him."

Fighting dizziness, I hoisted Seale over my shoulder and staggered from the laboratory. I slammed its door shut and prepared to grope my way toward the outer door. The lantern had been left behind in the burning lab, and the room was pitch dark. For an instant, I considered reopening the door of the lab so as to light my way, but was alert enough to reject the idea.

Twice I tripped on unseen objects and nearly fell, but finally reached the outer wall. Uncertain of the location of the door, I ran my hand along the wall, feeling for the doorframe. I bumped into something—probably the bookshelf I had noticed earlier—and tripped over it as it fell, nearly losing my grasp on Seale's limp form. Warm liquid ran down the side of my neck. I wondered how much blood he had lost, and how long it had been since the explosion. It felt like an eternity or two.

My hand bumped the doorframe. I groped farther down, seeking the door handle, hoping like hell Seale hadn't locked the door when we came in. There it was, but it wouldn't turn! I heard the crackle of burning wood. Orange light burst into the room and smoke billowed around me.

Desperate, I kicked at the door, all the while thinking I would have to lay Seale down and search his pockets for his keys. My kick must have dislodged something, though. The door gave way and swung open.

I had forgotten the stairs. With Seale's weight propelling me, I fell.

The Crossroads

We moved swiftly through lumpy, muddy terrain, a sense of imminent disaster poisoning the air. "Quick, boys—faster, faster!" said a commanding voice, and I urged my weary legs to a greater effort. The mud sucked at my boots, and I struggled to get good purchase for every step.

An intense, prolonged scream overhead, ending in a thud and an engulfing white light. Then chaos.

I awoke to thick darkness, earth beneath my hands and its dank smell in my nostrils. Groping about, I felt for Seale. We had to get going.

"Come on, Edwin—let's go!" I shook his arm, found his hand and pulled him to his feet. "This way."

"Where?" Seale's voice grated feebly. "I can't see anything."

"Hold on and come with me. I know this place. I've been here before."

First, the passage through darkness. The iron bridge rang under our feet. Below us seethed black waters, above us flapped black wings, and all around us the Abyss echoed and clanged.

Don't think about the depth of the chasm or the nature of its guardians.

"What's that noise? Where are we going?" Seale's hand tightened on mine.

"Don't worry, Edwin. Just keep putting one foot in front of the other."

After an unknown interval, something brushed my face, lightly groping. Circling my head, it chattered in my ear.

"Why are you here? Why do you traverse the Abyss?"

I raised my hands in a gesture of placation. "I bring a soul seeking passage. By favour of the Abyss, I will come and depart."

"Come, come, come! By all means come! But *depart*— we'll see about that!" The voice dissolved into shrieks and cackles.

A passageway opened before us. It ended at a stretch of sand with pale, water-smoothed pebbles here and there, barely visible in the dim light.

Until they weren't.

I stood with Edwin Seale by a tall stone that marked the place where three roads met. Seale was white-faced but calm. His small, rounded ears were evenly placed. I held out my hand to him.

"Edwin Seale, forgive me for using your body without your consent, and especially for pushing you into an impaired life that caused you grief and harm. I had no right to do that."

He took my hand, his grasp cold but firm. "Francis Dexter, I forgive you. And Herbert West as well." He smiled.

I bowed my head in acknowledgment. "And Herbert West as well. I thank you." I pointed down the road that led toward low hills, with a crescent moon descending into a ravel of dark clouds. "That way will bring you to the peace I stole from you."

He turned away and walked down the road. I watched him for a while, and then turned back to the place of brown sand and smooth pebbles.

"Pelican"

Now what? How do I get back?

I had been here before, in this place between life and death, where all ways begin and end. What did I do then? How did I recross the Abyss, from death to life? I knew a way existed, and hoped I would be shown it one more time.

I remembered it was not an easy road.

"Depart? You wish to depart? It's easy to come, hard to leave. Narrow is the way, and long. Cross, burrow and climb!" Again, the shrieks and echoes, the nameless heavings and convulsions in unimaginable depths.

"First, the bridge, the bridge! Narrow and long! Fragile but strong!"

Something formless pushed against me, and I stumbled onto wooden slats.

115

The bridge shuddered and swayed with every step, and its flimsy decking presented occasional foot-catching gaps. Phosphorescence glimmered here and there, hinting at, but not illuminating the enormous chasm I was traversing.

Don't look! Keep going! If you stop, you'll fall. Don't think, just walk!

Spongy shapes nudged me as I tottered along, grasping the ropes that served as handholds. Shrieks and laughter rang out at intervals, more than once startling me to the point I barely saved myself from falling.

After an unknown eternity, I felt solid ground under my feet.

A pinion sliced across my eyes, at once sharp and yielding, followed by a soft titter and the rustle of wings withdrawing.

"You will return. Oh yes, you *must* return. But first you will learn to love darkness." Followed by a chorus of cackling, *diminuendo.* "Darkness, darkness, darkness, soon, soon!"

What lies beyond the bridge? "Cross, burrow, and climb."

A tunnel, too low to stand up in, twisting through utter blackness. Upward through this stone intestine I crawled, scraping hands and knees, my progress impeded by occasional sharp protrusions. At long last, the tunnel ended at a vertical wall. Groping, I felt iron rungs.

Climb.

I climbed. I climbed until I forgot what it was not to climb. The smell of iron filled my nostrils as my hands bled upon the rungs. I hardly knew what to do when the ladder ended, but managed to scramble onto the level surface before me. My mind recoiled from the thought of the distance I had climbed, and the vast depth of the fall should I lose my balance.

I stepped forward, stretched out my left hand, and felt unbroken rock.

"The Word, the Word! Say it if you wish to proceed!" It was as though the rock itself spoke.

What word? I've forgotten it!

Don't think, Francis! You're doing what needs to be done. When the moment comes, speak from your heart.

I stood, listening to my heart beating, and far, far below me the slither and churn of the Abyss.

I've been here before. Alone. Standing between death and life, clutching a straw of hope and a fragment of love.

I struck my bloody fist on my breast and uttered the Word.

"Pelican."

The wall dissolved and something shoved me forward. Falling to my knees, I heard behind me the clang of a great door closing.

Until the next time.

The Hospital

Again, I awoke, this time to unfamiliar pain in a familiar atmosphere—a hospital—but in a bed in one of the wards. At first it was enough to catalogue the sources and intensities of my various pains—a heavy throb in my left ankle, sharp jabs from my lacerated face and hands, and dull rumbles from almost everywhere else, taking turns. For several days, I suffered a terrible weariness unaccounted for by the injuries I had sustained.

Over the course of those days, I was informed by physicians, visitors, and police that I had been found on the lower floor of a burning warehouse near the river, minutes before the upper floor collapsed. Near me was a dead man, who had apparently bled out from a wound in his throat. Several bodies were found buried in shallow graves in the building's courtyard, one of them the man who had recently worked as a janitor at the Antonescu Clinic. As far as could be determined, he and the other individuals had suffered mutilations and amputations, possibly before death, but more likely afterward.

I related to the police officers who questioned me how I had met Edwin Seale at the Blind Beggar, and had been sufficiently intrigued by things he had told me to accompany him to his home. I told them I had seen a half-full jug of ether on the premises. Unstable compounds would have formed on exposure to air and light. The jug had exploded, and an overturned lantern had started the fire.

But I did not tell them that Edwin Seale was one of the fourteen men I had revivified while serving at a military hospital in the Great War, when my name was Herbert West.

THE NIGHT JOURNEY OF FRANCIS DEXTER

A butler answered the door, an impeccably clad, stout, middle-aged butler with closely-trimmed mutton-chop whiskers. Like the elegant façade of the house, the butler's presence announced to the world that Edward Clapham-Lee was a successful man.

He awaited me in his study, positioned beneath a portrait of his father, the late Sir Eric Moreland Clapham-Lee, MBChB, FRCS. Stepping forward, he greeted me by name, the name I use now. Our hands met and parted for the briefest of moments.

Would he greet me so civilly, I wondered, if he knew what I intended to reveal to him?

Clapham-Lee gazed at me without speaking, long enough that the silence between us grew thicker, begging to be broken. His expression was appraising, as though I were a patient instead of a guest.

I was tempted to create a pressing reason to leave, but my host gestured toward a group of decanters on a sideboard. "Would you care for a drink?"

I accepted, shrugging off the apprehension that had weighed upon me since our chance meeting in the street two days earlier. After the brief ceremony of selection and pouring, we settled into the sort of conversation inevitable between men who have only their profession in common. From within the persona of Dr. Francis Dexter, eclectic physician and occasional surgeon, I chatted easily with Mr. Edward Clapham-Lee, neurosurgical specialist.

We proceeded from study to dining room, from *apéritifs* to a succession of wines and a progression of courses, delivered by the butler and a pair of stocky, businesslike waiters. Our talk touched lightly upon my work at the Antonescu Clinic and landed on Clapham-Lee's achievements in neurology, where it lingered. Once, when the Great War was mentioned, I thought we were approaching the point of opportunity. Did I have the resolve to speak, to reveal?

"You were acquainted with my father, weren't you?" said Clapham-Lee, looking up from his plate.

"Yes, we were at the same hospital for a time. The Number One General, at Étaples." How much more I could have said! But not yet. Not while we shared food and drink. Although I was too nervous to eat more than token morsels.

"That would have been just before his... disappearance, I imagine. In November of 1917. Nearly twenty years ago." Abruptly, he veered away from the topic, instead asking my opinion of the wine recently poured into my glass by the butler. The two of them exchanged a glance, and the butler nodded briefly and withdrew.

Clapham-Lee moved to a lengthy description of a procedure he had recently perfected to reduce involuntary tremors of the hand. Although familiar with the anatomy, I failed to appreciate the details of his explanation, suspecting it to be a bravura performance intended to elicit my awe.

"I don't imagine you've ever worked on the brain, have you, Dexter?" Clapham-Lee said, dissecting a chicken leg with exquisite finesse.

"The only 'work' I have done on the head has been on the outside, to restore or alter the external features."

"Of course." Clapham-Lee exposed long white teeth in a grin. Between bites, he went on to discuss his adventures within the brain, "the seat of all perception and knowledge," as he put it. "Not everyone has the *dexterity*"—he twitched an ironic eyebrow—"or, to put it plainly, the sheer *nerve* to delve beneath the cranium and manipulate the channels of crucial communication."

"Those channels do extend to the surface, as you know. My work requires a familiarity with the facial nerves," I said, nettled by his self-aggrandizement.

Clapham-Lee dismissed the facial nerves with a gesture of his knife. "Ah, but the brain is fundamental. Everything converges in the brain and radiates from it."

"It does, I suppose." I was getting tired of this pointless conversation, while the matter of primary importance lay between us untouched, as surely as the remains of the capon congealing on its platter. I prepared myself to speak again of the War, of his father, of deception. Of murder.

"Tell me, Dexter," Clapham-Lee interrupted, "do you actually do surgery in that clinic of yours? I thought its main purposes were delousing children and teaching basic hygiene to the indigent and ignorant."

"Come, Edward, you know better. The Antonescu Clinic serves the disadvantaged, but the cases range from simple to complex. And they are dealt with competently, I assure you." I immediately wished I hadn't said this. It sounded much too defensive.

Clapham-Lee smiled again, that slow, indulgent smile I was starting to hate. *Like father, like son.*

"Well, of course you would think so. And the Countess Antonescu too, I imagine. 'Countess.'" He snorted. "As if nobility could be acquired by marriage to some foreigner."

By now, dessert was in sight. A selection of fruits and cheeses arrived, along with a heavy torte and, of course, brandy and liqueurs. My anxiety had caused me to drink more than usual. I felt an all too familiar light-headedness and departure of inhibition, an approach of recklessness. It would serve. Now was the time. I drew in a breath.

"This is a very fine brandy," said Clapham-Lee. "You must try it." He offered a small decanter, and against my better judgment, I accepted. In the back of my mind, a quiet voice argued in favour of leaving the unspoken matter unspoken until some future occasion.

I sipped and appreciated, listening more to the hum of my own thoughts than to my host's discourses on his ever-expanding practice and his program of ambitious surgeries. I did not even try to follow him through a procession of -plastys, -otomies, and -ectomies.

Clapham-Lee set down his glass, its contents untasted, and stood. "I want to show you something," he said. "Come."

He turned, twitching his fingers in a beckoning gesture. At the doorway, he stopped and watched me get to my feet, a task I accomplished with a small lurch and struggle.

I concentrated on putting one foot in front of the other, and followed Clapham-Lee down a wide hallway, and then another, past closed doors and portrait-hung walls, no doubt displaying all of my host's eminent ancestors. Another turn led us to a more utilitarian passage. Surely we weren't going to the kitchen? He opened a door and revealed steps descending.

Many steps, and a long descent. I clutched the handrail and counted. I had reached sixteen when he stopped at the bottom, four steps below me.

"My private laboratory," he said, pulling keys from his pocket and unlocking a door. My mind danced with the idea of a private laboratory in a deep cellar. Was he playing games with me? For at one time I had such a facility. I, or rather, Herbert West. I was no longer that man, but I had dragged his misdeeds around the world with me, like a sack of shit. They were the reason I was here.

The place was clean and well-lit, equipped with the expected tools and furnishings. The latter included an operating table. Of course. My lab had one too.

"Very nice," I said, looking around, while my host stood and observed me. Perhaps he had brought me here for the express purpose of initiating our difficult conversation. But no, how would he know about the need for it? Dizzy and drink-fuddled, I floundered in confusion and wished myself elsewhere.

Clapham-Lee pulled open drawers, revealing arrays of tools for specialized surgeries. "With these," he said, "I could, in theory, transform an individual completely. You can relate to that, can't you, *Dexter*?"

Did I imagine the ironic emphasis on my present name? The light was suddenly too bright, bouncing off the white walls and ranks of glassware, stabbing my eyes and dulling my vision. My head felt disconnected from my body, twirling like a balloon in a breeze. I propped myself against the nearest solid object, which happened to be the operating table. All right, I would get it over with and conclude this fiasco. "Edward, I must tell you something. In the War, I…"

My tongue had become a lump of lead. I could no longer speak. Colours blurred and swam. I struggled to stay upright, swayed, slumped to the floor.

~oOo~

My eyelids cracked open, admitting blurred light. I tried to raise a hand and rub away whatever blocked my vision, but my arm weighed heavy as an anchor.

"He's coming around. Should I—?"

"Not yet. Never mind, he's not going anywhere."

Voices mumbled nearby, wavering, indistinct. Who were the speakers? Where was I? I lay on my back. Had I fallen ill? I forced my mind to focus. I had been dining at the home of Edward Clapham-Lee, hadn't I? How long ago? A day? A week? I tried to speak, but my lips were gummed shut. My mouth tasted of metal. The thin thread of consciousness slipped from my grasp, and I slid back into murk.

Until bright light glared my eyes open, its intense incandescence painful and disorienting. Behind it, someone spoke. Clapham-Lee's voice. "All right, we're ready. Let's have the gas."

Hands touched my face. Something that felt and smelled like rubber was placed over my mouth and nose. I jerked my arms to pluck it off, but they were clamped by my sides. My feet were similarly secured. Someone standing behind the glare pushed down on my shoulders and subdued my struggles. A shape descended, blocking the light. At last I could see. Despite the grotesque distortion of the upside-down view, I recognized the butler's face. Those sinuous whiskers were unmistakable.

124

"Come on, man! Put him out." Clapham-Lee's voice grated, at once strained and excited.

His face loomed over me. A set of magnifying goggles distorted his eyes into huge, misshapen marbles. His lips curved in a smile and flexed moistly as he spoke.

"Now you will *see*, Herbert West," he said. "Or rather, you won't."

That was the last.

Light invades my eyes. Searing, malignant light. White, yellow, red. Intense, destroying. A flood of blood surrounds, drowns, confounds...

~o0o~

My eyes were stuck shut. I forced them open and flexed my gummed eyelids. Open, close. Open, close. My eyelashes caught on something, a small, disturbing friction. I felt a bed or mattress beneath me. My fingers detected woven cloth, but iron clamps gripped my wrists and ankles.

Something terrible has happened to me.

I could not see. My wide-open eyes detected nothing but a blackness more profound than any I had ever experienced.

"Is anyone here?" Phlegm muffled my voice. I coughed and tried again. "Clapham-Lee. Edward. Are you here? Answer me. Please."

Silence.

From speaking to yelling to screaming to wailing and groaning. How long did that journey take? My ears grew tired of my voice. My throat burned. That long.

Blackness and silence.

I resorted to reason. I tried to think. Someone had brought me here. I was alive, and neither hungry nor thirsty. I felt no need to urinate. I had been attended to.

But I was imprisoned, and I was blind.

Terror. Panic. Screams. Back to black.

How many times did I traverse this cycle of reasoning, pleading, terror, panic, unconsciousness? A hundred? A thousand? Days? Nights? Weeks?

Finally, I heard the snick of a lock, followed by footsteps. A body displaced the air around my face. Someone stood near me, breathing, exuding a faint aroma of tobacco.

"Edward, is that you?"

No answer, but I knew he stood there, looking at me. Gloating.

"Who are you? I know there's someone here. Speak to me, for God's sake!" To my shame, my voice broke into wheezy shards.

He laughed. He laughed for a long time, pacing around in his excitement and triumph, the laughter growing louder and softer as he moved away from me and returned. I knew that excitement. I had felt it myself. Finally, he spoke.

"You have learned the first lesson, I see. Now you know what it is to be the subject of the experiment, rather than the experimenter."

"What sort of experiment are you doing?"

"You will see, Herbert West. Or rather, you won't."

"All right," I said, "you have me. I surrender. Now let justice be done. Turn me over to the police and the courts of law. Let them deal with me, but let me into the light again."

"The courts would be too lenient. I know them, and I know how persuasive you can be. I have dealt justice upon you with my own hands, for my father's sake. As for the light, you must learn to live without it. You will spend the rest of your life in darkness, and I hope it will be a long one."

"I'll see you again, Edward Clapham-Lee. I swear it." Weak bravado on my part, and both of us knew it.

He laughed again, and went away.

~oOo~

For several days, or weeks, or eternities, I remained there, in Edward Clapham-Lee's house. At regular intervals, he and his servants visited indignities upon me, to ensure my survival. Clapham-Lee ministered to the surgical wounds he had inflicted, while describing exactly what processes he had carried out on me. His minions forced some sort of nutrient solution down my esophagus and tended to matters of hygiene with clinical indifference. After one or two futile attempts at resistance, I stopped struggling. I was growing weaker, and I was completely blind.

Death was the only means of escape, but denied to me. It's impossible to will oneself to stop breathing. I could not even refuse nourishment; they forced it into me.

With my eyes useless, I explored my darkness. Like a trapped insect, I crawled inside the walls of my skull, revisiting memories of sight. Vivid images boiled up in my brain, like those pulsating globes of intense colour created by sunlight through closed eyelids. Images of myself, my choices, my motives, thoughts and deeds, in classrooms, in bedrooms, in laboratories, hospitals, and morgues, on public streets, in my secret laboratory, in the privacy of my inmost thoughts. Memories of sunrises and sunsets, firelit wine in a crystal glass, words written on a page, a beloved face in the ecstasies of love, the vivid red of arterial blood, the complex colours of intestines revealed by a stroke of the scalpel, a dead man struggling to life at my command, a living one dying by my will. I remembered the weight of the glass cylinder filled with the drug, the small resistance as the needle punctured living tissue, the faint grating of glass on glass as I dispensed death.

Only once. I did that only once.

Really? What about that travelling salesman, Robert Leavitt?

All right—twice. And it was for science, always for science.

With a smidgen of vengeance, in the case of Clapham-Lee the elder.

Enough of this intimate exhibition, this catalogue of my evil thoughts, my secrets and crimes. I had to find the trap door, to descend into my uttermost depths and swim through the abyss to freedom.

I searched my memories for friends. There was the one who, on a drunken night, confided to me a secret from the alchemist Paracelsus: "He who would enter the Kingdom of God must first enter with his body into his mother and there die." And had he done so? I asked him, but he rolled toward me the glassy eye of the inebriate and declared, "No, but you will." At which I laughed. Later, I learned that in the cryptic utterances of the alchemists, the word 'mother' referred to something in their bizarre procedures in search of enlightenment, or gold.

Mother. Did I cry out that name into the darkness? At the very extremity of endurance, almost everyone calls for their mother. I groped my way to memories of delirium, and a woman who came to me in a fever-dream to tell me of my mother's love. But my mother was not here now; that long-ago love was a rose-coloured pebble I lost long ago.

My memory-gropings snared another woman, a shaman who was able to detach from her body and travel the intangible realms between worlds, and who used dreams for healing.

"Mother?" They were all mothers, those women—my friend, the shaman, and my own mother, whom I lost in childhood and found decades later by unorthodox means. All had expelled living beings into the world.

Mother. I visualized the word being uttered. Lips shaped its syllables, a succession, a multitude of lips and mouths, revealing glimpses of teeth and tongues.

"Mother." I whispered the word, and then on the screen behind my skull, I saw lips again, enormous, flexing and stretching.

I discerned words. Discerned, not heard. They reverberated through my entire being.

"Your essence, your secrets, your crimes. Your essence, your secrets, your crimes. Come, come, come into me!" Followed by gurgling laughter, and the mouth an enormous gaping cave. A giant *maw.*

Was this the way out? I drove myself forward, through the fleshy portal, beneath the dental portcullis, along the ramp of the tongue, until I stood poised on the edge of a pulsating red funnel, a gaping pit with glistening sides.

And then I leaped.

Warm, viscid matter embraced me and whirled me in a circling pattern, a spiral, a downward gyre, toward the uttermost bottom of the ultimate abyss. It roared and echoed as it sucked me down. I tasted blood and acid, smelled yeast and fermentation. My substance thinned and stretched, even as part of me watched and *knew*. Knew the horror, and the reasons for it.

I was shunted along a soft, heaving tunnel that throbbed and gonged. Wormlike forms caressed my face and body, seeking, exploring. How long could I endure this? As long as I had to, for there was no returning. I clasped my arms over my head and pulled them into my body, knees to chest, head dropped forward, as though to burrow into myself. *Surrender, surrender, surrender.*

I enter the Egg. The Egg is black, smooth, solid. Here I will stay. There is no time within the Egg. Here I am safe, within the hum of Eternity.

Hmmmmmmmmmmmmmmmmmmmmmmmmm.

The Egg cracks.

I do not know where—

~o0o~

I didn't know how much time passed, or if I had left time behind, but I realized I no longer felt movement. I lay in a black void, encased in a soft, rhythmic throbbing. In this hot and fleshy cavern, eyes were an absurdity.

A voice reverberated. "I am the Abyss, the Mother of All, the Beginning and the End. Listen to me." And then, "Look."

Look! I tried to laugh, but She spoke again.

"Look."

I went through the motions of opening my eyes. At any rate, I twitched the relevant muscles, or pretended to.

"See," said the voice. And see I did. In some fashion, I saw.

I saw the body of Sir Eric Moreland Clapham-Lee, my enemy and my victim, suspended before me, as though on a hook. He was limp, dead without a doubt, a specimen displayed for my contemplation, twisting gently in a nonexistent breeze.

I remembered the thrill in my heart as I delivered his death, my satisfaction as his limbs ceased flailing and fell limp. And then the greater thrill of endowing him with an artificial existence as a mindless wreck. That was what he deserved, for trifling with Herbert West.

"That was a long time ago," I said, backing away from the corpse.

Silence.

"I've learned many hard lessons since then," I said.

Silence.

"I would never do such a thing now," I said.

Silence.

"What do you want from me? He's dead. By now, he would have been dead anyway, of natural causes. What am I supposed to do with him?"

"You know."

"So do you. Why am I here?"

"You know."

"All right! I'll say it to you—"

"No. Say it to *him*. Take his hand and say what you must."

I approached the hanging corpse. A bony finger grazed my cheek. Shuddering, I entwined the fingers of my left hand with the cold, stiff ones of the corpse. "Eric Clapham-Lee, I murdered you in cold blood and revivified you with evil intent.

I was delighted with the deed, but came to regret it bitterly. If you can, I ask you to forgive me."

I let go of the hand, but it did not release mine. Wrenching my fingers free, I came away with one of the distal phalanges, encased in dry, brittle skin.

"Keep it," said the Mother, juddering the world with laughter. "It's your token of forgiveness. You'll need it."

"I intended to confess the crime to his son, to atone, but he drugged and blinded me before I could speak. Wasn't his crime nearly as great as mine?"

"That's not your concern. This is the form of your atonement."

"But he did me a great injustice! He stole my sight!"

"Did you expect atonement to be easy? A few words of apology, and then back to your comfortable life? 'Oh, by the way, I killed your Dad. Sorry, old chap. Ta-ta.'" Her laughter gurgled. Clapham-Lee executed a little shimmy and faded away into velvet blackness.

"My life wasn't all that comfortable," I said. "The Countess could be difficult, but at least I was doing some good. Now I'm useless. Unless you can restore my sight, you may as well take my life; it's worthless to me now. 'May your life be a long one.' That's what he said to me, the bastard."

"Your life is already mine, Herbert West. Oh yes, it's Francis Dexter now, isn't it? Names don't matter here. Your life won't be so very long. A thousand days, during which you will serve me."

"I'll serve you? Doing what?"

"Healing those who may be healed, and conducting to me those who may not."

My sight would be restored! I would continue my life as a physician and surgeon; and perhaps, someday, I would get my revenge on Clapham-Lee. "All right. I'll do it."

"You'll do it. You know the road, and now you will have the key and the token. All right, here you go, out by the front door, not the back, you lucky devil." Her breath roared, drowning out the thunder of her heart, and the walls of the cavern gathered and pulsed, gathered and pulsed.

A gush of warm, salty liquid engulfed me, swelled to a flood, a cataract, and catapulted me through roaring gulfs. Ejected, I floated on the relentless tides of a nameless ocean.

My body ploughed through salty foam and came to rest, sand gritting under my palms and scraping my face. The tumult of waves faded, and I lay still. Under the fingers of my right hand, I felt a smooth, hard object. A wave-polished pebble. In my left hand, I grasped something small and knobbly. I hadn't lost Clapham-Lee Senior's finger bone after all. I clutched these things like instruments of salvation, tucked my right hand under my cheek, pressed my left to my heart, and gave myself up to whatever would happen next.

~oOo~

"Who's this, then?"

"Let's see. Gentleman, by the looks of him."

"No hat. Toffs always have toff hats."

"Blew away."

"Underdressed for the weather. Or he's been rolled already."

"Dead drunk, he is. Must have had quite the night. Let's see what's left in his pockets."

I lifted my head. Blackness of ebony night surrounded me. My outstretched palms met grit and unidentifiable debris, and then something that felt like a boot. I lay on wet pavement, and I could not see.

Hands fumbled at my clothing and turned me over.

"Look at his eyes! Something's bad here."

In hospital, as a patient, I accepted my blindness as complete and permanent. I made no accusation against Edward Clapham-Lee. In a sense, we're even—my sight for his father's life. But I know another force is at work, and I am content to be its instrument.

Now I see the past behind my right eye and the future through the left. I walk between worlds, a finger bone in one pocket, a smooth stone in the other. I visit the afflicted in their dreams and conduct the souls of the dead over the Abyss. On the edge of sleep, I lift my left eyelid ever so slightly and see endless streets of nighted cities and lines of grim-faced people marching with doomed purpose to nameless ends. Among them, I catch glimpses of familiar faces, but not that of Edward Clapham-Lee. Not yet.

But I have nine hundred days.

THE FINAL DEADLINE OF A.G. HALSEY

Milburn, Alma. Born Alma Gloria Halsey, January 23, 1886. Newspaperwoman. Died on July ~~20th~~ ~~22nd~~ 24th a date yet to be announced, 1963. Survived by her granddaughter, Francesca "France" Leighton, and her son, Nicholas St. George Leighton.

Except he's not officially her son, and the aforesaid Francesca isn't officially his daughter. And the aforesaid Alma Gloria (blame my father for that moniker!) was never officially married to Charles Milburn, nor to anyone else. To ~~heck~~ hell with officialdom.

People don't usually write their own obituaries, unless you consider some of the memoirs being published these days. Obituary writing is hack work anyway. I was lucky not to start out at that level. My own is the only obituary I'll ever write.

Why? Well, last week the doc finally gave me the bad news, or rather, confirmed the bad news my old body has been giving me for months. My cigarette habit has finally caught up with me. I have three months. So I have to organize my thoughts and write them down, along with the facts I've dug up, before I exit the scene. Or get too dozed up on pain drugs to think.

Old Reporter Writes Final Story

Editors never let us write our own headlines, but I'm my own editor now and can do whatever the hell I want. I have one last story to write before I close my typewriter for good. Some of the keys stick, but I'm pretty sure the ribbon will last.

I'll do this the way I once wrote to deadline. Treat each piece of the puzzle like a story and pound it out. Get the facts, string 'em together, dress them up in the right words. Then give the thing a pat on the bum and sent it out into the world I'm about to leave.

Except this story will have only one reader—my granddaughter Francesca. At least I hope she reads it. She will inherit this house and its contents. She will be, as the saying goes, comfortably well off. But she will also inherit more subtle things. The past has a way of reaching down the generations and she needs to know about it before I'm gone. She needs <u>facts</u>. Who and what and how and maybe why. Three W's and one H. She needs context. Context is all.

Francesca is 22, and thinks she knows more than her old grandmother. (Not that she calls me that. Being unofficial, I put my foot down the day she came to live here at age 12. "Alma" she called me then and still does. I was never a mother, except biologically, so have no claim to either title.) My job is to make her think about certain things before she makes a big mistake. I do know something about <u>that</u>.

Okay, where to begin?

```
Co-Ed Assists Investigation into Egypt
Murders
Miss    Francesca    Leighton    recently
returned    to    Providence    from    Luxor,
Egypt,    where    she    was    working    at    an
archaeological    dig.    While    there,    she
```

discovered a scene of murder. The bodies of Prof. William Stanton of Brown University, and Dr. James Dykstra, a Canadian geologist, were found in a tomb on the west bank of the Nile River near the town of Luxor. Questioned by police, Miss Leighton revealed that she had discovered Prof. Stanton's body while exploring a remote part of the Theban Necropolis. The crimes have been attributed to gangs of bandits who infest the west bank villages. Miss Leighton is recovering from her ordeal at the home of her grandmother, Mrs. Charles Milburn. She plans to resume her studies in archaeology.

Enough of that stuff. 'Mrs. Charles Milburn,' indeed! Isn't it time we stopped the absurd practice of calling women by their husbands' names? Especially absurd when the husband is dead. And you might say Francesca is recovering, but I wouldn't. She can't seem to make up her mind about anything. She got herself a job shelving books at the Brown University Library, but that's a dead end.

As for resuming her education, she talks about moving to England and trying for a scholarship to Oxford or Cambridge—someday. Nicholas has finally taken an interest in his illegitimate daughter and promised to help with money and influence, but Francesca hasn't written to him about her plans. Knowing Nicholas, I'm afraid he'll lose interest in her again, unless she reminds him of her existence. 'Someday' isn't good enough.

I'm too tired to keep pounding away. Time for a rest and a ~~little something~~ drink. One thing about being old and sick— you can forget about the damned yardarm.

Ever wonder how much sand is left in your personal hourglass? As I recall, the last little bit trickles out pretty fast. You've lost two days already, Alma! Let's try a little harder today, shall we?

> Egypt's Climate Destroys Antique Cello
> When Miss Francesca Leighton of Providence travelled to Luxor, Egypt last fall to work at an archaeological dig, she took with her a precious 18th century violoncello, a gift from her late grandfather. Unfortunately, exposure to the exceedingly dry climate of Luxor resulted in fatal cracks. The instrument shattered while Miss Leighton was playing it. The dry air of Egypt preserved fragile flower garlands in the tomb of Tutankhamen for 3,000 years. What irony that it destroyed a beautiful artifact of a more recent time.

Well, that was the story France (I see I'm starting to use the short form of her name, ~~darn~~ damn it!) told me when she arrived home in December. Dry climate, cracks, cello shattered while being played. She didn't tell me what she was playing or where. But this was Eudora. She and Charles named the cello when he gave it to her, and Francesca talked about it like it was another person. Talked to it, for all I know. Then she comes

138

home without it, tells me it dried out and cracked, too bad. As though she's too cool and sophisticated to care. I think she does care, but knows if she starts talking about it, she won't be able to stop.

I'm guessing a lot more happened to her in Egypt besides finding those bodies. Sex, for one thing. No, she didn't tell me, so how do I know? Call it mother's intuition —or grandmother's, to be accurate. The question is—with whom? She's told me about some of the men she met out there. I could tell by the way she talked about them they were just friends. Like the one named Jack, a red-haired fellow. Can't remember his last name, but he plays the violin. He came to tea one afternoon. Made me laugh.

So if not Jack, then who?

(I'm not so old I've forgotten what it's like. My first love affair was with Charles, of course. My best-beloved, whom I miss unbearably. It's just a year since he died. After we became lovers, I wanted to <u>tell</u> everyone—friends, colleagues, even my mother, if you can believe that! It was my happy secret, always wanting to burst out. It probably shone through my eyes, glowed through my skin. Ah, those lost young days!)

I've tried to entice Francesca to Tell All. Afternoon drinks, a relaxed atmosphere, reminiscing, confidences, girly-girly jokes, all that. No soap. Once or twice she's come close to opening up, but clamped it down. Still, those couple times she happened to let out a name: Adam Dexter.

I'm too tired to start on his story. Can't seem to catch my breath. Need a rest.

###

I've spent the last two weeks in bed, waited upon hand and foot by Lucy and Andre. I'm so lucky they decided to keep working for me. Francesca hovered around, visited, brought me weak tea (which I can't stand), and read the newspapers to me (which I appreciated). Needless to say, the poor old lungs weren't happy. Even the thought of typing made me short of breath. Now the doc sends his assistant every couple of days to drain excess fluid. He doesn't come so often himself, but then, I suspect he's a pessimist by nature.

The procedure is unpleasant, but it perks me up enough that I can spend an hour or two at my desk when no one is keeping watch and fussing. Too bad I can't muffle my typewriter. If the sound goes on too long, I get told to cease and desist. That's the trouble with devoted ~~servants~~ ~~employees~~ friends.

Now, back to Adam Dexter.

```
Nuclear Physicist Disappears in Egypt
A controversial scientist from
Providence has been declared a missing
person by Egyptian authorities. Adam
Dexter was invited to visit Egypt last
fall to advise its government on
peaceful applications of nuclear
energy. An enthusiastic advocate of
atom-splitting, Dexter met with
President Nasser in Cairo, and then
went on to Luxor, where he delivered a
lecture at a conference of scholars and
academics. He has not been seen since
the end of October. Rumors persist that
Dexter may have defected to the Soviet
Union in the aftermath of the Cuban
missile crisis. Inquiries continue.
```

I started investigating Adam Dexter after Francesca mentioned his name in a letter she wrote me from Luxor about mid-October. She'd had dinner with him and was bubbling over with excitement. A nuclear physicist! So charming, so intelligent! And she wondered if he might be a distant relative, because his surname was the same as her grandfather's (her real grandfather, Francis Dexter, of course).

There was nothing remarkable about Adam's early life, except his mother was Egyptian and the family travelled a lot. He showed no special interest in physics, nuclear or otherwise, through his college years. He studied medicine but never practiced as a physician. The closest he came to that was a position as a coroner's assistant in the early 1930s.

I managed to track down and interview that coroner. He remembered Adam Dexter because of a case Adam was assigned to investigate. A young man was found dead in a house on College Hill after an intense lightning storm.

"He wasn't the same after that," the coroner told me. "He completed his report and resigned. He didn't give me a reason. His manner was completely changed, like he decided he had better things to do. I wished him well and never saw him again."

As I was putting away my notebook, the man added, "It wasn't just the lightning that night, you know. Something strange was abroad. People talked about an explosion in the air near the house where that young fellow died, and foul smells, like some sort of gas was released. Some said it was the smell of evil. Maybe something noxious lingered at the scene of the death."

Adam left town, studied physics, and eventually became famous, or maybe notorious is a better word. That was the man France met in Luxor 28 years later. He was 57 at the time but looked much younger, or so France has assured me, with such a combination of anxiety, embarrassment, and defiance on her face that I'm almost certain she slept with him.

And now, it seems, he's disappeared. According to all the newspapers, he has failed to appear at several important meetings. When I mentioned this to France, she got a most peculiar expression on her face and started to say something, but stopped herself and started talking about her friend Willa instead.

We'll get to Willa later.

I found out that when Adam Dexter left Providence in the '30s, he broke off an engagement with a woman named Amelia Devlin. She's the same woman who sought out Francesca in Luxor less than a year ago. I actually helped her by giving her the address of the Stanton dig. Now I'm thinking that was a mistake, an error of judgment made in ignorance.

Enough of that, Alma! This is your body talking. The way I feel right now, I don't think I'll last another 2 months. And the way you're dithering, you'll take longer than that to get to the point. Focus!

Okay, okay! Amelia Devlin is a medium of sorts, a reader of the Tarot and a prognosticator. Perhaps she actually possesses some extra-sensory abilities (assuming such abilities exist).

In the early '30s, Amelia and her mother were living here in Providence. I gather they never stayed in any one place for long. They both worked, Amelia as a clerk at City Hall and her mother as a secretary to a firm of attorneys. They did seances in their spare time, maybe to supplement their incomes.

I admit I assumed (without evidence) that Amelia must have pursued Adam Dexter, rather than the other way around. She struck me as a dogged type the one time I met her in person. Did this doggedness include physically seducing Adam in order to become pregnant by him and strengthen his obligation to marry her? A risky move, and unfortunately for Amelia, she lost the bet.

Now we come to Willa. She is Amelia Devlin's daughter. Her full name is Willamina Devlin, after her grandmother. (It's interesting that all 3 of these ladies have the same surname, isn't it? Mustn't be catty, though, given my own mistake.) France met her in Egypt, and the two became friends. Willa stayed with us for a week back in January. I must say, I like her better than her mother. She appears guileless, but I wonder if Amelia encouraged the friendship so she could keep an eye on France through her daughter. Amelia did not, apparently, reveal to France her connection to Adam. What was her motive, and where are her loyalties?

And before anyone concludes I'm <u>paranoid</u> (how the terminology of psychology has seeped into everyday language!), I say only that just as I'm 100% certain Amelia is Adam Dexter's abandoned fiancée, I'm also 100% certain Willa is Adam Dexter's daughter. Having seen photographs of him in newspapers and magazines, I noted a resemblance while she was with us. So far, I haven't asked France if she has noticed it as well.

Why should all this worry me? So what if France is friends with the illegitimate daughter of a much older man with whom she had a brief affair? I have no idea if Amelia has told

Willa who her father is. I'm pretty sure France knows nothing about it. But it's an awkward piece of grit that could cause her distress if revealed the wrong way. As it might be, if Adam Dexter ever shows up here in Providence. He still has a house here; I interviewed its resident caretaker before I got too sick to go out. He told me, "You know, ma'am, I've never met Mr. Dexter, the owner, but that's fine as long as the bills are paid on time." So who's paying those bills?

Adam may have disappeared, he may even be dead (but in my experience, even those who have been declared dead aren't necessarily so). Amelia, with her connections to the occult, must know that too. So, for that matter, may her daughter, and even France herself. Her father, my son Nicholas, turned out perfectly ordinary (dull, even), but _his_ father, Francis Dexter (once known as Herbert West), certainly was not. What if France does have some sort of psychic talents? Is Amelia Devlin trying to recruit and corrupt her? And what (besides the obvious) attracted Adam to France?"

Now, old body, I have to stop. This marathon session has just about done me in. It's time for my next set of pills (thank God!) and something from my private stash to wash them down. After that, nap time. With luck, the nap won't be permanent.

###

Another week down the drain while I coughed, gagged, and puked, and rested up from coughing, gagging, and puking. There's not much of me left.

Francesca just told me she and Willa Devlin have plans to return to Luxor. "Unfinished business," she says, and even though she kept trying to change the subject, she had to admit it was something to do with Adam Dexter. I flat-out asked her if she was trying to find him, and she shuffled her feet and looked anywhere but at me. Finally, she said yes, she has some ideas about his disappearance. I reminded her he has been declared a missing person and may be a defector, or even dead. She said, "Maybe he is and maybe he isn't. I want to find out for sure. And we're going to do some other things too, like look up my friends at the dig, and see some sights. But don't worry, Alma. I've told Willa I can't go anywhere while you're still — while you're so sick."

I may be sick, but I caught that little slip of hers. "While you're still alive," she meant to say. So she won't go until — spit it out, old woman! — I'm dead. That means sooner rather than later, so I'd better get this done. Push, push, push!

I wish my health was better than shitty, so I could track down Amelia Devlin and ask her some pointed questions, especially now that my thoughts have taken a distinctly bizarre turn. Even though I didn't much like her, I'm beginning to think we have things in common. (~~Bastard~~ Illegitimate children, for example.)

```
Aging    Newspaperwoman    Becomes    a
Credulous Eccentric
A.G.  Halsey,  now  in  her  dotage  and
final  decline,  has  lost  her  mind  and
begun  to  entertain  peculiar  notions.
Fortunately,  she  is  no  longer  in  a
position   to   mislead   readers   by
spreading false news.
```

How my old newspaper colleagues would laugh (if most of them weren't dead, that is) if they knew into what dubious regions my recent investigations have led me. But I'm not writing this for publication.

Let's have a hard look at the facts. Let's lay them out and probe them with the sharp editorial pencil.

Item: my old enemy, then friend (and sometime lover), Herbert Francis West/Dexter returned from the dead in 1923, with the help of my old friend and best-beloved, Charles Milburn. Until his final death in 1939 he exercised inexplicable powers of healing.

Item: Adam Dexter also had/has (?) some sort of connection to realms beyond the ordinary. Beyond science, even. Something that relates to the fundamentals of <u>matter</u>. His origins are rooted in Egypt through his mother. France met him there, near a scene of murder, and was drawn into an intimate relationship with him. Now he has vanished.

Item: Amelia Devlin may have extra-sensory perception and was engaged to Adam Dexter. Her daughter Willa is also <u>his</u> daughter, which makes her an unknown quantity.

Item: Francesca Leighton experienced something in Egypt that altered her fundamentally, perhaps awakened latent abilities inherited from her grandfather. It made her devious and secretive. But I fear she may have acquired something dangerous as well.

France brought <u>objects</u> back from Egypt. Not just souvenirs. She acquired a pair of statuettes. They are small things, seven or eight inches tall, made of that glassy stuff called faience, blue in colour, with features and hieroglyphs painted on them in black. I saw them in her room soon after her return, and asked her about them.

146

France told me they're called <u>shabtis</u>, figurines that were deposited in ancient Egyptian tombs to work for the dead in the afterlife. Thousands and thousands of them were made over the centuries. I asked her whose tomb these two came from and would they work for that person even now? She got a funny look on her face for a few seconds. Then she said she doesn't know if they're ancient or just copies made for the souvenir trade. And anyway, she said, shabtis need a particular spell recited to make them work in the afterlife.

<u>But she talks to them</u>. I overheard her once, not long after she came back from Egypt. I don't think she knew I was in the house, because I'd gone out earlier and came back sooner than I'd told her. The door of her room was ajar but the hall carpet muffled my footsteps. I heard France's voice say, "But we don't know that." It startled me, not only because it seemed a strange thing to say just then, but because it sounded like she was arguing with someone. I stopped and stood there—and yes, I admit it—I listened.

"I didn't see him die," she said. "The cobra got him, but—" There was a silence, followed by a sigh. I heard a rustle of clothing as she moved, and got ready to retreat, but there were no more sounds. I peered into the room. France was sitting at her desk. Between her and the window, silhouetted against the light from outside, stood those two figurines, shaped like little Egyptian pharaohs, with the distinctive headdress and their arms crossed over their chests. It was like they were staring at her, watching and listening. I turned around and came back, shuffling my feet, saying, "France, I'm back early." She hustled out of the room and closed the door. I didn't dare ask her about what I'd heard and seen.

Another time, I was about to knock on her door, when I heard singing. No, maybe a better word is <u>chanting</u>. It was France's voice, for sure. Short phrases, in no language I could identify. A brief silence and more chanting, louder. Another silence, followed by "Damn it!" Then a few moments later, the sound of a door slamming shut.

I couldn't ask her about this without admitting I'd been eavesdropping. Maybe it was just her way of working out the aftereffects of what she'd experienced in Egypt. But I can't shake off the feeling that she brought <u>something unnatural</u> back with her.

Those statuettes are part of it, I'm sure. She came back from Egypt with those two objects instead of her precious cello. If I was able, I'd take them to an expert who could tell me more about them, but it's too late for that. At least I can take a good look at them. Interview them, you might say.

`News Flash! Sick Old Woman Undertakes`
`Perilous Journey Down Hallway`
Ha, ha! Not funny. But at least I've got my ducks in a row. One ducky, two duckies, three duckies, four... Not duckies. Two guys. Yes, I mean that—guys. They have personalities—evil, mischievous ones.

Begin at the beginning, Alma, even though you're at the end.

I'm never sure these days when France is in or out. Her job is part-time, with irregular shifts, but she did tell me she was going to a party on Saturday night. The trouble is when I wake up in the dark, I don't know if it's late today or early tomorrow.

Lightning and thunder dragged me out of sleep. I lay there watching tree-shadows thrashing around on the ceiling

148

and thinking it must still be Saturday night, since it felt like thunderstorm weather that evening. I made up my mind to investigate.

I managed to find the little flashlight in my bedside table's drawer. It wouldn't be a good idea to turn on the light in France's room, because it faces the street and she'd see it if she came home while I was snooping.

I shuffled down the hall and tapped on her door. Tap-tap. Wait. No response. Tap-tap, a bit louder. Wait. Nothing. Tap-tap-rap! Still nothing. I opened the door a crack. Silence.

The bed was flat and empty. No one home. Okay. I shone my light around, hoping the statuettes were sitting on the desk or dresser. No such luck. Then I remembered the slamming sound I heard while eavesdropping. What would make that sound?

I looked around, all the while listening for France coming home. The wardrobe had a pair of small doors near the bottom. I opened them and shone my light in. Three cardboard boxes sat there, looking anonymous.

My back hurt and I felt like lying down on the floor and giving up. I didn't like rifling through my granddaughter's things and maybe getting caught in the act. I grabbed a box at random, carried it over to the desk, and took off the lid. Photographs and letters.

I clapped the lid back on, returned it to its place, and tried another one. Turquoise scarf, lovely colour. I pressed down on it and felt something lumpy and vaguely cylindrical. Two somethings. Bingo.

I unwrapped the scarf and set the statuettes on the desk, side by side. A lightning flash jittered electricity into the room and brightened their blue colour. I sat and counted seconds.

"One thousand and one, one thousand and two, one thousand and three," and then thunder cracked, meaning it struck pretty close by. I peered at the figurines, my two eyes to their four. The guy on the left had a squint, the one on the right an evil grin. I could have sworn it smirked at me. Even worse, the other one stuck out its tongue. Then they looked at each other and back at me.

How could that be? Black paint on blue glaze can't smirk or move. Okay, the light wasn't the best—faint and shaky, like me. "Who are you?" I whispered.

In a hush between wind gusts, I heard a faint humming that grew to a buzz. There were words in it, I was certain. Words in a language I didn't know. The shabtis watched me as I listened, their black eyes intent. The air became hot and smelled of burning.

A tremendous bolt of lightning and nearly simultaneous roar of thunder shocked me out of my trance. I pushed myself up, knocking the statuettes over. I bundled the scarf around them, stuffed them back into their box, shoved the box into the cupboard, and slammed the doors shut.

Halfway down the hallway, one of my slippers tangled with the other, and something gave my shoulder a firm nudge. Or maybe I bumped into the wall. I went down hard and couldn't get back up. France found me when she got home. Now I'm stuck in bed for good.


```
The End of the Road
Alma    Halsey,    newspaperwoman,    is
gasping her last at age 77. The cancer
```

```
has done its work, probably helped by
a recent fall.
She's finished.
-30-
```

###

It has taken less time than I hoped, just six weeks since I got the bad news. At least France and I have had some Nice Talks. Yes, <u>nice</u>. It's sweet to see her become all protective of me, even while I'm telling her things she doesn't want to hear.

I've said what I needed to say, and she listened, or appeared to. And she has it in writing. I've met my deadline.

No more writing for me. No more typing. I'm on my deathbed. But the old brain still works, hurray! Too bad I can't add July 25th to that obituary. Or maybe the 26th. France will have to do it for me.

Enough of this. What will be, will be. Isn't that what the song says? It won't be for me to say, it won't be for me to do. I'm tired. I miss Charles. My body doesn't work anymore. I don't believe in heaven, and maybe not in hell either, but I hope my essence will once more touch his, before we merge into the world-soul together. And Herbert too. Herbert Francis, who returned from the dead once and died twice. Once is enough for me. If I see him again, maybe he'll tell me his secrets.

Oh—I forgot to ask France about the rose bush, the one that's had blue flowers ever since the year Francis died. It grows in the lower garden, by the spring that's never failed. I wasn't able to get down there one last time. I'll have to ask her.

The door to my room opens. I hear Francesca's voice, but I can't see her. Yes, the door is open. She's dressed in blue, but I can't see her face behind the blinding light.

SEVEN SPECULATIVE TALES

WELCOME TO THE WITCH HOUSE

Two character sketches for an unwritten novel

Arkham, Massachusetts, January 1925

The Ruminations of Walter Gilman

He turned up four months after I moved into the Witch House—fat Frank Elwood, from my home town of Haverhill, Massachusetts. When I saw him in the front hall, talking to landlord Dombrowski, it was like a chunk of that practical, shoe-obsessed city had tracked me down to Arkham, intent on dragging me back.

As if I hadn't had the devil of a time getting away from the place already. "Why do you have to go to Arkham?" My father must have asked me that a hundred times, alternating with "Why do you have to go to college? You can step into a good job right here and now, and when I die it will all be yours. You don't need college."

He was right, if all I wanted to do was spend the rest of my life among clanking, roaring machines and the louts who run them, cutting, stretching, shaping, stitching and glazing millions of receptacles for *feet*. Or if I was fascinated by the balance sheet and the ledger, the profit margin and the management of business.

But I am not. And unfortunately, my father managed to sire only one son. He will have to resign himself to a son-in-law as heir to his very own chunk of the Queen Slipper City of the World. Not everyone is content to fasten his nose to the grindstone and develop a fascination with grains of grit. The world is too wide and too strange for that.

The second thought that popped into my head when I saw Elwood looming over old Dombrowski was that my father had sent him to cajole or threaten me into quitting Miskatonic and going home. That was absurd, though. If he wanted to do that, he would do it himself, and even if he wanted to send an emissary, it wouldn't be Frank Elwood.

He was the son of a former foreman in Gilman's Excellent Boot and Shoe Company—former because he was dead, the result of an unfortunate encounter with one of the machines he was in charge of. His death was a considerable nuisance to my father, and even to me, because unrest among the workers and threats to form a union made Father decide it would be politic for the two of us to attend the funeral.

That was where I first saw Frank, glowering at me as I took a place in the pew across from the one he and his mother and sisters occupied. Maybe it was because we were close in age, but I felt him putting a mark on me, as though for future consideration. And now, here he was in Arkham, in the very place where I lived.

Some call it the Witch House, after one of the most famous denizens of witch-haunted Arkham—Keziah Mason, known to the initiate as Nahab. No one knows this (because I haven't told anyone), but she was my reason for choosing to live in this house, otherwise shunned by Miskatonians, faculty and students alike.

It's in the oldest part of the city, a huddle of sway-backed, gambrel-roofed structures that manage to stay standing after nearly three hundred years. I'm sure they were never meant to last that long by the honest Puritans who built them, nor to shelter some of the beings that have found homes within them over the years (and I don't mean the ubiquitous rats). Unless a house burns down or collapses from internal rot, they persist, growing ever more disreputable, like a group of drunks holding each other up as they lurch along.

I think the home folks finally gave up on me when I told them where I decided to live. "That horrible slum. Why, the people there aren't respectable. They're all foreigners and"—whispering –"*Catholics*." They decided I was doomed. The odd few times I went back home to visit they looked at me the way people look at condemned criminals or the terminally ill.

They would never have believed me if I had told them the simple truth—that Keziah Mason was part of my research, along with non-Euclidean calculus and quantum physics. In fact, I think that would have given my father grounds to ship me off to an asylum.

But what was Frank Elwood doing in the Witch House? That was the question.

He and Dombrowski looked up when they heard me close the door. "Oh, Mr. Gilman," intoned the landlord, scooping at the air with his hand, as though it was elastic and he could pull me closer. "Here is another man from the college, Mr. Alwood, his name. This is Mr. Walter Gilman. He lives in the room at the top of the house and has to climb up many, many stairs. You only have to go up to second floor." He beamed as though he'd said something profound.

Frank Elwood stood there looking at me like he was trying to figure something out, chewing over his thoughts like a cow with a cud. There actually was something bovine about him; he was big and solid and slow, with a heavy face and a wide forehead and a lot of thick brown hair. His eyes peered out like windows under a thatched roof.

Finally his mouth opened and words came out. "Walter Gilman. I know you."

I bowed in acknowledgement. "Perhaps, but I don't believe we've actually met."

This disconcerted him, as I intended. His face turned red and he looked at his feet (which were large like the rest of him and not particularly well-shod, surprising in a Haverhillian).

He raised his head and looked at me again. I could have sworn he was angry and trying not to show it. At me or at himself?

"We have now," he said and turned to Dombrowski again, and then back to me, as though he couldn't help himself.

"You live here?" he asked. "Here in this house?"

I smiled. "I do. Mr. Dombrowski was kind enough to rent me one of the rooms in the attic. A very special room. I have found it most satisfactory."

I had nothing more to say to either of them and headed for the stairs. The first set was relatively wide and gracious, except each step was bowed and hollowed from three centuries of use. I watched my feet move from one to the other and thought of all the hundreds and thousands of other feet that had preceded them—and whose they might have been. Keziah Mason's for sure. They must have trodden these steps many times, even the narrow ones from the second floor to the third, all the way up to the top of the house.

My room was larger than you would expect, but with the low ceiling typical of its location. It had a single eastward-facing window that was bright in the morning and dimmed gradually after noonday. Night came earlier there than in other places.

The real attraction didn't reveal itself to me until November, when, sick and feverish, I spent a couple of days in bed, dozing and staring at the ceiling, watching the watery sunlight traverse the room, lighting up now this wall, now that corner, a piece of the ceiling and then the opposite wall, before fading away and leaving my abode in soft, dusty shadow.

I thought about what we had been discussing in Prof. Upham's class before I'd been taken ill—the fourth dimension and possible freakish curvatures in space which may be used as points of contact with distant parts of the cosmos. I thought about Keziah Mason and what she had told Judge Hathorne at her trial in 1692, about *lines and curves* that led those who knew about them to spaces other than the known.

I fixed my eyes on the place where the north wall, slanting gently inward from its outer to its inner end, met the downward-slanting ceiling. The conjunction was an uneasy one, with peculiar angles. I thought of the equations I had pored over on many a long evening, and fancied I could see a sort of sliding or shifting of planes, as though a long-closed door was coming ever so slightly ajar. There's the gate, I thought muzzily. The portal. Right there. Then I fell asleep again and dreamed strange dreams.

The next day I was well enough to go back to class, but found it hard to concentrate. I could hardly wait to get back to the Witch House and take a good look at the north wall from the outside. As I expected, it was perfectly straight, and what was more, there had once been a window just where my room was. Judging by the carpentry, the window had been closed up a very long time ago, in the eighteenth century if not earlier. I wondered what might be found in the narrow triangular space between the inner and outer walls, where no light had entered for more than two centuries.

Then I grew curious about the loft above my ceiling, in the very peak of the roof, and borrowed a ladder from Dombrowski so I could get a closer look. Peering through festoons of cobwebs from the other end of the attic, I saw heavy planks and pegs similar to those that sealed the window, covering an aperture that must have led to a cramped space with a slanting floor directly above my room. I tried to persuade Dombrowski to let me open it up, but he refused outright, saying he had enough trouble keeping the rats under control. But he's a superstitious old loon, like all these Poles, and I thought I saw a nervous twitch in his eye. There was nothing I could say to make him change his mind.

The next time I saw Elwood, he was trying to manhandle a couple of suitcases up the stairs.

"It would be easier if you took them one at a time," I offered, earning myself a look like a clenched fist. I guessed he would have shaken one at me if his hands weren't full. That nearly made me laugh.

"Here, let me take one of them," I said and seized the handle. The thing weighed a lot more than I expected and nearly wrenched my arm off, but I didn't think Elwood saw that. We progressed up to the second floor and down the hall to his room. I landed the case and looked around. His room was bigger than mine and had a fireplace, but all the walls and ceilings met at the expected ninety degrees.

I thought a bit of conversation was the right thing for the occasion. "So what is it you're studying at Miskatonic?"

Elwood scowled and emitted a foggy grunt, as though this was the first time he'd spoken aloud all day. Clearing his throat, he tried again. "Medicine," he said. "Eventually. I'm taking a bachelor of science degree first, of course." A pause. "What about you?"

"Math and physics," I said. "And witchcraft, of a sort. Welcome to the Witch House, Elwood."

Then I turned and left.

~oOo~

The Account of Frank Elwood

I never intended to live in such a shabby part of Arkham. I didn't even think a college town would have a slum like that. Just about all the people who live there are poor, except Gilman, but he had his own reasons for being there.

My first semester at Miskatonic, I had a room close to the college, practically across the street, in fact. It was nice and clean and close to downtown as well. Right at the start I kicked up my heels a bit, seeing as I was away from home and didn't have to be the man of the house, as my mother called me.

But after a couple of months, I sat down and did some figuring, and the results of this effort were not good. I was living beyond my means. My scholarship wasn't enough to pay for everything and there was nothing to spare for me from my family. After counting up my remaining dollars I decided the only thing to do was find cheaper living quarters.

I didn't want to ask other students or my professors. No one likes to admit he's coming down in the world, not that I had a very long distance to slide before I hit the bottom. As luck would have it, I saw a notice in a cafeteria on Church Street — Room for Rent. It gave the address and the name John Dombrowski. I went over there right after classes the same day.

The house was brown and reminded me of an old person who used to be taller, with its little windows squinting out like bleary eyes. I stood in the street for a while, wondering if I really wanted to live there. It looked like it had rats. I hate rats. The truth was, though, I didn't have much choice.

Just then a fellow came out of the front door and grinned at me. "You looking for Dombrowski?" he asked, speaking with a thick Polish accent. "He's in his office. You just go in."

"I guess I will," I replied and walked inside.

Dombrowski was one of those short, fat Poles who smell like garlic. You see them everywhere now. A bunch of them were in my Dad's crew at the factory. He said they were good enough workers, once you pounded the right way to do things into their thick heads. I never figured one of them was going to be my landlord.

I asked about the room and he showed it to me. It was all right — on the second floor, not too small, with a bed, a wardrobe, a chair and a table. There was no bookcase, but what did I expect? There was a fireplace that looked like it hadn't been used in a long time, but most important, there didn't seem to be any active rat holes, although I could see a couple of stopped-up ones.

"Are rats a problem here?" I asked.

"No rats!" Dombrowski said, so quickly I knew he had to be lying. "I use traps, I use poison. No more rats!" I wasn't in a position to argue and Dombrowski, who knew his business, escorted me swiftly back to the front hall. He told me that for an extra twenty-five cents a day I could get a good breakfast. "Cooked by Mrs. Dombrowski; you can't find better anywhere." Just then, the door opened and someone came in. I expected to see another lodger, a stranger, but then I recognized him.

I had seen Walter Gilman around Haverhill when I was growing up there, but it wasn't like we were pals. He was the big boss's son and my Dad was just one of the workers. The last time I'd seen Walter was at my father's funeral, sitting next to his old man. I wanted to go up and slug them both, but that would have troubled my mother and probably landed me in jail, so I didn't.

I thought Walter was trying to dress like he belonged to one of the wilder college sets. He wore a fancy coat that looked like part of a costume, with a fringed scarf wrapped around his neck and a fedora in his hand. He was shorter than me and skinny, with almost-black hair that needed a trip to the barber and a little moustache I was sure he fussed over in front of a mirror, willing it to grow in thicker.

He closed the door and stood on the mat, looking at me like I was an exhibit in a museum. I could almost see the little wheels turning in his head: *there's that fellow whose father died in my dad's factory. Too bad. I had to take an afternoon to go to the funeral. What a bore. What's his name? Not important.*

Then Dombrowski got back into his song and dance, introducing us as though we were at a party. I guess to him we were two of a kind, both college students. People from Miskatonic probably didn't rent rooms from him often so he was delighted to have two of us at once. And I can't blame the man for what he couldn't possibly have known.

He couldn't have known that James Gilman, Walter's father, killed my Dad. All right, he didn't stick a knife into him or poison him or shoot him dead, but he was just as responsible for his death as if he'd done it deliberately.

Thomas Elwood, my father, was foreman on the leather cutting machines at Gilman's shoe factory. He'd worked his way up from the bottom and was proud of that. One day when he was clearing a fault in one of the machines, a belt pulled him into the blades and he was badly cut. He died a couple of hours later. If James Gilman hadn't been too cheap to install modern equipment with safety switches, my father would be alive today, my mother and sisters would have a comfortable life, and I wouldn't have to live in a rat-infested slum.

But never mind—once I earned my degrees and qualified as a doctor, things would change. As for Walter Gilman, I decided to stay out of his way. It would be easier if we didn't live in the same house, but it could be done.

Walking back to the college district, I started to wonder just what Gilman was doing in a place like Dombrowski's. It wasn't because he didn't have enough money; last time I looked, his old man was driving a Packard and the factory still didn't have a union. Well, he could keep his secrets to himself. I was going to avoid him.

This resolution was tested the very next day, when I moved my things into my new room. I had two big old suitcases that had belonged to my grandfather. He'd arrived in America with all his belongings in them and had done well. My worldly goods fitted into them with room to spare, so I suppose I had a job of work to catch up to Grandpa. The case with my books made for a heavy load, but I wanted to get the move done as fast as I could, so lugged both suitcases at once and was damn glad when I finally hauled them and myself onto the porch of Dombrowski's house.

I used the case with the books to hold the door open while I got the other one inside, and then picked them both up and started to hump them up the stairs to the second floor. It was harder work than I expected, but I couldn't go back and there was nowhere to put either case down. I was beginning to think I would have trouble with the corner at the top, when I heard a voice from below.

"You should have known better than to carry both of them at once." For a second I thought the labour of moving my possessions had rendered me light-headed, because I remembered my Dad saying things like, "Slow and steady wins the race, Frank," and, "Measure twice, cut once." Much as I admired my father, I have to admit these sayings sometimes got on my nerves. But now I wished it really was him even while I knew it wasn't.

I turned and saw Gilman standing at the bottom of the stairs with that stupid fedora in his hand, smirking under his moustache. Smirking at me. I was about to tell him to keep his advice to himself, when he ran up the stairs, holding out the hand that didn't have his hat in it. "Here, I'll take one of those cases."

I let him have the one with the books, hoping he'd drop it on his foot. It would serve him right, and besides, I couldn't hang onto it any more. He had a hard time with it at first but he was right behind me when we reached the top. He followed me into my room and dumped the case next to the one I had carried. Instead of leaving, he just stood there, looking around as though he was doing an inspection. I was about to ask him if he'd noticed rats in the house, but he spoke up first.

"So what is it you're studying, anyway?" he asked.

"Medicine," I said. Then, because I supposed I owed him something, "What about you?" trying to sound as though I cared.

"Mathematics and physics," he replied, in that la-de-dah way of his. Then he said something else, about witchcraft. "Welcome to the Witch House." He didn't wait for an answer but turned and left, flipping his fringed scarf over his shoulder.

Math and physics. Well, well. Sometimes I think the good Lord has a sense of humor. I was doing all right in my classes, except for math. One of the things that bothered me about moving farther from campus was there wouldn't be anyone handy to ask for help with math problems. But here was Walter Gilman, who was studying that very subject. Except I couldn't stand to look at his face and remember how he sat there at my Dad's funeral looking bored.

No—forget Gilman. I'd just have to work harder. I didn't want any more help from him.

The idea that I would end up helping him never entered my mind.

THE DELIVERER OF DELUSIONS

{With apologies to Robert W. Chambers}

The shop looked as I remembered it, with the same sign over the door. Hawberk, Armourer. A closer view revealed four more years of fade and peel. The same tinkling bell, though.

He looked up from his work with a blank-eyed stare. Then—"Ah, Miss Miranda. Miss Castaigne, I mean. My condolences. It's a sad return home for you."

"Thank you, Mr. Hawberk. I left Paris as soon as I received Louis's telegram, but it took me two weeks to get here."

"*Bienvenue à nouveau après toutes ces années, Mademoiselle.*" Followed by a courtly bow and a Gallic hand gesture that made a flash of reflected light from the ring on his right hand. It must have been the signet on which my brother Hildred had recognized the arms of some ancient English family—one of the reasons he found Hawberk and his shop so fascinating.

"*Merci, Monsieur.*" As always, suits of armour stood around the shop, in various stages of completeness, some shiny, some rusty—customers who did not mind waiting. "I gather it happened here? That last incident, when Hildred was... taken into custody?"

"Not here in the shop, no, but in this building. In Mr. Wilde's rooms, upstairs."

"Mr. Wilde—he was the man who died? Whom Hildred was supposed to have murdered?"

"He lived upstairs, yes."

"May I see…? I'm trying to put it all together, his last days. How it happened."

"I understand." He rummaged in a drawer and brought out a key.

The stairs were steep, brown and narrow. Hawberk struggled awhile with the key before the door opened with a screech. "Reminds me of Wilde's cat," Hawberk said. "Savage creature, but he liked her."

Mr. Wilde's rooms were empty of visible life—bare bookshelves, a curious high desk and matching tall chair with a set of ladder-like rungs. Dust and nameless scraps lay on the floor. A signboard leaned against the wall. I turned my head sideways to read it. "Repairer of Reputations. What's that?"

"Mr. Wilde was eccentric."

Watery sunlight from the small-paned window drew a scintillation from something on the floor. I bent and extracted a bit of glass from a crack between two boards. A scrap of paper lying nearby caught my eye, my own surname unlikely in this dreary place. "…only son of Hildred Castaigne and Edythe…" and, on the line below that, "…in the succession."

I slipped the scrap into my pocket and examined what proved to be more than a piece of broken glass. Intricately cut facets made a small brilliance on my palm. I held it out to Hawberk. "What do you suppose this is?"

"It looks like a diamond. Couldn't be real, though." He looked up at me. "It might have come from that diadem."

"Diadem? Did Mr. Wilde collect such things, as well as repairing reputations?"

"No. Mr. Castaigne brought it with him, that night."

"My brother had a *diadem* with him?"

"Yes. Made to look like gold and diamonds. Couldn't have been real. With everything that happened, I didn't get a good look at it, but I supposed it had something to do with his interest in heraldry, royal symbols, all that. You didn't know about it?"

"No!" *The succession.* I looked at the diamond again. Real or paste? "So what happened to this diadem?"

Hawberk creased his brow and looked toward the window, where a fly buzzed against the panes. "I really don't know. Perhaps the police took it away as evidence."

There was nothing more to say. The musty smell of the place and the buzzing fly oppressed me. "I've taken up enough of your time, Mr. Hawberk."

But at the door of the shop, I paused. "Do you think my brother was insane?"

He examined the key to Wilde's door, rubbing it with his thumb. "I really can't say, Miss Castaigne. He didn't seem so, all those years, but something strange happened to him at the end."

"Goodbye, Mr. Hawberk. And thank you for being kind to Hildred. He loved your shop."

~o0o~

Upon his removal from Dr. Archer's care six months after his riding accident, Hildred had moved to the Benedick apartments in Washington Square. For an entire year, I had called on him

169

every day, often tracking him down in Hawberk's shop, where he went to listen to the music of metal on metal and lose himself in scintillations of light on the armour plates. Then the call of Paris and adventure had grown too strong for me to ignore. An opportunity presented itself and I took it, telling myself that Hildred was well again, even if other interests had supplanted his former pastimes of fishing, yachting and riding. And our cousin Louis was near enough to keep an eye on him.

I was gone for more than three years—golden years! They fled by so quickly, until Louis's telegram came. "Hildred dead in asylum for insane." By the time I arrived in New York City, Louis too was far away. His regiment had been posted to San Francisco. He had married Constance Hawberk and departed. Was I unjust in suspecting him of undue haste? No matter—he was only a cousin. I was Hildred's sister.

The concierge at the Benedick admitted me quite readily when I identified myself. I felt a moment of dread before unlocking the door to Hildred's rooms, anticipating sorrow at the sight of his possessions bereft of his presence. But a surprise greeted me instead—the rooms were empty. Not only of Hildred, but of furniture, books, carpets and ornaments. Only the curtains remained, their velvet folds hanging mutely, as though in helpless apology.

No books on the shelves. No shelves. No papers on the desk. No desk. No clothes in the wardrobe. No wardrobe. Where was everything? The concierge hadn't said anything about this removal. The rooms were still Hildred Castaigne's. He was gone, but his possessions should have remained.

I returned to the sitting-room and took the tour again. Study, bedroom, sitting-room. Back to the study, floors creaking, steps echoing. He was gone. Gone completely. His mortal remains rested in our family's cemetery plot. I had hoped to capture something of his spirit here, in the last place he had lived, but it was an empty shell.

The concierge was still in his office. "Can you tell me who removed Mr. Castaigne's possessions? And when?"

"Not exactly, Miss. Some men came, a couple of weeks ago. Said they had the family's permission."

"I am his family. His sister. I gave no permission. And a couple of weeks ago I was in Paris."

He shrugged. "Well, that's what they said. And where? I think I heard them say Madison Avenue."

My heart sank. Madison Avenue was a long street. I pulled my wallet from my handbag and held out several dollars. "Please, can you remember anything else?"

The man took the currency and counted it. "Maybe," he said, smirking. "Make it an even ten and we'll see."

I produced two more dollars.

"Dr. John Archer," he said.

~oOo~

A muscular servant admitted me into Dr. Archer's establishment. "One moment, Miss Castaigne." He vanished down a plushly carpeted hallway, bearing my card.

I was studying some prints of the Hudson River Valley on the walls of the foyer when a small cough startled me. I had not heard the man's return.

But it wasn't the servant. Behind me stood a figure of grey and silver—silver hair, pale skin, grey eyes, grey suit. "Miss Castaigne," he murmured, extending a hand. "I am John Archer. He clasped my hand in both of his. "I am happy to meet you at last, Miranda Castaigne, despite the sad reason for your presence."

"Thank you, Dr. Archer." I extracted my hand. The hall was dimly lit, but did that account for the squinting right eye, a darker colour than its mate? A substitute for the original, perhaps?

"Come into my office, Miss Castaigne." He applied his hand to the back of my arm. "This way, please."

Seated in a chair opposite Dr. Archer's desk, I told him I was seeking a coherent account of Hildred's last days. "The person at the Asylum said only that he threw himself down a flight of stairs. He had been brought there the previous night, after an incident where a man had been murdered. It was assumed Hildred had committed the crime. I find that hard to believe. My brother was never a violent person."

The burly manservant entered, bearing a tray with teapot and cups. Dr. Archer poured out. "Some tea, Miss Castaigne?" With his back to the windows, the disturbing squint was no longer visible.

"Miss Castaigne," Dr. Archer said, "an injury to the brain, such as your brother sustained in the fall from his horse, can cause unpredictable, and indeed violent behaviour."

"But that fall was more than four years ago! And you declared him cured. He wrote to me months ago, saying he had, as he put it, 'paid my tuition to Dr. Archer.'"

The doctor's lips stretched and thinned into a smile. "Yes, I remember that. Indeed, for several years Mr. Castaigne was in most respects as sane as anyone, but such injuries have lasting effects. That is why I insisted he visit me regularly after he left my direct care; and why I hired one or two individuals to keep a watch over him, especially after you left the country."

172

"You had him watched! So how do you explain these events? Hildred is dead! How could he go from 'as sane as anyone' to dead—and in such a terrible way?"

"Calm yourself, Miss Castaigne." The smile had vanished. "Clearly, some external event triggered a swift return to an irrational state and set off the sequence of events leading to his death. Do you have any idea what that trigger may have been?"

I took a sip of tea. It was delicious, sweet and fragrant. "I don't know. I've been abroad for the past three years. Hildred and I corresponded, of course. He did mention, last spring, that our cousin Louis and Miss Hawberk were likely to marry, but—
"

"Indeed. That may have had a profound effect on young Mr. Castaigne. Perhaps he, too, entertained romantic feelings for this young woman? He did, after all, frequent her father's shop."

"No. He never so much as hinted at such a thing. Dr. Archer, my brother Hildred was a... dreamy young man. Impractical, even before his injury. After it, he developed intense interests in particular topics, such as heraldry and Napoleon. He became something of a recluse, but a violent attack on another person—that was entirely unlike him!" I set down the now empty teacup, my hand shaking a little.

"You were not in personal contact with him at the time, though. Subtle changes are not conveyed in letters, I fear."

From a lazy young man about town, I have become active, energetic, temperate, and, above all—oh, above all else—ambitious. I remembered this sentence from one of Hildred's last letters to me. Hildred, ambitious? God help me, I had smiled. And I had dismissed as a harmless whim the fact that he had begun dating his letters as though they came from the future—1920.

All this was overwhelming. I felt a little dizzy and decided it was time to end the conversation.

"May I ask, Miss Castaigne—what was the reason for your extended absence?" Dr. Archer folded his hands together on the desk and leaned forward slightly. The squint I thought I had seen in his right eye was no longer evident; perhaps I had been mistaken. There was no sense of urgency about him. He was prepared to listen. And I—oh, there was so much I could say! About the death of my father, which launched my mother into rural seclusion. Then Hildred's accident and transformation and my decision to run away to Paris, comforting myself with the hope that he would someday return to his former self.

"I went to Paris to study art," I replied, thinking how frivolous that sounded. "There are many Americans there. I became part of that group. It was a very... productive environment." I felt myself blushing, as though Dr. Archer could see the memories behind my words—days of work and nights of debate and merriment, ramblings beneath the sun, in bird-haunted meadows, on crystalline lakes. The meshing of personalities and aspirations. And Jack Scott.

"Art," said Dr. Archer, tilting his head and smiling. "Painting, sketching, charcoal, pastels, oils?"

"Printmaking," I replied. "Lithography."

"Ah." He smiled again, without blinking. "And what led you to that medium?"

"Being around others who worked in it, I suppose." My ears buzzed and my head felt as though it wanted to float away. I hoped I wasn't becoming ill.

"You were influenced." He removed his hands from the desk and turned his chair slightly.

"I suppose so. Dr. Archer, I think I have taken up enough of your time—"

"But you want to know what happened to Hildred, do you not? Well, I can show you." He stood. "Come with me."

I stood too, and almost sat back down. My legs felt like wet ribbons. Dr. Archer grasped my arm firmly and conducted me farther down the hallway, to a small elevator. The same muscular servant—or was he an orderly?—opened the sliding gate and heavy door. The conveyance carried us some unknown distance upward, or perhaps downward? I was unfamiliar with these machines. Once the sensation of motion ceased, the man opened the door and gate to another narrow hallway. The carpet here was thin and worn.

Without a word, Dr. Archer led me to an open door. Entering the room beyond it, I looked around me, astonished.

I was in Hildred's rooms as I remembered them. There stood the furniture, there hung the familiar pictures. Not at the Benedick, of course, but here, in Dr. Archer's house on Madison Avenue. If I looked out the window, I would not see the fountain playing or nursemaids wheeling infants along the paved walks. What would I see? Unsteadily, I moved forward, intending to part the nearest set of garnet-coloured curtains, but a large metal box caught my eye. About the size of a biscuit-tin, it had been fitted with metal knobs of some sort.

"What's that?" I asked. My lips felt slightly numb. "And why did you bring Hildred's things here?"

"I hoped to resume treating him, when I heard of his arrest and confinement. Unfortunately, his accident prevented that."

175

"It wasn't an accident," I muttered. "But his belongings... Why?"

"I wished to create a congenial, welcoming atmosphere."

"So he was to be brought here from the Asylum?"

"Yes. I saw Hildred at the Asylum, soon after his arrest and confinement, and offered to take charge of his case. They know me at the Asylum." He smiled again, like one who holds all the cards, squinting both his eyes. "I immediately arranged for his possessions to be moved here and placed as you see them before he arrived."

"Except he killed himself first." My head was full of fog and I found it hard to think.

"Miss Castaigne, you are quite pale." He indicated an armchair. "Have a seat here. Pretend you are visiting Hildred. Miss Castaigne, are you familiar with crypto-mesmerism?"

"What?" Still thinking about what he had just told me, I sank onto the chair. "Crypto—I've never heard of it."

"As I thought. Crypto-mesmerism is the effect of art upon susceptible minds. Certain pictures or writings may have a profound influence upon those who view or read them."

"I suppose, but what—?"

"Artistic temperaments especially lend themselves to the study of this effect. Your brother Hildred had such a temperament, unrealized though it was. He proved exquisitely susceptible, at least to one particular book."

He went to a bookcase filled with what I had already recognized as Hildred's collection of Napoleon books. Ignoring these, he drew out from among them a slender volume, which he handed to me. Swirls of yellow outlined in black adorned the cover. Among them was the title — *The King in Yellow.*

"I've heard of... this book," I said, my tongue slow and awkward in my mouth. "What sort of inf... influence did it have... on Hildred?"

Dr. Archer went to Hildred's desk and removed a paper from its surface. He handed it to me. "This was one effect."

On the paper were two words in my brother's handwriting, repeated many times. Dozens of times. *Hildred Rex.* "What does this mean?"

"He thought he would be King. The lost King of America. Mr. Wilde, who was once a patient of mine, aided in my diagnosis and treatment."

"And that's why Hildred murdered him?"

A nod. "And now, Miss Castaigne, we have much to do. I've sent my man to your hotel for your baggage, as I'm sure you would not want to wear your brother's clothes. Please make yourself comfortable." He gestured toward the bed, whose plump pillows looked most inviting.

"But why—?"

"You will be my guest for a while, Miranda Castaigne." Dr. Archer smiled broadly now, showing large yellow teeth. "Your brother is dead and your cousin Louis is temperamentally impossible. But you—you definitely have potential." He grasped my arm yet again and led me toward the bed.

"Potential for what? What will I do here?"

"You will sleep. And when you wake, you will read *The King in Yellow*. Then we shall see."

I fell onto the bed. Black wings enfolded me and a voice intoned, "...a Consort of the true Blood to serve Him..."

THE ICE CREAM TRUCK FROM HELL

Music. A happy, merry tune, growing fainter with distance and then coming back. Will Todd knew the tune, even though he couldn't remember its name. The sound of an ice cream truck meant it was summer and everything was all right. They were still living in their old house. Will wouldn't be going to a new school where he didn't know anyone. It was summer and he could have ice cream for breakfast.

Then he woke up. Even in a dream he'd never be allowed to have ice cream for breakfast. His mom might say okay, but not his dad.

Leaning out his window, Will thought he could still hear the music floating through the air. He kept listening for it, but it was just a siren far away or a car stereo beating out a rhythm.

~o0o~

September became October and the rawness of seventh grade at a new school wore off. Late one afternoon Will heard the music again, for real. From far away, maybe four or five blocks, it came, that jolly, happy music. He stood and listened, trying to follow the tune, until moms started calling kids in for supper. Until kids knew they'd get heck if they came home late, to chilling soup and congealing gravy and stern lectures from dads.

"I heard an ice cream truck," said Will, sitting down to meat loaf and mashed potatoes that had stopped steaming but weren't cold yet. "I wanted to get a look at it, so I waited, but it went away."

"It can't be an ice cream truck," Will's dad said. "Not in October. Not this time of day. You should know better than that, son."

"Probably somebody's radio," said his mom. "Now eat your supper."

"But it was—"

Will's dad looked up from the book next to his plate, held open with his knife laid across the pages. "You heard your mother. Eat your supper." He was using his college professor voice. Will shut up.

But he kept the argument going in his head while he chewed meat loaf and green beans. No one played music like that on the radio, the same tune over and over, in the same tinkly, wheezy style. It had to be an ice cream truck, cruising the neighbourhoods in the dying day. But the music he'd heard wasn't "Pop Goes the Weasel" or "Turkey in the Straw" or "Little Brown Jug." It was a familiar tune, but with something wrong about it. Will wondered what kind of ice cream the truck sold.

Doof might know. He always knew stuff. Doof was the only kid Will had managed to make friends with. He was the class weirdo, but at least he didn't look at Will like he was a new kind of bug, the way the other kids did. If Doof was at school next day and felt like talking, Will would ask him if he'd heard the ice cream truck. Some days Doof just wouldn't talk. When

Will asked him why, Doof threatened to squash Will's nose so he wouldn't go sticking it into other people's business.

His real name was Harold Duffy, but no one called him Harold except teachers. Doof was short for 'Doofus,' and even though that wasn't exactly a compliment, it was better than Harold.

Doof was good at getting into trouble. He'd crack jokes in class and talk too loudly. Other days he was grumpy or wild, picking fights for no reason. He usually had an array of bruises, in a range of colours from purple to yellow, green, and brown. Every now and then he'd show up with a black eye.

"Got beat up by some big kids," he said, when Will asked him where he'd gotten the shiner. "They thought I was trying to move in on their territory."

"What territory?"

"Never mind. Let's check out the creek."

That was another thing about Doof. He knew all the interesting places. The creek with a knotted rope on a tree, where you could swing out over the water like Tarzan. A little house where no one lived that was stuffed full of old tires. Shortcuts to everywhere, through alleys and vacant lots.

Just before he fell asleep that night, Will thought he heard music again, faint and far away. He listened but couldn't pick up the tune. Out in the hallway, the night light cast its dim glow. Will was glad to see that little light. Then he was asleep.

~o0o~

Doof wasn't at school the next day, but on his way home, Will saw him standing on a corner looking up at the sky.

"Hey!" said Will, sneaking up behind him.

181

"Geez, Will! Don't do that to a guy!"

"Looking for Santa? Too early by a couple months. What'cha doing?"

Doof wound up a punch, but stopped halfway and held up a finger. "Listen!"

A sound floated toward them. Music, coming closer.

"You know what that is?" Doof's eyes narrowed.

"It's that ice cream truck!" said Will.

"There it is!" Doof pointed and ran, and Will followed. He'd be late for supper again, but this was important.

The ice cream truck turned onto the street two blocks ahead of them, braying its incongruously cheerful tune.

"It's purple!" said Will. "Weird." All the ice cream trucks he'd ever seen were white or painted in bright, summery colours like pink or yellow. This one was a solid, dark purple, a night colour. On the roof, a lit-up plastic ice cream cone twirled bright red stripes.

"That's not all that's weird about it," said Doof, puffing a bit. "Come on, hurry up!"

But they couldn't catch it. The ice cream truck was speeding toward downtown, its taillights glowing an intense red. Will thought he saw orange and purple sparks coming out of the tailpipe. As it went around a corner and out of sight, Will almost remembered the tune, some kind of lullaby, but played so fast it sounded anything but soothing.

"It's a *special* ice cream truck," Doof said, as the two of them stood catching their breaths. "It goes out at night. I'll bet it's got special ice cream and maybe other stuff. It's only for grownups, or kids who don't go running home to Mommy just 'cause it's getting dark." Doof jerked his head, flinging his mop of hair back, and grinned at Will while he put his baseball cap back on.

"My dad says there can't be an ice cream truck now that it's getting cold out, and who wants ice cream at night?"

"Why not? All kinds of things happen at night." Doof hummed the *Jaws* theme. "Doo, doo, doo, doo, woo! Boogeyman gonna get ya, Willy!"

Will laughed and punched him on the arm. "How do you know so much about that ice cream truck, anyway?"

"I go places you don't and keep my eyes open while I'm there." Doof flapped his ball cap at Will.

"Have you had any ice cream from it?"

"Not yet," said Doof, "but I'm going to."

"Hey, how about if you come home with me for supper?" Will thought he wouldn't get into as much trouble for being late if he had a friend with him. And his dad had been asking if he'd made any friends yet, so bringing Doof home would show him.

Doof shifted from one foot to the other, twirling his cap around his finger. "I dunno. Maybe your mom wouldn't like that."

"She won't mind. She always cooks lots of food. Come on." Will led the way at a brisk trot. They had followed the ice cream truck farther than he'd realized.

Will's house was warm and full of good smells. Will showed Doof the bathroom so he could wash his hands and went to tell his mom about his guest.

Will's dad was standing by his chair at the head of the table when the boys came into the dining room. Will carried an extra plate, glass, and cutlery for Doof. "Will, you know it's disrespectful to be late for supper. This is the second time this week."

"I'm sorry, Dad. This is my friend Doo—uh, Harold. Harold Duffy." Will shifted his plate over and put the extras on the table. "This is my dad."

Doof and Will's dad stared at each other. "Pleased to meet you, Mr. Todd." Doof stuck out a hand, but Will's dad ignored it.

"That's *Professor* Todd," he said and turned to Will, eyebrows crumpled. "This boy is joining us for the meal? Does your mother know?"

"She says it's okay."

Doof was backing up like he was planning to run out the door. Will pulled one of the spare chairs over and put it in place. "It's okay. You can sit here."

Will's dad nodded and they all sat down.

While they ate pot roast, mashed potatoes and broccoli, Will couldn't help noticing things about Doof that didn't seem to matter before. His shirt had holes in the elbows and wasn't too clean. There was a fading bruise on one of his wrists. Without his baseball cap on, you could tell he needed a haircut.

Will's mom kept a kind of conversation going by asking Doof things like how did he like school and what sports did he play and did he have any pets. Doof did okay answering her questions, didn't even talk with his mouth full, used his napkin properly, ate up everything on his plate, and accepted seconds.

"I have a dog," said Doof, answering the pet question. "Well, he's not really my dog, but he's my pal, you know."

"It'd be cool to have a dog," said Will.

Will's dad cleared his throat. "We're not getting a dog, Will. I don't care for dogs. What does your father do, Harold?"

184

Doof didn't reply right away. He lowered his glass of milk and looked like he was consulting an inner authority. "Business," he said finally.

"What kind of business?" asked Will's dad.

"All kinds," said Doof. "It depends."

"Where do you live, Harold?"

For a couple of seconds Will thought he would say, "None of your business," but instead Doof gave a little one-sided smile and said, "Walnut Hill."

The best neighbourhood in town, where all the rich people lived. Will was pretty sure Doof was lying, but at least Will's dad stopped asking questions.

Dessert was apple pie and ice cream. As soon as he was finished, Doof put his folded napkin on his plate. "May I be excused?" he said. "I have to go home now. Thank you for supper, Mrs. Todd. Good night, *Professor* Todd." He was out the door before anyone got up to see him out. Will ran after him, but all he saw was the pale blur of Doof's shirt fading into the dark.

When he got back to the table, his father gave him a look. "That the only friend you managed to make at school? Can't you do any better?"

"The boy was hungry," said Will's mom. "Did you see how much he ate? I wonder if he's getting proper meals at home. His table manners were good, though."

~oOo~

"Do you really live in Walnut Hill?" Will asked Doof at recess the next day.

Doof narrowed his eyes. "What do you think?"

"I think you were lying."

"Two points for Willy! Yeah, I lied to *Professor* Todd. So what? Don't you ever lie to your dad? Or don't you dare?"

Will shrugged, blushing. "So what kind of business does your dad do?"

"It depends," said Doof,

"My dad said he figured it was probably funny business."

Doof's face turned red. "Your dad thinks he knows everything, doesn't he?"

"Well, he is a professor." Will paused. "But he doesn't know about that ice cream truck."

Doof threw a rock at a bird sitting on the schoolyard fence. The rock missed. The bird flew away. "Race you back to school." He took off.

By the time Will caught up, Doof had a grin on his face. "I dare you," he said.

"Dare me what?"

"Find that ice cream truck. Tonight."

"After supper? I'm not allowed—"

"'I'm not allowed! My daddy won't let me!'" Doof mocked, his voice high and whining. "That's why I'm daring you, Willy. And not just after supper. I'm talking real night time. Midnight. Are you up for it?"

"Midnight! That's stupid. Nobody's going to be selling ice cream then."

"I'll bet that ice cream truck does," said Doof. "I've heard its music at night. So've you."

"Yeah, but—"

"But nothing! Are you with me or not? 'Cause I'm going anyway."

186

"Tonight?"

"You bet! Big ol' Friday night."

Luckily, Will's dad was a fan of "Early to bed, early to rise," and packed it in right after the ten o'clock news. His mom didn't watch the news because it gave her nightmares, but she liked to read in bed. Their light was always off by eleven, though. Another lucky thing was that Will's room was close to the stairs. He tested them for squeaky spots that evening, while his parents were watching TV. All okay, except for the fourth from the top and the third from the bottom.

Right after his mom kissed him goodnight and left the room, Will changed from his pjs to regular clothes and got under the covers. It felt weird to be wearing jeans and a shirt and sweater in bed, but his dad sometimes checked on him, so everything had to look normal. Then he got scared he'd fall asleep and not wake up until morning. Doof would tease him mercilessly about that. Will could almost hear him singing "Rock-a-bye baby" or some other lullaby.

Finally, the clock beside Will's bed said 11:30. He was supposed to meet Doof at the corner of 12th and Maple at midnight. Normally it would take fifteen minutes to get there, but this wasn't normal.

The stairs had developed a lot of fresh squeaks and creaks. Will froze after each one, a story about needing a drink of water ready on his lips. Except how would he explain being fully dressed? But nothing happened. Going out the back door, he realized he hadn't thought about getting back inside. He'd have to leave the door unlocked. If a burglar came in and stole something, it would be his fault.

Thinking about what his dad would say if that happened, Will almost changed his mind. But then he thought

I don't care what he says. I'm going. He closed the door softly and crept down the driveway to the street.

Doof wasn't at 12th and Maple. No one was. Parked cars sat there, reflecting the street lights. Will stood on the sidewalk, wondering how long he should wait before he gave up. He'd never been out this late before, not even on Halloween. The trees rustled quietly, as though they were telling each other secrets.

"Gotcha!" Hands grabbed Will's shoulders from behind. He screamed.

"Quiet!" Doof clamped a palm over Will's mouth.

Will shook him off and pushed him away, nerves jangling. "What did you do that for?"

"Just testing your reflexes, pal." Doof giggled. "Testing, testing, one, two, three. You ready?"

"Not if you're going to be a jerk," said Will.

"Not me! Everything's cool. Hey, listen!"

Music. A faraway sound, getting closer, the way a siren gets closer and louder. Except this wasn't a siren. It was the ice cream truck's tune, frantic and jolly.

"Let's go!"

They ran down Maple street. The numbers on the cross streets got smaller. As they crossed 1st Street, Will noticed they weren't on Maple anymore; the street sign said Railway Avenue. He'd never been here before. The houses were much older than in his neighbourhood, and then there were no houses, only business buildings. Ahead, train tracks gleamed silver-blue under the street lights. On the other side of them was a gas station.

The lights on the pumps were off, but a yellow light shone in the garage. A couple of cars were parked outside its open door and a few dark figures stood around. Guys. Strangers. They had beer bottles in their hands and talked in low voices, punctuated with bursts of laughter.

Will stopped. "Are we going over there? Where are we going, anyway?"

"Don't be a dummy. We're going to get us some ice cream. Come on!" Doof set off across the tracks.

"Are those guys waiting for it too?" Will asked.

Doof didn't get a chance to answer. One of the guys by the gas station saw them and came over. He wasn't a kid. Not even a high school kid. "What're you kids doing here?" He didn't sound friendly.

"What's it to you?" Doof stuck his chin out.

"This isn't a good place for kids—"

The ice cream truck's music sounded really close, but they couldn't see it.

"It's over there! Come on!" Doof took off, running hard.

The guy from the gas station noticed Will for the first time. "That kid a friend of yours?"

Will nodded.

"You know what's making that sound?"

Will nodded again.

"Then you better keep him away from it." The guy turned and went back to the gas station, where the light in the garage suddenly looked warm and friendly.

The music brayed and wheezed, only a couple of blocks away. The tune's words popped into Will's head. Lullaby and good *night*, soon you'll *be* sleeping tight. He turned and ran after Doof, just in time to see him go around a corner two blocks away.

Will pelted down the street and around the corner. Doof was a block ahead of him. The ice cream truck pulled over to the kerb by a vacant lot and stopped. The music faded to a growl.

Will almost ran into Doof by some bushes. He felt suffocated from holding his breath. Both of them were panting. "Maybe they're waiting for us," said Doof.

"Let's not get too close to it at first," said Will. "That guy by the gas station said to stay away from it." For once, Doof didn't argue.

The ice cream truck sat by the side of the road, music cranked low, the ice cream cone on its roof spinning and flashing a kaleidoscope of colours against the truck's dark purple. Up close like this, the cone didn't look like plastic with a light bulb inside. It glowed all over like it was molten, with a spiral of dark red lava from top to bottom.

The door slid open and someone jumped out. The driver. There was something spidery about the figure, something not right about its proportions.

"Heya, hey!" it said, in a voice that sounded like an amplified buzz. "Come on, you kids!"

Will's stomach lurched. Was it talking to them? If Doof hadn't been there, for sure he would have run away.

But no, the spidery figure was turned away from them. "Get busy!" it buzzed. "I feel customers coming!"

The service window in the side of the ice cream truck clattered open. Red lights showed a menu board and a couple of employees getting ready to sell whatever kind of ice cream and treats the truck had on offer. The employees were short; only their heads showed above the counter.

"They're just kids. Let's go see what they've got." Doof stood, but Will pulled him back.

"Maybe they're kids, but that other guy isn't. Didn't you see him? He's really weird looking."

A gang of teenagers jostled down the road and stopped in front of the ice cream truck, yelling orders for Frosty Flamesicle and Sulphur Surprise. Just like the cone on top of the truck, the treats glowed like hot coals. The teenagers waved their popsicles and ice creams, tracing lines of light, laughing and daring each other to eat them. One took a lick and then another.

"Oh man, that smarts! Love it!"

"I'm gonna catch fire! More, more, more!"

"This one's wild!"

"Look, I'm a fire-breathing dragon!"

Their exclamations faded away as they moved down the road. "See, it's okay," Doof said, jumping up. "Say, have you got any money?"

Will didn't want to get any closer, but Doof was more than halfway across the street.

"Doof! Wait, come back!" Will's voice felt as though it was being sucked away. Doof didn't stop but slowed, his shape blending into the dusk. Will stomped down his fear and ran after him.

"Look, it's a dog!" said Doof. A black form near the truck unfolded into a dog shape and turned its head toward them. A big head on a big body. Really big.

Dogs loved Doof. He was always making friends with random dogs. But this was no ordinary dog. Dark orange flames floated behind it. Sparks shot from its studded collar.

Doof started toward the dog. "Hey, boy," he said. "Come here."

It shambled toward them. Its eyes glowed and little sparks popped out from its fur, like one of those happy birthday sparklers.

Will grabbed for Doof's arm, but he was too far away. The dog came closer. He didn't look mean, just weird, with the cloud of little lights around him, like dust.

"Come on, boy!" said Doof. "It's okay, I won't hurt you."

Then the spidery guy looked over at them.

"Heya, heya, heya! Dog!" The voice rose to a buzzing screech that hurt Will's ears. It did something to the dog too. He stopped and whined.

"Heya, heya, heya! Boys!" The tall black figure glided toward Will and Doof. It looked like it was put together from pieces, arms and legs loose-jointed, head bobbling on top. Its movements were both smooth and jerky, like it was worked with strings.

"Heya, heya, heya! We got treats for you!" Its voice twisted like wires, wrapping around Will's head.

"Doof, let's get out of here! Let's go!"

Doof looked back at Will, his eyes wide and wild. "But the dog—"

"Never mind the dog. He's *their* dog. Come on!"

The dog lurched toward them, jaws open and dripping fire.

"*Run!*" Will yelled. But Doof just stood there, watching the dog.

Then the spidery guy moved, snapping a whip that shot purple sparks. The dog shambled slowly toward him. Doof finally turned and ran. The dog howled, a sound of empty loneliness that froze Will's heart.

Three blocks later, Will sneaked a glance over his shoulder. No one there, just a faint glow of departing taillights. The ice cream truck was gone. So was the dog.

Neither of them said anything until they were back at the corner of 12th and Maple, where a streetlight shed its cold light on the pavement.

"What is it?" asked Will. "It's not really an ice cream truck. Who was that... guy? And that dog came after us."

Doof had been looking at his shoes while Will was talking, but now he jerked his head up. "The dog was trying to get away. I'm going to go back and help him."

"Whaa—? That's stupid! He was helping that weird guy. They were trying to catch us."

"No, he wasn't. That dog needs help." Doof sounded a lot older, almost like a grownup. "You'd better go home, Willy. You'll get in shit for being late."

"I'll be in sh— shit for being out at all," said Will. "Don't your parents mind you being out late like this?"

"Parent. Just my dad. He doesn't care much."

Will thought about Doof's weird lunches and frequent absences from school, his lack of concern about being late for meals. "Where's your mom?"

"Gone," said Doof. "Since last summer."

"You mean... she died?" Will found himself whispering the last word.

Doof jerked his head up. "No, Willy, she didn't *die*. She's just gone." He shrugged. "I dunno where."

"Geez," Will breathed. He couldn't think what else to say.

"Okay, now you know. So how about if you go home."

"But you can't stay out all night! Come home with me. You can sleep in my room. Mom won't mind."

Doof made a sound that wasn't really a laugh. "Maybe not, but what about your dad?"

Will didn't say anything.

"Go home, Willy."

~oOo~

Doof wasn't at school on Monday. Or Tuesday. On Wednesday, Will went to the school's office to ask if Doof had been reported sick. The lady who usually sat in the office wasn't there, but Will heard people talking in the Principal's room, whose door was open.

"I think it's time we did something about the Duffy boy." Will's ears pricked. The Duffy boy, that was Doof. "He's missed three days already this week and I'm pretty sure I know why." Will recognized the voice of Ms. Lacy, the school's guidance counsellor.

A man rumbled an answer. Will couldn't understand what he said, but he knew it was Mr. Springer, the Principal. "What about the mother?" Mr. Springer must have turned or talked louder, because Will heard this just fine.

"She's not in the picture," said Ms. Lacy. "I gather she's left the home. It's just Harold and his father. They live at that Shady Grove Trailer Park. Not a great place. I think something bad happened last summer. I think that boy is in trouble."

"We don't want to act prematurely," said Mr. Springer.

"Better to deal with the child welfare people than the police."

194

Ms. Lacy appeared in the doorway of the principal's room. Will ducked behind the counter and out of the office before she saw him. Was Doof in some sort of trouble? Why would Ms. Lacy think they might have to deal with the police?

After school, Will decided to go to Doof's house and see if he was okay. Maybe he had a bad stomach bug and no mom to look after him. Or maybe he'd gone back to the ice cream truck and the driver had done something to him. The Shady Grove Trailer Park was in the opposite direction from Will's house, in the part of town Will's dad called a slum.

The trailer park's name was the nicest thing about it. The trailers were old and looked like they were sinking into the ground. A few of them had little patches of grass and flowers outside, but most were surrounded by weeds and junk. Will asked an old lady if she knew where Mr. Duffy lived. She stopped sweeping her walk and stared at him.

"What you want with him? He's kinda mean."

"Well, actually, I'm looking for Doof, uh, Harold. His son."

She frowned, clutching the broom. "Haven't seen him around the last few days. Maybe he run off too. Wouldn't be surprised. Tom Duffy's trailer's right at the back." She pointed and snorted. "End of the road. That's the right place for him, all right."

Doof's dad's trailer made the others look good. It had once been white, but now was a mottled grey. Bags of garbage slouched against the broken steps, and a rusty barbecue with a missing wheel leaned nearby. A couple of crooked posts held up a dirty sheet of corrugated fiberglass over the entryway.

Will stepped up to the dented door and knocked. Nothing happened. He made himself knock again, louder, and waited. A wreck of a car peeked out of a thicket of bramble bushes. Behind the car, an old brown blanket hung from the branch of a tree. Something about its shape bothered him, but before he could get a better look, a couple of thumps sounded from inside the trailer, followed by shuffling. The door creaked open.

Mr. Duffy loomed over Will like the moon, a T-shirt cratered with stains and holes stretched over his pot belly. "Who're you and what do you want?" Mr. Duffy's voice sounded like it came out of a bowl of thick oatmeal.

"Uh, I'm Will. I'm looking for Doo—Harold."

"Don't know where he is. Little bugger should be at school. You too, kid."

"School's out for the day. He hasn't been there all week. I wondered if he's sick or something."

"'Or something.' That kid's never sick, except in the head. He's not here."

"I guess he's missing then. Don't you think you'd better call the police?"

"I don't talk to cops. Don't you sic the cops on me. Kid's probably gone to visit grandma. Now get lost!" He started to close the door.

Will felt a kind of sneaky relief. He'd tried. Now he could go home. But Doof had never mentioned a grandma.

"Mr. Duffy, did you know that Doof—I mean Harold— he really wants a dog?" The words popped out of Will's mouth before he knew it.

"Dog!" Mr. Duffy made a gargling laugh. "No damned dog here. Not any more. I don't like dogs, I don't like cops, and I don't like you either. Get lost before I run you off!" He slammed the door so hard, the posts holding up the fiberglass shuddered and a clump of rotten pine needles fell off.

Will could go home now. Except he wasn't done. He had to find Doof. That meant telling the police. Or finding the ice cream truck again.

At home, Will charged himself up with a glass of milk and three cookies. Then he knocked on the door of his dad's office.

"It's me, Dad. Can I talk to you about something?"

"Yes, you *may*, Will." His dad looked at him over his glasses from behind a big pile of students' papers. "What is it? I'm pretty busy."

"Doof's gone missing. He hasn't been at school since last week. I'm kind of worried about him."

"Doof?"

"My friend Harold Duffy. He came for supper one day, remember? Doof is his nickname."

"I don't approve of nicknames, Will. And I don't approve of that boy, either. He struck me as a questionable type. I'm not surprised he's left school. You'd best find some better friends."

Will shrugged. "Doof's my friend right *now*. I want to make sure he's all right. Do you think I should tell the police that he's a missing person?"

Will's dad shook his head. "Waste of time. The police won't listen to you. The boy's parents are the ones to report him missing. But I'm sure he's all right. That type is always all right, as much as they care to be. Don't waste your time worrying about him. I very much doubt if he's giving you much thought. Now, please excuse me, young man. I have work to do."

~oOo~

Will dreamed a dog was barking, barking, barking. Then he was awake. His clock said 3:09. *What a weird time to be awake.* He didn't have to pee, but he went and did that anyway, to make being awake feel normal. Before getting back into bed, he looked out the window. Just in case.

Faintly illuminated by the light on the street, a dog sat on the front walk. A big dog, really big, wearing a collar that glowed in the dark.

The dog from the ice cream truck.

Will pushed the window open and leaned out. The dog raised its head and looked right at him with eyes that glowed like a flashlight whose battery was almost dead. It had something in its mouth. It dropped the thing onto the pavement, a dark object, not very big. The dog nosed and pawed it into a recognizable shape.

A baseball cap. Doof's ball cap?

"Doof?" Will hung out of his window and looked around. Why would the dog have Doof's cap? The dog settled down on its haunches again, like it was waiting. Waiting for Will.

Will pulled on some clothes and crept down the stairs, just like the night he'd sneaked out to meet Doof and look for the ice cream truck. The dog met him halfway between the back door and the driveway, carrying Doof's cap again.

The dog's collar glowed the same dull orange as its eyes. "Do you know where Doof is?" asked Will. The dog turned and trotted toward the street, stopped and looked back. Will followed.

The dog loped purposefully along, heading toward that fringe of downtown where the boys had seen the ice cream truck. Tonight, the gas station was closed and dark. No one was around. They crossed the train tracks and headed toward the empty lot.

There stood the ice cream truck, with its kaleidoscope of flashing lights. Will stopped and stared at it, but the dog kept going. When it realized Will was no longer following, it turned and shambled toward him. It thrust its snoot up and shook the baseball cap. Its eyes glowed dark orange, but Will thought they looked sad. Sad and impatient, as though the dog wanted to say, "How long are you going to stand there?"

"Okay," he said, "I'm coming."

As they approached the ice cream truck, a figure detached itself from its black shadow. The dog lurched into a run. Doof wore black clothes that looked like some sort of uniform.

"Hey, Will," said Doof. "You got my message. Good boy, Gryph!" This to the dog, who capered around him. Doof took the ball cap from its mouth. He held a popsicle that glowed like it was red hot, but he put it in his mouth and licked it. He grinned. "Delicious."

"What… what's it taste like?" said Will.

"Red hot cherry ice," said Doof. "Want to try?" He held out the popsicle.

"No. No, I don't. Did you buy it?"

"Nope. It was free." Doof gestured toward the ice cream truck, whose lights dappled the trees, the grass, and the pavement with splotches of yellow, orange, and red. Music welled from the truck, low and menacing.

"I thought something bad happened to you," said Will.

199

"Something bad, something good." Doof took another lick of the fiery popsicle. Little drops of molten flame dripped from it, hissing when they hit the grass.

"I even went to your house—I mean, your dad's house. His house trailer."

Doof pulled the popsicle from his mouth. "You saw my *dad*? Talked to him?"

"I thought you might be sick or something."

"Sick! I would have been, if I'd stayed with that bastard. Maybe even dead. I know places to go. I can look after myself. I have friends."

"You mean those guys?" Will pointed to a couple of shapes standing near the ice cream truck.

"Yeah, and this guy for sure." Doof put his hand on the dog's head.

"I told your dad you wanted a dog," Will said. "He started yelling at me to get lost. I ran away. I was scared."

"He *killed* my dog," said Doof, throwing the popsicle stick into the bushes. It burst into a shower of sparks that lasted for a few seconds and winked out one by one. "That night we came out here. Okay, he wasn't really my dog. He just hung around the trailer park, but he was my pal, you know? My dad—that bastard killed him and hung him up behind the trailer. I saw him hanging there when I got home. That was it for me."

"Geez, Doof. I'm sorry. I didn't know." He thought of the brown thing he'd seen hanging. Not a blanket.

"Things are different now. I have my pal here. Name's Gryphon, Gryph for short. Come and have a popsicle. Or an ice cream. First one's always free."

"You sound like you work for... them. Whoever they are."

Doof grinned. "I sure do. Come on."

Three shapes surrounded them as they approached the ice cream truck. In the multicoloured whirl of lights from the ice cream cone on top of the truck, it was hard to make out their faces. All three wore black coveralls with a red symbol on the breast pocket, the same outfit as Doof's.

I'm dreaming, thought Will. *This is a dream, so don't worry, just go with the flow.*

"Blaze, Pyro, and Ember," said Doof, pointing to each of them in turn. "This is my friend Will."

"Another new hand?" said Blaze. He pushed his face close to Will's, close enough that Will smelled something like hot motor oil and saw a tiny tattoo on the boy's cheek. Three points joined at the bottom. A trident, same as the symbol on their uniforms.

"N-no! Not me!" Will backed up a couple of steps. "I was just talking to Doof."

"Doof! That's not his name. He's Ash."

"I got a new name. That's part of the deal." Doof was still wearing that goofy grin.

"Okay, Ash, how about we get your friend a treat? What would you like, Will? Popsicle or ice cream cone?" Ember was a girl. She had a trident tattoo as well.

Remember, you're dreaming. "I'll have an ice cream, please."

Ember jumped into the back door of the ice cream truck and appeared in the sales window. The red light showed a dark bruise on her right cheek. "I recommend Cinnamon Glow. It's one of our starter flavours. You wouldn't be able to handle

Sulphur Surprise, never mind a Brimstone Sundae!" She popped a scoop of bright red ice cream into a black cone. As she handed it to Will, her sleeve pulled up, revealing an iron bracelet that looked too heavy for her wrist.

The ice cream glowed like a live coal but felt cold on his tongue. As Will swallowed, his sinuses filled up with hot cinnamon, like he'd just swallowed a handful of those red heart-shaped candies. He shuddered and took another lick. He couldn't stop.

"Who do you guys work for?" asked Will.

Blaze, Pyro, and Ember looked at each other. "The Boss," said Blaze.

"The man downstairs," said Pyro.

"Mr. Phlogisto!" said Ember.

"Heya, heya, kids!" said a buzzing voice from behind the truck. "Time to pack up! Nothing doing here." The driver's spidery shape came toward them. It was freakishly tall, with two upward-pointing projections on its head.

"Is that him?" asked Will.

Blaze and Pyro scrambled toward the truck.

"No, that's Scorch. He's, like, our supervisor." said Ember. She touched her bruised face.

"Gotta go, Will." Doof 's head swivelled back and forth between Will and the ice cream truck's driver. "You coming with us?"

"No!" Will threw the remains of his ice cream cone on the ground, where it burst into flame and vanished. He turned to Doof.

"Do you know where this ice cream truck comes from?"

Doof nodded.

"Doesn't that bother you?"

"Not as much as seeing that dog hung up dead."

"Well, I guess I won't be seeing you at school anymore," said Will.

Doof nodded again, with a smirk.

"Do you get paid? Like a real job?"

"Room and board," said Doof. "But that's not all—"

A sharp snap-crack sounded nearby.

"Hey Ash! Time to go. He's getting mad. 'Bye, Will!" Will wasn't sure who said what as Blaze and Pyro piled into the truck and Ember slammed down the service window. Doors banged shut.

"Okay, coming! Not *just* room and board," said Doof, "They grant wishes! I wished for a dog. And something else too." He glanced at the truck, whose engine fired up, shooting flames out both tailpipes. "'Bye, Will. Maybe I'll see you again someday." Doof held out a hand and they shook. He wore a bracelet just like Ember's.

"C'mon, Gryph!" Doof ran to the truck and jumped in the back, the dog hot on his heels.

The driver's door opened and Scorch spidered out. A pair of glowing red eyes focussed on Will. Their heat moved around his face, exploring and memorizing. The figure lifted a hand and pointed at him. A grin appeared below the eyes and a whip cracked, shooting purple sparks into the air. "Wishes!" said Scorch, his voice buzzing like an evil bee. "Only for those who deserve it, boy. Remember that."

A dream, it's only a dream. But something curled around Will's ankle, hot and stinging. He turned and ran until his chest was about to explode and he tripped and fell.

Will lay on the ground quivering, alternately hot and cold. The ice cream truck's frenetic music floated back to him, fading into the distance. *Lullaby and good night. Did we give you a fright? We've got fire and ice. You don't have to be nice...* The music turned into a siren, like the ice cream truck was an ambulance from hell. Its mission was hurting, not helping. *Only those who deserve it.*

Will got to his feet and shambled homeward. It seemed a lot farther than he remembered. A patrolling policeman spotted him and took him home.

~oOo~

Will's Mom kept him home from school the next day. His head ached and his stomach roiled queasily. It was almost supper time when he felt well enough to get up. Putting on his socks, he noticed a narrow red line around his left ankle. It tingled when he rubbed it.

Will's dad lowered the newspaper he was reading when Will came into the living room. "Feeling better, son?"

Will nodded.

"Ready to tell me what you were doing last night?"

Will shrugged. "Not really."

Will's dad folded his newspaper and stood. "Answer me properly. You were with that lowlife kid, weren't you? Harold somebody. Am I right?"

Will stared at a headline. *Fire at Shady Grove Trailer Park. One Man Dead.*

"Actually, Dad, you're wrong."

THE COLOUR OF MAGIC

In September, Marc's Mom had to go to Italy. Construction work had uncovered a previously unknown temple, and Dr. Dupplin's expertise in Late Empire ceramics was urgently needed.

"It's not a problem," Eleanor Dupplin declared in a hastily summoned Family Meeting, attended by both members of the family. "You'll be here anyway. All you have to do is welcome her and show her the ropes."

"Hopefully it won't come to ropes," said Marc.

Eleanor flapped a tea towel at her son. "Oh, you know what I mean. I've written up a list of rules you can give her."

"This lady needs rules? I thought you said she was older."

"She's my age, Marc."

"Right, older."

Another flap of the towel.

"I hope she doesn't need a lot of helping out. Second year is a lot tougher than first."

"Suck it up, buttercup. Remember who you're named for."

Marc's Dad had been a great fan of Marcus Aurelius, the stoic emperor.

Second year was just getting under way and Marc had a scholarship to maintain. That was a big part of the plan he and his Mom had drawn up three years ago, when Paul Dupplin, aka Dad, had collapsed and died while participating in an Iron Man competition. The plan was simple. Get undergrad degree. Get master's degree. Get PhD. Become a professor, like Mom.

The tenant would be moving in the week after Mom left. She had stocked the freezer with survival rations and left lists of Things to Check and Things to Remember as well as a list of emergency numbers and email addresses and names.

As far as Mom was concerned, Marc was all set.

The suite in the basement was pretty nice—bedroom, bathroom, kitchen, and living room. It had its own semi-private entrance by way of the shared laundry room and a private patio, if you could dignify a 6x10 concrete slab with such a label. When Marc started college, he had hoped to move into the suite, but Mom nixed that idea. "You don't need an apartment yet. You have it pretty good living up here, and we can make the suite available to someone who really needs it. And bring in some extra money too."

"Someone who really needs it" meant a series of Dr. Dupplin's grad students. They mostly ignored Marc; after all, he was just a kid. They were boring anyway, obsessed with their schedules and theses and running errands for Marc's Mom. A couple of the women students were pretty hot, but Marc's attempts to have serious conversations with them went nowhere.

The new tenant was different. "She's making some changes in her life, I gather. Probably one of those older divorcees. She's ditched the old man and wants a second chance at life."

"Like taking courses in ancient history?" Marc said.

206

"Exploring new interests is always a good idea. She needs a place to live for a while and really liked our suite. And the yard too. In fact, that seemed to be the clincher for her, after she took a walk up to the back."

"Is yard work part of the deal?" Some of the grad students let themselves be dragooned into mowing grass or raking leaves.

"No, that's your job," Mom said with a grin. "I didn't even suggest it. Give her some space if you find her back there communing with nature when you're busy raking. She struck me as the cosmic type—you know, yoga and stuff."

~o0o~

A few days after his Mom left for Rome, Marc decided to take a walk around what his Dad had called "Gnome Home." Soon he would be sharing it with a stranger, a stranger who found their back yard attractive.

The front of the lot was like any other suburban yard, with a lawn and the survivors of a bed of roses Paul Dupplin put in one year as an anniversary present for an astonished Eleanor. The back yard had a clothesline on a pulley, an unused brick barbecue, and a lawn with a couple of weedy raised beds.

Marc tried to see everything through the eyes of a stranger. The brick barbecue might have been an ancient ruin and the raised beds scenes of unknown rituals. Beyond the mowed lawn, a narrow trail twisted upward among huddles of shrubs and trees to a ravine with a seasonal creek at the bottom, a trickle that was sometimes transformed by rain or melting snow into a temporary torrent.

In summer, the place was a leafy mystery, but now the autumnal foliage had thinned enough to show the bones of the trees. The day's watery sunlight, uncertain and shifting, filtered through fading leaves. Marc's feet fell soundless on the soft, woodsy duff, layers upon layers of leaves, twigs, and bits of bark. Moss cushioned the sides of the path; mushrooms clustered nearby. Trees leaned toward each other across the ravine, as though discussing secrets. On the ravine's far side, a chain-link fence bordered the main road to the campus.

Marc remembered long-ago summer days when he and other kids had chased each other around here and constructed "hideouts" in which to eat picnic lunches and discuss important matters. The ravine was pretty small, really, not the lawless place full of lurking hazards Marc remembered. The trees on its far side had grown since he was there last. He could barely hear the swish of passing cars on the road, never mind see them.

Marc's stomach rumbled, reminding him it was well past lunchtime. He turned and loped back to the house, entering through the basement laundry room. On its far side was the door of the soon to be occupied basement suite. Once Ms. Stone—that was her name—was in residence, he would have to follow landlord-tenant protocols before he could go through that door.

On an impulse, Marc crossed the room and opened the door of the suite, just because he still could. The kitchen was bare, clean, and empty. *Nothing to see here, folks*. Beyond it, the beige living room with its tired sofa and a couple of mismatched armchairs. A computer desk and bookshelves acknowledged the academic endeavours of the suite's usual occupants.

A slant of yellow light beckoned Marc to the bedroom. Its ceiling sloped to accommodate furnace ducts, creating odd proportions and walls of different heights. Otherwise, it was as neutral as the rest of the suite, painted a pale non-colour.

It would be hard to wake up early here, Marc thought. This room would be dark until late morning, especially in winter. Maybe he was better off upstairs in his old room.

"Excuse me?"

Startled, Marc whirled around. A woman stood in the doorway.

"Oh, I'm sorry! The outside door was open, so I came in."

She was of the class of women he thought of as 'moms.' Her shoulder length hair was silver and her figure solid. Not fat, exactly, but comfortably upholstered. In the second it took him to notice all this, his brain came up with who she must be.

"Oh, you're the—"

At the same moment, she stepped toward him, holding out a hand. "I'm Merlyn Stone."

"You're the tenant." Mark finished his sentence. "You're renting the suite."

Her face relaxed into a smile. "I'm supposed to move in tomorrow, but I'm hoping it's okay if I come today. Right now, in fact."

Marc realized she must have thought he was living in the suite. "I'm Marc. Marc Dupplin. I guess my Mom showed you the place. She's out of the country for a few weeks, but I can help you out. I mean, show you where things are. You're moving in right now?"

She had no luggage, just a leather shoulder bag. "My things are outside. I don't have much. The suite's fully furnished, isn't it? I mean dishes and so on. Dr. Dupplin said it was, I believe."

"I think so," said Marc. "Let's see." He followed her into the kitchen, where a look into cupboards revealed assorted plates, cups, and cooking pots. "If you need anything, I can lend you some of our stuff."

"Oh, I don't think that will be necessary," said Ms. Stone, "but thanks for the offer."

A rolling suitcase sat just outside the door and beside it, a sturdy wooden case. The case's corners were reinforced with copper and a handle had been bolted to the top.

"I can take that inside for you. It looks heavy." Mark reached for the case, but Ms. Stone beat him to it.

"That's okay. It's not that heavy, but maybe you could manage the suitcase." She hefted the wooden case off the floor and went back into the suite.

The suitcase was fairly heavy, but rolled along easily once he got it going. Ms. Stone carried the wooden case into the bedroom. "That's fine right there," she said, as Marc approached with the suitcase. "Thanks for all your help."

"No problem." The suite was *her* place now. He didn't belong here. "I guess you want to get settled," he said. "Let me know if you need anything."

Upstairs, he realized he hadn't followed Mom's checklist for welcoming the new tenant. There it was, on the fridge. He hadn't even given Ms. Stone the keys. They were still in the envelope marked "Tenant" on Mom's desk.

Marc dashed into the office, grabbed the envelope, and hustled back to the basement. The door to the suite was closed. It looked sealed, somehow. Marc told himself to stop being silly and tapped on it.

The door opened immediately, as though Merlyn Stone had been standing right there, waiting for him to knock. Her eyes were sharp, focussed, ready to face an enemy.

"I forgot to give you this," Marc said, holding out the envelope "The keys are inside. One's to this door and the other's to the outside one. And some notes my Mom wanted you to have."

"Oh, okay, thanks." Ms. Stone's face relaxed again, just like when she realized he hadn't taken over the space she had rented.

"Sorry to bother you."

Back in his own part of the house, Marc realized he'd forgotten all about lunch. He heated up some pizza and sat down to a game of Terraformer Megaplanet.

That evening, in the intervals of quiet between running the microwave or dishwasher, when he didn't have music on and wasn't concentrating on homework, Marc found himself listening. What would Ms. Stone be doing? Talking on the phone, telling her friends about her new place? Did she have a computer? Or maybe a sewing machine? Maybe that was what was in that wooden box with the handle. Except he didn't hear the small, dense sound a sewing machine would make. But then, she'd just moved in. Maybe she was doing yoga. That wouldn't make any noise at all.

A sound broke his thoughts, a rapid, high-pitched beep-beep-beep-beep-beep coming from inside the house, from the basement.

A smoke alarm.

Heart pounding, brain churning, Marc clattered down the stairs. *Should have taken my phone, called 911, what's she doing, is the house on fire?*

He raced across the laundry room and grabbed the doorknob of the suite. It wasn't warm, so maybe the fire wasn't too big. But the door was locked. He hammered on it. "Are you okay in there? Ms. Stone?" Maybe she couldn't hear him over the noise of the alarm, which was still shrilling, drilling into his head.

The noise stopped, leaving his eardrums sizzling. The door opened. Merlyn Stone stood there, clutching something black and smoky.

"Is there a fire? Are you okay?"

"No, no fire. I'm all right. I should have realized about the smoke detector." Her face was red. "It took me a while to find it and push the button." She gestured with the smoking bundle of stuff in her hand. "I was burning some herbs. Cleansing the atmosphere."

"Oh." *Shit, she's a nut case! There's a crazy woman in my house.*

Ms. Stone twitched a little smile. "Okay, it must seem like a weird thing to do. These herbs—lavender and sage—they symbolically clean the atmosphere. Every time I move into a new place, I like to do that. I just didn't think of the smoke detector. I'm tired, I guess."

She didn't look tired. She looked rattled.

"Well, okay," Marc said. "Um, are you finished... cleaning? Because the alarm'll likely go off again in a few minutes. The upstairs one did when I burned something on the stove once and it took a while to stop smoking."

Ms. Stone looked at the blackened stalks in her hand. "Well, no—I'll have to start all over again, after I've calmed down and centred myself. Luckily, I have a good supply of cleansing herbs."

"Um, how about if you take the battery out of the smoke detector until you're done? But only 'til then," he added, thinking about what his Mom would say if she was here. *She'd be having a fit.*

"Good idea. I'll make sure to put it back in and test it when I'm done."

Marc went back to his assignment, but couldn't concentrate. He couldn't sleep either, kept waking up anticipating another alarm, wondering if he should phone his Mom and tell her she'd made a mistake with this tenant.

~oOo~

He slept in the next morning, missed his first class of the day, and had to stay late to catch up.

He got home at sunset. The leaves of the boulevard trees echoed the western sky in vermilion and orange. Behind the house glowed a band of cold crimson, scrawled with the intricate black silhouettes of trees at the top of the hill. Marc stood on the front walk, shivering slightly, while the sun's furnace flared and faded. It was hard to believe that behind the hill was the familiar campus, not some alien, fantastic realm. A whiff of wood smoke tickled his nose. Someone had a fire going in their fireplace. Cozy warmth, mugs of cocoa... His Dad had been big on that stuff, but Mom was usually too busy or tired to bother.

A figure emerged from behind the house, black on dark blue. Fear jolted Marc until he recognized Merlyn Stone. She raised a hand in greeting. Her palm glittered under the street light.

She noticed Marc's gaze. "Oh, will you look at that?" she said, pulling a tissue from her pants pocket and dabbing at her hand. "I was working on a craft project and some of it stayed with me. Would you like a coffee?"

Marc blinked. "Sure, okay, I'll go make some."

"No, I mean at my place. I owe you one after last night."

"Oh, all right. Thanks." Too late to refuse.

Merlyn's kitchen smelled of fresh coffee. Two mugs and a cream pitcher stood on the tiny table. Ms. Stone bustled around, assembling spoons, napkins, a plate of cookies.

Just like Mom when I was a kid home from school.

There was something in the kitchen window—a pattern of knotted strings, blue and purple, in a kind of spiderweb shape, with an intricate knot in the middle.

"So you're at the university too," said Ms. Stone, pouring coffee. Marc relaxed into the kind of conversation he had with his Mom's friends, about his studies and plans for the future. The coffee wasn't bad and the cookies made up for his missing supper.

"What are you studying?" he asked, not because he was interested, just to be polite.

"Life," said Ms. Stone.

Right. And you burn herbs to clean the atmosphere. "Oh, I thought you were taking courses in archaeology. My Mom's department."

She looked into her mug for a couple of seconds. "I saw the poster she put up in the hallway near that department," she said, jerking her head up and fixing Marc with a focussed stare, as though daring him to argue. Her eyes, he saw now, were light blue, a quiet colour, maybe the wrong colour for her. "Do you see many strangers here?" she asked.

214

The question set off Marc's weirdo alarm again. This was a lady who hung purple fake spider webs in her window weeks before Halloween.

"Strangers? No, just people who live on our street. It's a dead end, a cul-de-sac. Sometimes people who're lost use our driveway to turn around."

"Dead end," Ms. Stone muttered, staring into her mug again. When she looked up, the combative stare was gone, replaced by something else. "I wonder, if you see anyone who doesn't look like they belong here, would you please let me know?"

"Well, sure, okay, but... would it be someone specific? Someone who's, like, stalking you?"

Ms. Stone let out a little laugh and swirled her mug. "No, it's not exactly like that. I meant if you see someone... *strange*. You'll know if you see one."

I think I'm seeing one right now. Marc washed down the last cookie and stood. "Strange strangers. Okay, I'll tell you I see any."

Ms. Stone stood too. "There's one more thing. I have to paint the bedroom."

"Paint? Uh, does it need painting?"

"Technically, no, but I need a bedroom that's a particular colour. I sleep much better that way." She picked up the mugs and put them in the sink. "I'm sure I mentioned that to your mother."

"Well, I think I'd better check with her. She didn't say anything about it to me. I'll call her, or text maybe. She's in Rome."

"Doing as the Romans do? Okay, I can wait for a day or so." She reached out and adjusted the strands of purple string in the window over the sink.

With the nine-hour time difference, it would be well after midnight in Rome, so he texted. "Question from tenant. Phone me 1st thing tomorrow."

Which his Mom did, just as he was falling asleep. Of course, her first thing tomorrow was his middle of the night. He scrabbled for his phone and picked up on the fourth ring. After the usual stuff ("Yes, I'm eating right and sleeping fine, don't worry"), Marc got to the point.

"The tenant, Ms. Stone, she wants to paint the bedroom."

"But I had the whole place painted last year!"

"Well, she says it's the wrong colour. She'll sleep better after she repaints it."

"*She's* going to paint it?" Rustling and clunking in the background.

"I guess so. I didn't ask."

Mom sighed. "*Tenants.* I thought she'd be fine, but... Okay, let her go ahead, but a couple things—Marc, are you listening?"

"Sure I am."

"You go with her to wherever she's planning to get the paint. In fact, offer to drive her. Paint cans are heavy."

"Except I can't use the car."

"This is a one-time exception. If you don't get in an accident, the insurance guys won't know. Make sure she doesn't pick some godawful colour like bright pink or screaming orange. Or black, for Pete's sake. You never know with people. Tell her I'd prefer a neutral shade. Or pastel, at least. And help her with the painting."

216

"But I've got midterms coming up!"

"It shouldn't take that long, especially with two of you. I want you to make sure she doesn't mess up. Get a drop cloth. Are you writing this down?"

~o0o~

Ms. Stone didn't want to buy her paint just anywhere. Only a particular store would do.

"I've got the address here," she said, fastening her seatbelt. She took a folded piece of paper from her shoulder bag. "Please call me Merlyn, by the way."

"Okay—Merlyn. And I'm Marc."

"I knew that."

The place was downtown. Not downtown proper, but an industrial area beyond it, a warren of narrow streets among old brick buildings and warehouses near the waterfront.

The correct street was empty and peaceful, dreaming a Sunday morning dream, even though it was Friday. Over a shop door hung a sign. Elemental Colours Expert Formulations J. Farber, prop.

In the display spaces on either side of the door sat a mortar and pestle and a set of bristle brushes, fanned out in order of size. Peeling tape held a faded help wanted sign to one of the windows.

Inside were no displays of paint cans, rollers and brushes, no spectrum of paint sample cards under fluorescent lights. A counter divided the front of the shop from a doorway into a dim space behind. A brass bell with a wooden handle sat on the counter next to an old-fashioned cash register. The place smelled old—old wood, old dust, organic oils, something metallic and something else that reminded Marc of incense in an old church.

Merlyn knocked on the counter. Tap, tap, tap. Tap-tap, tap, tap. Then she picked up the brass bell and shook it, releasing bright notes into the still, musty air.

A man emerged through the doorway. Tall, thin, with black hair parted in the middle and pulled back. A white face, white as his shirt, but his arms below the rolled-up sleeves were blue. No—they were tattooed, right down to the backs of his hands. He sure isn't like the guys at Quality Paints, thought Marc.

Merlyn spoke to the man, a low, rapid flow of words. He nodded and murmured a reply. Marc wandered around, looking at things on the narrow shelves that lined the walls between the counter and the storefront. The place was a museum. Glass jars and vials held powdered pigments arranged to form a subdued rainbow—garnet and cinnabar, ochre and umber, jade and malachite, ultramarine and violet. Other jars contained oils that ranged in colour from almost clear to dark amber. There were even some chunks of rock-like stuff whose colours were dull echoes of the prepared pigments, except for one that was a sparkling white.

A metallic clink drew Marc's attention toward the counter. Merlyn counted coins from a small leather bag and placed them on the proprietor's palm. The man deposited them into an old-fashioned till, wrote something on a piece of paper, and vanished into the workroom.

Merlyn came over to Marc. "It'll take a little while. I told him we'd wait."

Sounds of grinding and clanking came from the back room. Marc remembered his Mom's caution about discouraging bad choices. "How did you pick the colour? There aren't any of those sample cards."

"Oh, I know exactly what I need and described it precisely." Merlyn smiled. "Don't worry, it won't be garish. It's a nice pastel shade. You can reassure your mother on that point."

Marc's face grew hot, even though he hadn't said what he was really thinking. Could Merlyn have overheard his conversation with Mom?

"What colour is it, anyway? Does it have a name?"

Merlyn smiled. "You mean like 'bluegrass green' or 'fuzzy mitten white'?"

"Something like that."

"Well," she said, "Jordyn in there"—she waved at the workroom—"would call it some complicated formula, but I think of it as the colour of magic. You'll see how it looks when we paint. It's a *light* colour. Very light."

She hadn't actually answered the question. "Okay," Marc said, "but why did we have to get it here? Our house is just an '80s split level. This place looks like it caters to people with heritage houses who want to be period authentic."

"This is the only place that can supply the paint I need." Again that glacial stare. Marc glanced toward the workroom, from which issued a liquid gurgling, soon followed by the reassuringly normal sounds of a can being tapped shut and a paint shaking machine running.

Then a voice chanted. Three notes, repeated three times. Again. And again.

"That's so— What's he doing?" Marc asked.

Merlyn touched his arm lightly. "It's okay. I think he's nearly finished."

The shaker ran for at least another full minute, accompanied by further bursts of chanting, before the proprietor emerged with a surprisingly small can. There was no wrap-around label on it with instructions and safety warnings, just a sticker with the name of the shop and something scribbled by hand. He handed it to Merlyn, along with two little brushes and a stirring-stick tied together with string. For the first time he looked at Marc directly and nodded. "You will be helping her paint?" he said, his voice low and confidential.

"Yes, I will."

The man clasped his hands together and made a small bow. "Blessings upon the work."

Going out the shop's door, Marc noticed something he'd missed coming in. After 'Help Wanted' on the sign in the window was a question mark, in faint violet pencil or crayon.

On the way home they stopped at a normal hardware store for a couple of drop cloths. Marc suggested paint rollers, but Merlyn shook her head. "No. This paint has to be applied with the brushes that came with it."

Shit, this job is going to take forever, Marc thought, remembering the size of the brushes. "What about surface prep? Mom says you have to wash down the old paint with something called TSP."

"Oh, I've already done that. Not with TSP, but the surfaces are sufficiently prepped, believe me."

Merlyn carried the paint can into the house, clutched to her chest like something precious. Marc followed with the drop cloths and brushes. Both living room windows had the same kind of purple knotwork decorations as the one in the kitchen. So did the window in the bedroom.

He hovered in the bedroom's doorway. This was where Ms. Stone slept and dreamt, where she got naked to change into pjs (if she wore them). He shouldn't be thinking about this stuff. His ears felt pink. She'd guess.

Merlyn had already moved the lighter furniture away from two of the walls. While Marc spread out the drop cloths, she took a Swiss Army knife from her pocket and unfolded the screwdriver. She pried the lid off the can of paint and untied the string around the brushes and stirring stick.

Merlyn dipped the stirrer—which looked like a trimmed and polished branch from a tree, not the usual flat piece of wood—into the liquid. She stirred three times in one direction and then three in the other, muttering something under her breath. "That should be right," she said, letting the excess paint from the stick run back into the can. She straightened up and handed Marc one of the brushes. "Okay, let's get started."

Marc was taller, so he painted the ceiling, standing on a step-stool. The paint went on a bright, greyish-white. It felt light, almost insubstantial, but the blah beige vanished beneath it as Marc moved his brush back and forth. "Do you think it'll need two coats?"

Merlyn dipped her brush and resumed painting before she answered. "Not really, but we'll just keep painting until it's all used up."

"What kind of paint is it?" Marc asked. "Latex or something?"

"Or something," said Merlyn. "It doesn't matter, Marc. Just keep painting."

They kept painting. The job seemed to do itself. The paint floated onto the ceiling and walls with almost no pressure from the brush. It sparkled a little as it spread out over the surfaces, as though it contained tiny crystals. The colour was hard to describe. Off-white? Pale grey? A tinge of violet, maybe? Some paints changed colour as they dried, but this stuff seemed to dry instantly, almost to go on dry, more like a powder than a liquid.

With two walls and half the ceiling done, they moved the bed and chest of drawers to provide access to the remainder. The ceiling was lower here, which made the rest of the job go faster. With all surfaces coated, a little paint remained in the can. "I'll finish that up tomorrow, when I second coat the bit behind where the bed goes," said Merlyn, pressing the lid closed.

"Why not right now? It won't take much longer."

"It has to dry overnight."

"But it's dry already." Marc reached out to apply a finger to the section of wall nearest him.

"No, don't!" Merlyn grabbed his hand. "Sorry, but it has to stay untouched until it… sets."

"Sets. Okay. So you'll finish it up tomorrow?"

She gave him an apologetic look. "Would you mind helping me move the furniture back after I'm done? It'll be okay where it is until then."

"I have a study session with some friends at the library tomorrow morning. We should be done by lunch time."

"That'll be perfect."

The study session wrapped up at one. Arriving home, Marc remembered his furniture moving commitment. He tapped on the door of the suite.

"Oh, hi Marc!" Merlyn wore a loose purple velvet shirt over black leggings and looked more relaxed than he'd ever seen her.

"It looks great," said Marc, once they had shifted the bed and chest of drawers into their places. The room now had a faint but distinct violet tinge, especially near the bed, where the sloping ceiling met the converging walls. The colour was almost like a mist there, in the shadows. The lines where the planes met dissolved, vanished...

"Marc?"

He turned toward Merlyn, who was looking at him with curiosity.

"Uh, I was just thinking how good the paint job looks. Especially for a couple of amateurs. Or maybe you've done this kind of thing before?"

"Just call me a Jill of all trades. But I appreciated your help."

Marc pulled out his phone. "Is it okay if I get a picture to send my Mom? So she can see what a great job we did?"

Merlyn made a face. "I'd like to say yes, but, well, it's my bedroom. It's... personal."

"Yeah, okay, I can see that." He pocketed the phone. Was there a smell of some sort in the room? He hadn't noticed it while they were painting, but it was certainly there now—not really a perfume, maybe a herbal smell. Had Merlyn been doing something with herbs to welcome the new paint? Or maybe it was just soap.

"I'm sorry," said Merlyn.

Marc shrugged. "No problem. Well, see you later."

~o0o~

A week went by and then another. Midterms came and went. Marc shuttled through his routine of classes, library, gym, friends. He shared a few stories with them about Ms. Merlyn, the 'woo-woo' tenant with her knots and herbs and strange ideas about paint. But all that faded into the background as October chugged along.

Marc said hello to Merlyn a few times, stopped to talk once or twice, heard music from her place—exactly what he expected—chanting, flutes, plaintive songs. Once, taking out some garbage after dark, he noticed purple light leaking out from behind the blinds in one of the rooms of the basement suite. Wasn't that the bedroom he'd helped to paint? Black light, maybe? Weird, but at least it wouldn't start a fire.

On Halloween, Marc went to a party at a friend's place. No way he was going to do the trick or treat scene at home. That was his Mom's thing and she wasn't here. He wasn't in costume, but on his way to the bus stop, he passed a tiny pirate and a giant ladybug and their parents.

The party was okay—the usual gang, a lot of drink, a bit of smoke, a couple movies. He got the last bus home. A block from his house, lurching along, hearing firecrackers faking war in the distance, he almost bumped into someone. Someone wearing a dark hoody. He couldn't see a face. *Pretty late to be out trick or treating.*

"Excuse, please." A low, toneless voice issued from inside the hood.

"Huh?" *Who is this guy?*

"I require information."

"What kind of information?"

"I am seeking a person called Stone. A female person."

I don't know what you're up to, but you're creeping me out.
"Sorry, I can't help you. Good night."

Marc quickened his steps and was happy not to hear any behind him. At his front walk, he stopped and looked back. He couldn't see the guy, but then he'd been pretty much black on black.

A dozen quick strides got Marc to the door. He locked it behind him and peered out the window. No one there.

That was one strange dude.

He slept late the next day and woke up groggy. The previous night's encounter felt like a dream, but the memory niggled all day. *I'd better tell her.*

Coming home from classes, he detoured to Merlyn's place.

"Hi, Marc. Nice to see you."

"You asked me to tell you if I saw anyone... strange in the neighbourhood."

Her forehead crinkled. "And have you?"

"Uh, I'm not sure, but I met someone on the street last night. They asked if I knew a woman named Stone." He described the encounter, reliving it, realizing how few details there were, despite the creepiness. "The guy—I guess it was a guy—had a weird voice. Sort of an accent, but not really. I couldn't see their face."

Merlyn stood between Marc and the closed door of the suite, clasping her hands together, tapping one finger against another. Her lips moved as though she was carrying on a silent conversation.

"You don't look well, Marc."

"I had a late night." He rubbed his face. "Too much beer."

"I have just the thing for that." Merlyn opened a cupboard. Before Marc could say anything, she was running water, setting out a mug, and spooning dried leaves from a jar into an infuser.

"Hey, it's okay, I'm fine, really. Don't bother."

"Oh, this is no bother, believe me. I owe you something for helping me out."

"I haven't done that much, really." Marc didn't even like tea, but maybe there'd be cookies with it.

The kettle steamed and whistled. Merlyn poured the hot water right into the mug. No teapot this time. That barely registered before the tea's aroma filled the room.

It smelled wonderful. Oranges on steroids. Maybe rose petals. Can you harvest sunshine and blue sky? He wrapped his fingers around the mug and inhaled the fragrant steam. He forgot he was hungry. He forgot to wonder why Merlyn insisted on making him tea but didn't have any herself.

Merlyn sidled over to the window and peered between the slats of the venetian blind. "I have to make some plans."

Her voice filtered through Marc's reverie. The tea had cooled enough to drink. He took a gulp. It smelled way better than it tasted. No sunshine or oranges, just watery warmth and a slight bitterness. He took another few sips for politeness. "I'd better get going."

He floated to his feet. "Is everything okay, Merlyn?" Her face was taut and worried. She should have some of that tea, Marc thought. Slipping behind her, he tipped what was left of it into the sink and parked the mug on the counter.

"It will be," said Merlyn. Her hand gripped his arm as she steered him to the door. "Thanks for everything, Marc."

~oOo~

He didn't remember going to bed, but he woke up there, dragging a dream with him, full of vibration and words in an unknown language, spoken by giants wearing big red boots.

Pitch dark, except for the clock by his bed glowing 12:12. Music somewhere in the house. No, someone singing. A woman's voice, but he couldn't make out the words. "Alla-ama-lala-mala-matta-matta-mala-lala."

Merlyn?

Marc jumped out of bed—good, he still had clothes on—and ran for the basement stairs, skidding down them in his socks. A movement outside the laundry room window caught his eye—something huge out there, blocking the light from the street. Pin-pricks of orange light, like eyes peering in.

Marc lunged for the door of the suite, pounded on it, fell through as it opened. Not locked or even latched.

The singing was louder down here, with a throbbing rhythm. The suite was dark, except for a violet glow coming from the bedroom. Marc stopped in the doorway.

What the f is that?

Instead of walls, a depthless violet mist surrounded him, as though the paint he and Merlyn had applied was vaporizing.

Marc stepped forward. "Merlyn! Are you here?" His voice sounded like it was muffled in wool. An irregular hole gaped on the far side of the bed, where the northwest corner had been when the room had corners. Its margins pulsated in rhythm with the chanting.

A blur of flesh and hair moved within the hole—Merlyn, naked, a many-rayed star tattooed on one shoulder. She turned back, mouth gaping. "Marc! No!"

She vanished into the purple mist. Marc took three strides and pushed into the gap. Something soft but resistant enveloped him, blocking his forward motion. As though through a veil he saw Merlyn, her shape embraced by a swirl of similar shapes.

Marc raised his hands shoulder high, grasped at whatever blocked the gap, and hauled backwards, as though executing a breast stroke. Something ripped, his arms broke through, and then the rest of him fell—into his own back yard. There was the lawn, the patio, the clothesline, and the hill sloping up to trees. But it was another world. A crowd of dancing figures, their long hair intermingling, swayed behind Merlyn.

She came toward him, her body swathed in a rainbow of shifting colours.

"Marc, you shouldn't be here! I must have miscalculated the dose."

She was gorgeous. No longer his mother's age or older, but ageless and beautiful with a beauty beyond age. She took his hands. "You have to go back."

"Why?" A rich, golden light, the colour of a harvest moon, illuminated the hillside. Fireflies danced among the trees. A crowd jostled, of human shapes, some of them winged and antlered. Near the trees, one figure waved an arm. Its face was familiar, was—

"That's Dad! My Dad's up there!" Marc lunged forward.

Merlyn pressed her palms against his chest. "You shouldn't be here." She turned and spoke to those behind her.

The words she uttered were lost to Marc, but he thought she asked them to wait.

"I'm sorry, my dear, but this is wrong," Merlyn said. "I don't know how you managed to break through, but it's perilous for you to be here, just as it is for me to remain in your world. You're too young, too young by many lives. They won't let you stay."

Shapes approached him and bright eyes peered inquisitively. "But I—my dad's here! I want to talk with him." There was Dad, his arm still raised, like a statue's. He stood, staring beyond Marc, beyond everything.

Is that really Dad?

Merlyn's voice interrupted.

"Marc. Someday, perhaps, you will be permitted here. When Time yields to you, instead of the other way around, you may find your way here. But now you must leave—quickly, before the portal closes."

"But you're—going? Why?"

"I must. I can't explain. I made a big mistake. I've made enemies. This is the only way out and now is my best chance. That entity you saw, it was an emissary. Master Jordyn knows about these things. Ask him when you go back."

The Dad-shape was gone. Down the hill came a jostle of dark forms with glowing eyes, accompanied by canine shapes with jaws of flame.

Merlyn turned toward them. "No! He's going!" She shoved, and Marc fell backwards. Something cold and slimy slapped against his face and a cracking sound exploded in his head. Eardrums throbbing, he landed with a thud on something soft.

~oOo~

Dr. Eleanor Dupplin came home to a world of trouble. The tenant in her basement suite, Merlyn Stone, had gone missing. She had not been seen since November 1st. Three weeks later, there was still no sign of her. Marc had reported her as a missing person and dealt with the police until she got home.

Marc! That son of hers! She had self-congratulated on escaping the usual ructions of the teenage years, but now the boy—okay, at almost twenty, he was technically a man—had decided to go back to adolescence.

He'd cooperated with the cops, saying over and over that both the door of the basement suite and the outside door were open on the morning of November 2nd. Ms. Stone wasn't in the suite, so he had searched the property for her and reported her absence to the police.

Eventually, the cops left them alone and removed Ms. Stone's belongings, which she had apparently packed before disappearing. A suitcase and a leather satchel were found near the door, as though ready to go. The satchel contained her phone and wallet, complete with identification, credit cards, and cash.

The only reminders of Ms. Stone left in the suite were those weird purple knots and strings in the windows. They were still there, because as soon as the cops were finished with the basement suite, Marc had moved into it. On Eleanor's return, he declared that if his Mom wanted to rent space to her grad students, there was the spare bedroom upstairs and Marc's old room. He had a job now and could pay rent. Her normally cooperative son had become surprisingly stubborn in just a few weeks.

He had a *job*. Prof. Dupplin shook her head. He had dropped out of college. He said he might go back someday, but first he wanted to do other stuff. When he'd saved up enough money he was going to travel. *Good luck with that one, son. How much are you saving? Your job at that paint store can't be paying more than minimum wage.*

Okay, it was a delayed flare-up of adolescence. She could only hope Marc didn't start wearing a hoody and slinking around like those kids she kept seeing in the neighbourhood.

And at least the paint colour Ms. Stone had chosen was a nice, warm beige. Not too different from the original.

~o0o~

When Marc moved into the basement suite, he shifted the furniture in the bedroom so the chest of drawers hid the northwest corner.

On the morning of November 2nd, he had woken up in that very room, on Merlyn Stone's bed, now his bed. His clothes smelled smoky, as though he'd been camping. There were scuff marks on his arms and a small purple bruise on his chest. The scrapes eventually healed, but the purple mark was still there. More and more it looked like a twelve-pointed star.

He knew it was irrational, but the first thing he did that morning was go to the place in the back yard where he thought he'd seen Dad. Nothing there, except for patches of shiny stuff, like silvery glitter, that disappeared when he touched it. Just for the hell of it, he kept on going all the way up to the ravine. *Like Dad's going to be there, right.*

Dad wasn't there, and Merlyn was gone. Her suitcase and shoulder bag stood near the door, packed and ready. On the kitchen table was a note. "Marc, please repaint the bedroom asap. You must close the portal. Leave the protective knots in place. <u>This is important</u>!! Get the paint from the same place. Jordyn will be expecting you. Please take the wooden case to him too. Thank you for all your help."

Marc did not touch Merlyn's suitcase or shoulder bag, but he did open the wooden case. No sewing machine inside; it contained books. Some of them looked ancient.

When Marc went back to Elemental Colours, J. Farber, prop., the help wanted sign with the purple question mark was still there.

Jordyn Farber recognized him right away. In fact, he had a can of protective beige ready for him, with instructions on how to apply it on the day before the dark of the moon. Marc followed them precisely, except he left a two-by-three-foot patch of wall untouched. Just in case.

When Marc offered to pay for the paint, Jordyn refused and offered him a job instead. Marc had learned a lot since then. With Jordyn's guidance, he had begun reading Merlyn's books. Maybe it wouldn't be all that long before Time yielded to him.

A HOWLING IN THE WOODS

Todd stepped over another fallen tree and stopped.

"Come on, don't dick around. Keep moving." Doug gave him a little shove. There he was, dragging his feet again. Shit— the kid wasn't even overloaded. When Doug was ten, his dad made him hike all day with thirty pounds on his back.

Todd took a few lurching steps and stopped. "Wait, Dad," he said. "What's that?"

"What's what? Say what you mean."

"That noise. Did you hear it?"

"All I hear is you talking. Let's get going." Doug's dad had always made Doug carry part of the kill, too. That wasn't a problem for Toddy-boy, though, since they hadn't managed to track down the elk Doug had taken a shot at. The kid was too goddamn slow and the animal had gotten away.

His son got moving, picking his way through the underbrush. He raised a hand and pointed. "There it is again. That sound."

Both of them stopped and listened, their breaths curling steam into the frosty air. In the Vancouver Island bush, snow in November wasn't out of the question.

"It's someone yelling. Like it really hurts." Todd glanced at his father and spoke louder. "Can't you hear it, Dad?"

"Nope." Doug shook his head. "Lots of things howl out here. If you hear something growling, it's my stomach. It's another hour to the truck, so let's get a move on. We can't stop to listen to every little sound." If he'd gone out by himself, he would have bagged that elk. That's all he got for trying to be pals with his son—nothing.

Doug's pack and rifle got heavier. All the deadfalls didn't help any. Climbing over them wore a guy out. Too bad about that elk. Waste of meat if it died out here in the bush. With his job on the line, it would have helped to have it in the freezer.

The sun hung low in the sky by the time they reached the creek they'd crossed in the morning. The mud still showed their boot prints. Cedars stood black against the orange sky behind the swampy little lake the creek fed into.

Doug looked back. Todd had stopped again, yards behind. He just stood there, arms out in front of him, staring toward the lake. Holding up his phone. Taking a picture? Playing with that goddamn phone was more fun than doing things with his old man.

Doug opened his mouth to tell the kid to get a move on, but shut it again. A sound came from the woods on the far side of the lake. It increased in pitch and volume, built up, died down, started again. A split second of silence, and then it came again. And again.

Doug wanted it to stop. Listening to it made his stomach clench. It sounded like the noise you'd make if you were being turned inside out.

He punched that thought down as Todd scrambled over to him, holding out his phone. "Dad, Dad, I got it! It's a lot louder here."

234

He fell silent as the sound came again. A screaming roar or roaring scream. Something was having a big emergency out here in the woods.

"Goddamn it, Todd, let's go!" The kid was still holding up his phone, biting his lip.

The woods were quiet again, but the sound had left part of itself behind, like a bad smell.

Doug's pickup sat in a clearing off the logging road. They stowed their gear and climbed in. While the truck was warming up, Doug poured himself a coffee from the thermos he always left for the trip home and handed Todd the can of pop saved for the same purpose.

Doug put the truck in gear and got rolling. What was that screeching? *Don't tell me the truck's crapping out too.* Then he realized the sound was coming from Todd's precious phone, probably a game of some sort.

"You think it's that elk, Dad? The one that got away?"

"What?"

"You know—that noise we heard. This one." Todd held up his phone.

The roar filled the truck's cab. Then Todd's voice, excited. "Dad, Dad, I got it! It's a lot louder here." The roar again, then Doug, sounding fuzzy and far away, telling the kid to get going. Then the howl, even louder, like whatever made it was catching up to them.

"What're you listening to that for? And why'd you even record it?"

"Because it's so *weird*. It's not that elk, is it? I was thinking, you hit it and it's, like dying, and—"

"That's no elk. You should know better. Cougar, maybe, not elk."

"But it's *dying*. Hurt really bad."

"That wasn't an elk. And we don't even know if I hit it. You got all whiny and wanted to quit when we went to see, remember?"

For a few seconds, the only sounds were the truck's engine running and the clunks when they hit potholes in the road.

"So what do *you* think it was?"

"Geez, Todd, just drop it, okay? It wasn't anything."

"But it *was*! Just listen." Todd played the recording again, turning up the volume. Channeled through the electronic device, the noise had an edge Doug hadn't noticed in the woods, crackly and full of urgency. His son's voice and then his, sounding dumb, the way recorded voices always did. Then that goddamn howl again.

"Maybe it's a sasquatch. Dad, you think it might be a sasquatch? They live here, don't they?"

"Get off it, Todd. There aren't any sasquatches. That's just a myth. I've spent half my life in the bush and I've never seen a sasquatch."

"Maybe the sasquatch was telling us we shouldn't have been trying to shoot that elk."

Where did the kid get these stupid notions? Those teachers at his school, going on about animal rights, for God's sake. "Look, Todd, it was just a cougar or a wolf howling. It wasn't telling us anything. And there are no such things as sasquatches."

The sound played again—a long, drawn out scream, roar, howl.

"I bet it was a sasquatch. Maybe he's mad about people cutting down trees. That's what you do, Dad. You kill trees."

Doug barely heard the words. Todd whispered them to his phone. Maybe he didn't mean for his dad to hear. But he did.

Doug stomped on the brake. The truck stopped in the middle of the road. "*What* did you say?"

Todd looked up, eyes wide. "You cut down trees, Dad. Kill them."

"Goddamn right. It's called logging, and that's what pays for that fucking phone you love so much." Doug practically had to yell over the howling sound coming from the phone. Todd must have turned up the volume. "Turn off that damn thing! Right now!"

"Okay, Dad, but I was just thinking, you know. Maybe it's like, the trees crying."

Doug shot out an arm and grabbed the phone from his son's hands. "You're the one who's gonna be crying now, Todd. Or you can just get out and walk home."

"Dad! I was just—"

"Out! Now!" Doug clutched the phone in his raised fist. "Or I'll smash this damn thing on your head."

Todd opened the door, slipped out of the truck, and ran into the darkening woods.

Doug threw the truck in gear and drove away.

~o0o~

Todd ran. He ran and ran, feet sinking into moss, twigs snapping. Trees stood watching. Trees ahead of him too, with the last dull red of sunset behind them. He ran toward the light, because he didn't know where he was going, and at least that looked different.

His feet slipped and he crashed into a skinny fallen tree held off the ground by its own stump and a fishbone of branches at the other end. Forearms on the crumbling bark, Todd hung there, panting. He couldn't hear the truck. He couldn't hear his dad coming to get him. Just his own breathing.

Then, another sound, from where the red sun-glow faded to grey.

Todd listened. He nodded. Then he got going.

~oOo~

The sight of the stop sign where the logging road joined the highway snapped Doug out of his rage. He'd left his ten-year-old kid alone in the bush. In the dark. In the bush where something howled like nothing Doug had ever heard before.

He stopped short of the intersection, turned around and stomped on the gas. Too bad he hadn't paid attention to the kilometres on the trip meter. He knew darn well how hard it was to find a particular spot along these roads, even in daylight. Everything looked the same. Trees all looked the same. So did the potholes. The only things that were different were the numbers on posts showing how many kilometres to the next junction, and he hadn't noticed those either. Too busy arguing with his kid.

That attitude of Todd's! Like the goddamn woods were screaming because they were mad at loggers.

Doug stuffed that thought. He had to go back and get his kid. Todd would be on the side of the road, waiting for him, scared shitless. He drove slowly, keeping an eye out for Todd's orange jacket.

He stopped where he thought they'd left the truck that morning. That would be the logical starting point. He parked and found a flashlight in the glove box, hoping the batteries still worked. They did, but for how long? He headed into the bush, looking for footprints. Two sets of two, one big, one small, plain to see in the flashlight's beam. Okay, this was his starting point.

Doug got back in the truck and drove slowly to where he figured he'd kicked Todd out, and turned so the headlights shone into the bush. He got out and hollered, "Todd, come back! Can you hear me? Come on, Toddy, it's okay. I'm not mad at you. Just get your ass back here!"

Half a dozen episodes of shouting in half a dozen random spots along the road produced zero results. The goddamn kid wasn't there. Was he hiding, laying low in the bush just to yank his bad old dad's chain? Doug didn't think Todd had the guts for that.

So where was he?

Doug shone his flashlight around. Its beam was weaker than when he started, too faint to show up any footprints. He yelled again. "Todd, come here, buddy. It's okay. Don't worry. We need to get home. Toddy, can you hear me? To-odd," he called, stretching out the name. Then the whole song and dance all over again, until his throat hurt.

Doug stood and listened. Nothing. Not even that weird howl again, thank God. He turned and tramped back to the truck. It was time to get help.

~o0o~

From under a swag of cedar boughs, Todd watched the flashlight's beam darting around and listened to his dad calling and calling, yelling his name, making promises he wouldn't keep. Todd knew better now. He'd heard a different voice.

~oOo~

"You did *what*? Left him alone in the *bush*? At *night*?"

Doug suppressed an urge to slap his wife. Loreen's voice had risen to the screeching point. Okay, she had a reason to screech—her husband had abandoned their ten-year-old son in the woods—but her voice scraped his already strained nerves.

"We had an argument and I told him to get out of the truck. I didn't mean to leave him there, but he ran off. I turned around a little while later,"—*sure, like half an hour*—"and went back for him, but he wasn't by the road. Maybe he decided to camp out, make himself some kind of shelter. Anyway, I've called some of the guys. We're going to get a search going at dawn, so—"

"What kind of argument? You didn't hit him, did you, Doug? What was he scared of?"

"I didn't hit him. Look, I had a headache and he was being a pain, saying all kinds of dumb stuff. You know, what he learns at school about loggers being evil monsters killing the planet. I just lost it and yelled at him to get out and walk."

"You shouldn't have." Her lower lip trembled.

"Right, I shouldn't have. But I did." He grabbed her shoulders and gave her a little shake. "Listen to me—we're going to find him. He can't be that far from the road. As soon as it's light we'll go find him. He'll probably be on the road, waiting. Cold and sorry for himself. Don't worry."

"'Don't worry.' A ten-year-old out all night in the bush. I'm calling the police." She pressed her lips into a thin line and reached for the phone.

~oOo~

Doug stood in a mud puddle at the side of the logging road. The map in his hands was wilting, the lines and circles he'd drawn on it fading away. Lines and circles showing where they'd searched. They would have covered more ground if not for that prick coordinating the local search and rescue volunteers, who were there because Loreen called the goddamn cops. The guy was one of those know-it-alls with safety on the brain. There he was in his hi-vis jacket, talking into a VHF radio and pointing in all directions like a frigging weathervane.

Mike came over. "They're calling off the search 'til tomorrow. You want to pack it in too?" Rain dripped off the bill of his cap.

"No way." Doug tried to fold his map, gave up, crumpled it up and shoved it in a coat pocket. He'd get a new one tomorrow. "Figures those wimps would let a little rain stop them. They're on a picnic but I'm gonna find my son. Let's keep going. There's a couple hours of light yet."

"Okay, you're the boss." Mike shambled over to the other guys in their group, while Doug talked to Mr. Search and Rescue Robert about their plans for the next day. He almost told them to stay home, but figured having a few more bodies out there wouldn't hurt. Unless they found Todd today.

The volunteers drifted toward their vehicles. Doug and his friends headed back into the woods, shrouded in rain and late afternoon gloom.

~oOo~

In deep moss, on wet rock, where roots wound down to hidden springs, where mats of fungal mycelium shuttled nutrients and messages from above and afar, the boy rested and dreamed.

~oOo~

Doug pushed his plate away, his supper half-eaten. He wanted to sleep. He wanted to go back to the search. He wanted to cry. He put his elbows on the table and clutched his forehead.

"He still has his phone, doesn't he?"

It took a while for Loreen's voice to make it through the fog. She'd been giving him the silent treatment since he'd come home last night and told her about Todd. That was one good thing about Loreen, she didn't harp. "What?"

"Todd's phone! He has it with him. Why didn't we think of calling him? Do it now!"

"Loreen, there's no service up there. It would just go to voice mail. And it's probably out of juice anyway."

"Well, it wouldn't hurt to *try*. Come on, Doug!"

So he 'tried.' As he went through the motions, he realized Todd's phone must be in the truck. He'd grabbed it just before he ordered Todd to get out.

The call went to voice mail. He held up the phone to Loreen's ear so she'd hear it. "Told you, didn't I?"

She didn't say a word, just picked up the plates and took them to the kitchen.

Doug went out to the truck and had a look. There was Todd's phone, on the passenger side floor mat, where it must have landed when he threw it. The battery was flat; he'd been right about that.

Back inside, he got a charger and plugged the phone into an outlet in his basement workshop. Out of Loreen's sight; he didn't want any more questions from her. Some time after midnight, unable to sleep, counting the hours to dawn, he went back down there.

The phone was fully charged. He called Todd's number, even though he knew that was stupid—the phone was right here in his hand! He ended the call before it started to ring.

Doug sat there, looking at his woodworking tools, old paint cans, creased sheets of sandpaper, a toaster he'd meant to fix someday. He picked up Todd's phone and touched the video icon.

Trees, just like the ones he'd been seeing way too much of lately. Jiggling and shaking a little, moving from side to side. But Todd hadn't been videoing; he'd been recording that sound. The howling. Doug listened. In the basement of his home, surrounded by his old stuff, Doug listened.

It howled. It screamed. That voice came from *something*. Some creature.

"Dad, Dad, I got it! It's a lot louder here." Todd's voice, young and excited. Doug jerked and almost dropped the phone. He'd forgotten their voices were also in the recording. He turned it off before he could hear himself swearing.

The next day, when he went back to the search, Doug took Todd's phone with him.

~o0o~

"Hey Doug, what'cha doing here? I thought you were going to be on the other side of the ridge."

Doug looked up from the phone to see Mike's bearded face and almost said, "None of your business. Get lost." But Mike was a friend and was helping him look for his son.

"Getting a vid of the place? Think that might help?" Mike looked at him sideways, like he wanted to say something else but decided not to.

"Okay, did you ever hear anything like this?" Doug pushed the 'play' button again and handed Todd's phone to Mike.

The sound again, the sound Doug was trying to figure out. To *get*. He was going to get it. He had to, if he wanted to find Todd.

"What the heck is this? You playing some kind of game with me? Come on, man, we have to go find your kid."

"Did you ever hear a sound like that before? Out here in the bush? I'm not joshing you. Todd made that video just before he… went missing."

Mike shoved the phone at him like it was red hot. "Nope, never heard anything like that before. You know kids— he was probably just trying you on. Okay, I'm going to take another look along the creek here, like I said before. See you back at base."

Doug walked. He was on the right path now, he knew it. For sure this was the way he and Todd had gone that day. The day Doug was going to show that son of his a few things— how to find your way in the bush. How to track and shoot an animal. How to make a good, clean kill and bring the meat home.

He could see their footprints in the moss, a big set and a small set. In places, the moss had been scuffed up in clumps. Recently snapped branches hung along tree trunks, like signals. This little rise—he remembered them hiking up it, knapsacks firm against their backs, rifles snugged under their arms. Father and son out for a day's hunting.

Doug stopped in mid-stride and looked at Todd's phone clutched in his hand. The screen was black; he'd turned it off to preserve the battery. So what was he hearing?

That sound. That *voice*. Not small and tinny like in the recording, but wide and deep, a roar like a river. Except rivers didn't have throats, couldn't *express* the way this did. It sounded the way Doug's heart felt these last few days—like something living being ripped to shreds.

Doug stood and listened. He didn't know how long, but when the sound faded to a growl, he realized the sky behind the trees was glowing red. Another day was ending and Todd was still missing.

Except Doug was on the right trail now. Wherever that sound came from, that was the place. He was almost there. He just had to keep going. Once he found Todd, the two of them could hunker down somewhere to wait for morning. One of those cedars with branches hanging down like a tent. He'd cut some fir boughs and make a bed. He'd build a fire. He knew how to do that stuff. He'd keep his boy safe.

The sound started up again, softer now but closer. As though it was telling him something. Listening carefully, he heard another voice joining it, high-pitched and shrill. Todd's voice.

Doug broke into a run, jumping, tripping, falling, rising again and running through the bush. Every now and then he stopped to listen, holding his breath so his panting wouldn't block out the voices.

~o0o~

Something jiggled his shoulder. Glaring light cracked open his eyelids.

"Doug. Hey, man, wake up."

Doug shifted his head and blinked. His face rubbed on something wet that smelled like dirt. Moss. He was on the ground.

"Whaa—?"

"It's okay, Doug. It's me, Mike. Can you get up? Good news! We found him."

Doug heaved himself into a sitting position. "Mike?" He squinted up at the shape behind the flashlight's glare. "What did you say?"

Mike squatted next to him, laughing. "Boy, you're a mess. We had a heck of a time finding you. What made you come all the way out here, anyway?"

"Did you say… you found Todd?"

"Yeah! We did. That's why we had to find you too." Mike stood and grabbed Doug's hand, pulling him to his feet. "Come on, let's go. It's a bit of a hike." A radio crackled behind him and someone mumbled something.

"…found him. Seems fine. We'll be back at base… Better wait." Sure enough, there was that busybody search and rescue guy, Robert something-or-other. He came over, stared at Doug, shone his damned flashlight in Doug's face, and asked a few stupid questions.

246

"Where'd you find him?" asked Doug, once they were under way, tromping along with flashlights showing up the trees, the ferns, the moss.

"About five klicks northwest of the base," said Robert. "Far side of that ridge by Wolf Lake."

"Is he okay?" Doug directed his question to Mike.

"Yeah, he looks great. Really good, in fact. Better than you. Said he found a shelter or something. Said he was 'inside,' anyway. He'll tell you all about it, I'm sure."

An hour later, they saw lights in the distance. Camping lanterns, the really bright kind, more flashlights, even a campfire. A tent had been pitched beside the tarp shelter Robert had insisted on. Robert hurried forward and started talking to some people.

"Where's Todd?" asked Doug. "Where is he?"

Mike pointed. "Resting in that tent, I think."

~o0o~

The tent's flaps were closed. Doug stood for a moment. Poor Todd, he thought—all these strangers around, instead of his own dad. He must be confused and scared. And he'd been alone all that time, in the woods where something howled.

Before he could reach it, the tent flaps opened and Todd stepped out. He stood and looked at his father. He didn't look confused or scared. He smiled.

Doug felt tears squirting out of his eyes. He held out his arms to his son. "Toddy, I'm so glad you're safe! Look, kid, I have to say, I'm sorry. I shouldn't have kicked you out of the truck. I'm just glad you're okay."

"Hi Dad," said Todd. He didn't move toward his father. "It's okay. I'm fine."

Doug's arms sank back to his sides. He realized everyone—his friends, the search and rescue people—were standing and watching, as though he and Todd were actors in a play.

Todd didn't look like a kid who'd been lost in the bush for two days and nights. Doug didn't recognize the clothes he was wearing—black jeans and a dark green hoody. Someone must have lent them to him.

Todd looked taller than he'd been three days ago. Doug felt like Rip Van Winkle, like he'd been out of touch for 48 years instead of 48 hours. He pulled Todd's phone from his pocket. "Here's your phone. I'll bet you're glad to have it back."

Todd took the phone and stuck it in a pocket without looking at it. "Did you listen to it?" he asked.

"Listen to what? Oh, you mean that sound? I heard it when I was looking for you, thought you must have been pretty scared."

"But you told me it was nothing," said Todd, coming closer.

God, the kid looks different. His eyes... something about his eyes. Doug stepped back. Behind him, people muttered and coughed.

"Okay," he said. "I think—I know I was wrong. But hey, we can talk abut all that later. Now let's get you home."

"I *am* home," said Todd.

"Come on, Toddy, no jokes. Your Mom's all worried about you. So was I." He hesitated. "Did you did hear that sound while you were lost?"

"I did," said Todd. "And I wasn't lost. You were."

248

"Whatever." Doug waved a hand. "Do you know what was making it?"

Todd grinned. "I do. Let's go tell Mom I'm okay. And let's come back here next weekend. Then you'll know too."

THE GLAMOUR

Toast jumped from the toaster.

"Butter that, please, Ann," said Mom.

Ann slouched over to the counter, pulled the hot slices from the toaster, and reached for the butter dish. She scrabbled in the dish drainer for a knife and dragged butter over the bread, churning up crumbs. The kitchen TV contributed its usual background babble of local news and views.

"Hurry up, there. Your father's eggs are getting cold. And don't step on that bug." Mom bent over, slid a piece of paper under the bug and tipped it out the window.

My Mom, the bug rescue lady, thought Ann, bringing the plate of toast to the table. "Here you are."

Dad set down the newspaper and reached for a piece of toast. "Thanks, Punkin."

"Welcome." Ann forked scrambled eggs. On the TV screen, a smiling couple held up one of those giant cheques people seemed to think were the way to show how important they were. "Gabriel and Patricia Desmarais have worked extremely hard to raise funds for the Roxham Hospital Foundation," a chirpy voice proclaimed, "and we are pleased to have them here this morning."

"Pass the ketchup?" Ann's brother Lucas reached out a hand.

"Pass the ketchup, *please,*" echoed Mom.

"Sure thing," Lucas said, squirting ketchup on bacon.

On TV, the smiling couple talked about their fundraising efforts. That didn't interest Ann, but the couple did.

Elegant. That was the only word to describe them. So different from Randy and Donna Brown. 'Brown'—what a boring name. Not like 'Desmarais,' which sounded totally grand. Gabriel Desmarais wore a suit, and his wife a dark red dress whose draped neckline tapered to a fitted waist with a narrow belt. Elegant.

Their voices were what Ann thought of as 'cultivated,' their gestures graceful. Patricia's chestnut-coloured hair was perfectly arranged in a chignon. Her husband's carefully shaped black beard made him look like a magician. They smiled and nodded, cool and relaxed.

I'll bet those two don't make a big fuss over toast, thought Ann. She tried to imagine breakfast at the Desmarais' place, probably in a breakfast room, not crammed into the kitchen with the TV blaring and the stink of frying bacon. For sure Mrs. Desmarais didn't rescue bugs. Ann frowned as Lucas crammed his fourth piece of toast into his mouth, hair flopping into his eyes. She wondered if Mr. and Mrs. Desmarais had kids.

A commercial came on. Ann's Mom clicked off the TV. "Bloody waste of time," she muttered.

Ann glanced at her Dad, who shrugged. A headline on the newspaper by his plate caught her eye. "Scandal at Roxham Hospital." Ann pulled the paper toward her and read the story. DNA tests had proved that a pair of local men were not the children of the people who had raised them. When they were born, someone in the hospital's neonatal unit had sent each of them home with the wrong parents. The rest of the story was about the shock and sadness the discovery had caused, because all four parents had since died. Lawsuits were planned.

"Come on, you guys, you don't want to be late for church," said Mom. She stood and gathered empty plates. "Ann, are you going to finish that? You know I hate wasting food."

"I'm not hungry," said Ann. She took her plate to the scrap bucket and scraped her leftovers into it.

"Well, well, aren't we a princess! Where do you think that food came from? Your father and I worked hard for that, not to mention the effort of cooking it."

"Sorry," Ann muttered, heading for her bedroom. *What's with Mom, anyway? She's a real grouch today.*

A princess. Ann knew there were no real princesses left in the world. Look at the clothes she was getting into for church—no lace or velvet, just stretchy cotton poly. She did the best she could with the long black skirt and purple scoop-necked top by adding her silver and amethyst pendant and matching earrings. She pulled her hair back and up, securing it with a purple velvet scrunchie. After a look in the mirror, she added a lavender-coloured fringed scarf. Her shoes weren't right, of course, but then, shoes never were. Good shoes were too expensive.

Ann and Lucas got into the back seat of the car. Dad tooted the horn to tell Mom they were ready to roll. She finally emerged, still wearing her bathrobe. "I'm not going. I told you I'm not feeling great." Her face was red and her eyes looked small and mean. "Just go without me."

"Okay, honey. Hope you feel better soon," said Dad. Mom waved a hand and went back inside. Ann threw Lucas a questioning look. He shrugged.

By the time they arrived at church, the Mass was about to start, so they had to sit in the overflow area at the side.

Ann liked Mass. She liked the vestments and the ritual, the music and the solemnity. It would have been cool if it was still in Latin. During the homily, which was boring, she looked at the people in the regular pews across the aisle. They were at a ninety-degree angle to the overflow ones, so she could see other people's faces, not just the backs of their heads.

A woman with hair gathered into a chignon turned her head and whispered something to two children beside her. The boy and girl looked like twins, and were as elegantly dressed as the woman, who must have been their mother. The woman was Mrs. Desmarais. For the rest of the sermon, Ann stole glances at the family. She wondered why Mr. Desmarais wasn't there. Maybe he wasn't feeling well, like Ann's Mom.

During Communion, Ann noticed another girl, who had been sitting on the far side of Mrs. Desmarais. She was tall and gangly, with light brown hair that fell below her shoulders. Unlike her elegant mother and the neatly dressed twins, she wore blue jeans and a sweatshirt. *She doesn't fit,* thought Ann. *Like me, only in reverse.*

At the church door after Mass, the priest asked about Ann's Mom. Dad, blushing a bit, said, "She's feeling under the weather today." Ann thought of black clouds and thunder.

As they stepped out of the church, a dark blue car pulled up. Mrs. Desmarais and her three kids walked toward it. Ann wondered if the driver was Mr. Desmarais. The person's face was hidden by reflections, so she couldn't tell. Maybe he wasn't Catholic.

The boy opened the front passenger door for his mother and all three kids piled into the back seat, the tall girl last.

254

Patricia Desmarais stood as though waiting for something, her pale, carved face turned toward Ann. Had she noticed her staring at them during Mass? Ann blushed. Mrs. Desmarais held her gaze for a full second, a little frown on her face. Then she stepped into the car and closed the door with a thunk.

"Ann?" Her Dad waved his hand toward the parking lot and their car.

"She's come unplugged." Lucas made a face and sniggered.

"Was that someone you know?" asked Dad as he fastened his seatbelt. "That woman you were looking at just now?"

"I don't know her," said Ann. "I just thought her outfit was cool. Hey Dad—what's wrong with Mom? She's acting kind of weird."

Dad sighed. "She's just… having a hard time right now. You guys have to cut her some slack." But later that day, Ann heard her parents having a big argument in their bedroom.

~oOo~

After that Sunday, it was like an itch. Every time her Mom got all pissy, it itched even more.

Fact: Ann was short and slight. The rest of her family were tall and big-boned. Her hair was dark, almost black, while they were blondy-brown.

Fact: Patricia Desmarais and her two younger kids were dark-haired and petite, but that other girl, the older one who went to church dressed like a slob, was tall with light brown hair. She looked more like Ann's brother Lucas than the twins or Mrs. Desmarais.

Fact: That tall girl looked about the same age as Ann.

Fact: Babies born in the Roxham hospital had been switched. If it happened once, it could have happened twice.

Fact? Ann was the daughter of Gabriel and Patricia Desmarais, not Randy and Donna Brown.

Well, she had to investigate, didn't she?

The computers at school had blocking programs to keep kids safe, but Ann knew they sometimes blocked good information. She didn't want to miss anything. She needed to *know*. There was no way her brother would let her touch his precious laptop, and the computers Mom and Dad used for their accounting business were also out of the question. So Ann did her research using 30-minute time slots on a free computer in the public library after school, sitting next to poor people and other teenagers.

Searching on the names 'Gabriel Desmarais' and 'Patricia Desmarais' brought up an avalanche of information, most of it useless. What she really needed to know was when and where their oldest daughter was born. Instead, she found out that Gabriel Desmarais was a professor of entomology at the local college. Entomology—the study of insects. Okay, bugs weren't glamorous, but he was a *scientist*, not an accountant like Dad.

Patricia was on a lot of boards and committees of charitable and cultural organizations. Ann found story after story about her appearances at galas and fundraisers, always with pictures. There she was, smiling and shaking hands with the mayor and other important people, cutting ribbons, planting trees—or at least holding a shovel spray-painted gold, with a ribbon tied around it. Smiling, always smiling and looking great, neat and fashionable at the same time. Not like

Ann's Mom, who schlepped around the house without a bra, her hair messy, rubber clogs on her feet.

Was Patricia Desmarais Ann's real mother? Ann even dressed like she was *her* daughter instead of Donna Brown's. Ann loved clothes, kept her hair and nails nice, even when the family teased her about being a slave to fashion.

Ann's googling didn't yield that much about Prof. Desmarais—stuff about his research, like naming some new kinds of beetles found in the tropics, and boring things he did at the college. A long story popped up about him donating 'artifacts' to the local museum, meaning old things that had belonged to the professor's great-great-grandfather, who had been a sea captain. He'd sailed to the South Seas a couple of hundred years ago, from Queenshaven, a little town on the coast. Ann knew Queenshaven. Her Mom's family came from there, and her grandpa said his grandpa used to talk about the old days of sailing ships.

The story included pictures of the artifacts, including a ship's figurehead, a wooden thing that looked like a monster woman. Gabriel Desmarais and the museum director stood on either side of it, smiling. Ann peered at his face, trying to see if there was a resemblance to her, but the photo was too fuzzy.

Her searching did yield the older girl's name. Melissa. Melissa Desmarais. *That could have been my name. That tall girl— she should have been plain old Ann Brown. Just 'Ann,' without the 'e' that would have made it almost okay.* In a story from the local newspaper, there was a picture of Melissa lunging for a basketball in a game against another private school. It turned out she was captain of the Roxham Academy junior team. The story said she was fifteen. *Yes! She's the same age as me.*

What to do now? A DNA sample would clinch it, but how could she possibly get one from Melissa? You needed saliva or hair or something, and they didn't even go to the same school. Well, but she could get samples from her parents, couldn't she? That would prove they weren't related to her. She checked websites for companies that did those tests and told you where your ancestors came from. Would that work? The trouble was, they were pretty expensive.

If she could get close to Mrs. Desmarais, talk to her, that might do the trick. Surely a mother would instinctively recognize her own daughter. What about that look she gave Ann after church?

The woman Ann called "Mom" surely acted like a stranger these days. She didn't talk much, but when she did, it meant trouble. Ann and Lucas weren't pulling their weight around the house. Dad was working too much, or on the wrong projects. They had some pretty loud discussions in their office. Discussions? No—fights. These days, Mom was nicer to bugs that got in the house than to her own family.

Ann's friends Darcy and Sarah had it all figured out. "She's going through menopause, that's all," said Darcy. "The Big M. My Mom did that last year. She was a real bitch. Okay, she still is, but not as bad."

"Menopause? That's when your periods stop, right? Wouldn't it be, like, a relief?" Ann had been having periods long enough to think they were a royal pain in the ass.

Darcy and Sarah looked at each other in that knowing way that bugged Ann. So what if they were a couple of months older than her? That didn't mean they knew everything, but they acted as though they did.

"Well," Sarah said, "maybe it's a relief, but it does something to your hormones. You know—sex chemicals in your brain. Then you get something called hot flashes and mood swings."

Ann thought about the way her Mom's face got all red sometimes. And her moods surely did swing, from bad to worse. But she was embarrassed to ask Mom about that stuff, and it would be useless to talk to Dad. He wouldn't have a clue.

~oOo~

Hands on hips, Ann's Mom looked her daughter up and down. "Why are you all dressed up like that for school? It's Friday, for Pete's sake!"

"Oh, Mom! I just don't want to look like a slob." *Like you.*

Mom grabbed Ann's wrist and stared at her. "Don't you roll those big green eyes at me! You think you know everything, don't you? Okay, go on, get out of here!" She dropped Ann's arm, gave her a little push and stomped back to the kitchen.

She'd get out, all right. The trouble was, she didn't know where her real family lived. You couldn't get someone's home address from the internet. On the way home from school, she remembered the phone book, remembered Mom and Dad joking about how the only use for it anymore was to prop up a wonky table. Or it might come in handy if they ran out of toilet paper. It was a long time since she'd heard them joking like that.

The phone book was in the living room, under a bunch of old magazines. She yanked it out and took it to her room. There it was—"Desmarais, G." and "205 High St." And the phone book even had a map. It was small and the print fuzzy, but it showed High Street in the old part of town, near the

Cathedral. Ann sat down and drew herself a map on a piece of paper.

On Saturday night, her Mom settled in front of the TV with a glass of wine, and Dad disappeared into the office.

"I'm going to Darcy's, okay?" Ann had her hand on the doorknob.

"Fine," said Mom, eyes on the screen where people were running around in the dark, with ominous music. "Be back by eleven, okay?"

"Yep. Love ya." That popped out automatically, even though it wasn't true anymore.

Ann jogged around the block before heading for the bus stop, which was in the opposite direction to Darcy's house.

As the bus entered downtown, the old brick buildings glowed invitingly in the golden light of the late May evening. Ann rang the bell for the next stop. She hardly ever went to the old part of downtown, and never by herself. The streets were narrow, full of funky little shops. Even the streetlights were old fashioned.

Passing the Cathedral, she wondered why Mrs. Desmarais and her kids went to the suburban church where she had seen them. Ann had been inside the Cathedral only a few times, but remembered carved stone and wood, stained glass, and the mysterious smell of incense. *I'd go here all the time if I had a choice*, she thought. *And maybe I will.*

By the time she found High Street and started climbing the hill it was named for, the sun had slipped behind the tall buildings of downtown, turning them into crisp black cutouts silhouetted against the orange sky. A golden haze lingered in the air. The edges of things—wrought iron gates under trailing vines, stone urns, blooming shrubs—grew soft, as though they weren't quite real, a curtain about to be lifted on another world. Ann couldn't help skipping as she counted the house numbers to 205.

There it was, carved into a stone pillar next to a driveway. Giant elms arched overhead. The air smelled of springtime and mystery. It felt softer than the air around her house, the house she'd lived in all her life, which wasn't her home. Was this?

A car came up the hill and turned into the driveway. Ann slipped behind a big tree. After the car passed, she stepped out and started to follow it, but then another car purred by. Ann darted behind a bush whose white flowers exuded a heavy perfume. She hoped no one had noticed her, and counted to a hundred before emerging.

The house's lights shone behind a lacy tracery of new leaves on the surrounding trees. Ann pressed herself against a tree trunk and watched people getting out of the second car — two couples, one young, the other elderly. The younger man supported the older woman. Both women wore long dresses. The four of them made a slow procession up the wide steps to the front door.

Chimes rang and the door opened, spilling golden light. Voices chorused in greeting. The guests went in. The door closed.

For one wild and crazy moment, Ann thought of going up to that big old door and ringing the doorbell, making those chimes chime. When someone—who might it be?—opened it, she would say, "Hi, I'm Ann. I belong here."

But that would be dumb. It would just get her into trouble. So what should she do? What did she want?

First, to get a better look at the family. Surely, if Gabriel and Patricia Desmarais were her real parents, she'd see a resemblance. She had to get face-to-face, though, and if there was a formal party happening tonight, maybe it wasn't the best time to try.

She could at least get a look through a window. She left the shelter of the tree and stepped cautiously across the lawn. A planting of shrubs near the house provided cover, but the only thing Ann could see through the tall windows was a grand piano and frustratingly brief glimpses of people moving around.

She had to get inside.

Ann wriggled out of the sheltering shrubs and returned to the front walk. At the bottom of the steps leading to the house's entrance, another walk branched off toward the side of the house. Ann followed it past more big bushes to a stone-paved patio. Or, no—here it would be called a 'terrace,' wouldn't it? Patios were for backyard barbecues. The Desmarais family would take tea on the terrace.

On the far side of the paved area was a set of glass-paned doors. *This is it. Do or die.* Ann took a gulp of air, crossed the terrace and pressed the latch. She was ready for a quick retreat if necessary, but the latch yielded to her touch and the door opened.

Ann leaned into the room but pulled back abruptly, startled by the touch of filmy fabric against her face. A curtain. She hesitated a moment and pushed it aside.

The room was dim but not yet dark, full of the soft, dying light of the vanished sun, like a warm fog. Ann slipped inside, pulled the door closed, and replaced the sheer curtain. She stood there for a few moments to get a feel of the room.

It smelled old. Not crummy old, but expensive old, antique old, old and rare old. Leather and smoke and furniture polish. Fine books, pipe tobacco and woodsmoke, velvet jackets, mysteries and secrets. From somewhere in the house, faintly, she could hear music.

The room had to be a library. Cool—a whole room just for books. Between tall bookshelves hung pictures, with little lights glowing above them. Portraits in fancy gold frames, one of a man with whiskers and watch chain, and another of a woman in a low-cut dress edged with lace, her hair pulled up and curled.

Something else hung over the fireplace mantel, a metal sculpture of a winged creature that wasn't a bird. Those were wings, weren't they? It had six legs and antennae. A giant bug? Okay, Mr. Desmarais—no, *Professor* Desmarais—was a bug expert, wasn't he? But this couldn't be a real insect; maybe he'd had an artist make it for him. It *was* sort of gorgeous, with its burnished colours—fiery red, glowing green, metallic blue.

In a nearby nook were glass cases of real insects, mostly beetles. Another of those little lights lit up an old map that hung above them. It showed a group of islands, an archipelago. Ann leaned close to it, but the only thing she could read of the spidery script was *Le jardin de la Reine* on the largest island. A few spots were marked with some sort of symbol. A bug? A skull? It looked like a treasure map. Maybe Mr. Desmarais' ancestors were pirates.

Next to a sofa was a small table with several framed photographs. Ann picked up one that showed a group of people dressed up for a party. Recognition tickled her consciousness as she scanned the faces, but she couldn't see details in the failing light.

As she fumbled for the switch on a nearby lamp, a latch clicked and a beam of light shone into the room. A long shadow stretched across the polished floor.

Ann froze and clutched the photograph to her chest. A woman swathed in white closed the door and glided toward her.

"Welcome." Her voice was soft and fuzzy, like gauze.

"Uh, excuse me." Ann's voice shook. She laid the photo on the table with the lamp and edged toward the French doors. "I'd better go."

"Oh, but you don't want to miss the party."

Who is she? Aloud, Ann said, "I wasn't invited to the party. I made a mistake." At least this lady didn't seem to mind her trespassing.

The woman waved a hand. "That doesn't matter. It's Melissa's birthday. Sweet sixteen." She tittered softly. "Let's help her celebrate."

Birthday. Ann's birthday was in October. So much for her switched-at-birth theory.

The woman in white came closer. She wore gloves, the long gloves that went with evening gowns, and a kind of turban on her head. Maybe she had no hair.

"I'm not wearing the right clothes for a party," said Ann, gesturing toward her black leggings and hoody, her worn sneakers.

The woman's dress was a strange style, wrapped rather than draped. Even her face was veiled, blurring her features. And there was a smell Ann hadn't noticed before. A smell out of place in this room, like bread dough left to rise in a morning kitchen.

"You'll be fine as you are. But let's introduce ourselves," the woman said, extending one of her gloved hands. "I am Esmerelda Desmarais, Melissa's grandmother. I am Oldest."

"I'm Ann. Just Ann. How do you do, Mrs. Desmarais." The woman's hand felt as soft as her voice, an empty glove, but under the fabric there was... something. More like sticks than fingers. Ann pulled her hand back. *So weird!*

"All right, Just Ann. Now we know each other. You're one of us. I can tell." She pointed to the giant beetle sculpture over the mantel. "Isn't it beautiful? A family heirloom." She tittered again. "They must be dancing now. Soon they will utter the chant. Ee-yah, ee-yah, ee-yah." She clapped her hands soundlessly in rhythm with the words and cross-stepped toward the French doors.

No escape through there, Ann thought. She pivoted toward the door into the hallway, opened it and slipped through.

A few metres away, a wide doorway on her right spilled light and sound, and beyond it was the house's main door. Ann sidled along the wall and peered cautiously into the large room.

Several couples whirled in a full Viennese waltz, the women's skirts sweeping the floor. Beyond them, silhouetted against the room's large windows, the Desmarais twins played piano and violin. The boy leaned into the keyboard and looked up to smile at his twin, who dipped gracefully toward him.

In the centre of the dancers, Melissa, tall in peach-coloured ruffles, her curly brown hair cascading over her shoulders, danced with her father. Gabriel Desmarais, black haired and black-bearded, twirled his daughter around the floor and then stepped back to let her dance free and alone. He raised his arms over his head and clapped his hands together.

The music stopped. The other dancers slowed and stopped, forming a circle around the pair.

Everyone clapped. Everyone except the tall girl in the middle of the room. A chorus of "Happy Birthday" broke out. Melissa smiled, her face pink, turning from one side to the other, finally twirling again, her skirt belling out, as the song ended. "Ee-yah, ee-yah, ee-yah," everyone cried, encircling the girl and uttering words Ann couldn't understand.

"It goes on," came a whisper in her ear. "She is Becoming, as one does when young. And I am Becoming, as one does when old. As you will too, in time."

A claw-like hand dragged Ann through the doorway and into the ballroom. In the dazzling light, she *saw*. Saw a woman-shape swathed in gossamer silk, but not a dress, not really. The bread dough smell grew stronger.

Becoming.

The veil ripped and split, revealing a face of immense age, only the eyes alive. Dark green eyes that gazed into Ann's. Under the thin, white skin, something inhuman pulsed and vibrated with incipient life. The face fell away and another shape emerged. Mouth parts stirred. Antennae twitched. Burnished wings spread and flexed

Ann screamed. People rushed over and surrounded the monster, resuming the chant with different words. The birthday girl, Melissa, grabbed Ann's arm. "Who *are* you?" For a second, they stared at each other. *She looks just like Lucas*, Ann thought.

"Happy birthday," she said, and fled.

~o0o~

Ann burst through the front door and ran—down the long, curving driveway, down steep High Street, across the road at the bottom of the hill, through the Cathedral grounds and the park. She ran through the old part of downtown, ignoring shouts of "Hey, girlie!" and "What's your hurry?"

She thought about waiting for the bus, but couldn't make herself stop. The only safe thing to do was run. Home.

Where the streets widened out and the trees were smaller, the houses closer together, she slowed down. There was the strip mall and the grocery store. There was the gas station. *Nearly there, Ann!* She pushed herself for two more blocks, until she reached her own house.

Ann stopped to catch her breath, bent over and clutching her knees the way she did after a long run in phys ed class. She straightened and circled her arms, walked up and down the driveway, cooling down.

Our birthdays are different. That's not my family. Thank God!

The street was empty and quiet. A single lamp shone in the living room. Was someone still up, or did Mom leave it on for her?

The TV was on without sound. A bottle and empty glass sat on the little table next to the couch and a book splayed open on the floor. Mom got up from the couch as Ann came in.

"Ann, honey, are you okay?"

Ann was still puffing a bit. "Yeah. Yeah, I'm okay." She snorted out a little laugh to show how okay she was. "We watched a stupid scary movie. Really scary. About a woman who turned into some sort of monster."

Her Mom's arm around her, they settled on the couch, sinking into the familiar lumpy cushions. A warm, winy smell surrounded them. Mom must have drunk quite a bit of that bottle.

"You kids just love those horror movies, don't you? Until they're too scary. I'm glad you're home."

"Me too." Ann smiled at her Mom. *Maybe she's okay again.* Her face looked normal—high forehead, long nose, firm chin. And her dark green eyes, just like Ann's.

THE BLUE ROSE

Black. *Again.* Every bloom on the rose was black, grotesque, and necrotic. His latest formula had failed, just like all its predecessors.

Banging shut the glasshouse door with an oath, Deon whirled through his tiny laboratory and out into the courtyard, not bothering to stopper and put away the flasks on the workbench.

"All right, it's time."

Deon made for the canal-side street with only one thought in mind. *Sylvius.* He'd promised.

Fragrant blooms of the callimandra tree mingled their scent with the rankness of the black canal water. Waxy white petals floated on the turbid surface, accepted along with all the muck of the lower town.

Intent on his goal, Deon ignored the scents, both rank and sweet, as he made for the East Funicular. Seeing a long queue of sweepers, runners and leaf-gatherers waiting to board, he decided to run the stairs instead. Only nine flights to Sylvius' house. Nine long, steep flights.

Deon retraced his steps to the canal and the First Stair, pausing when a callimandra bloom, spent and heavy with pollen, brushed his cheek and landed on the stones at his feet. He stooped and picked it up, remembering the old maxim,

"Callimandra's kiss brings luck to the daring." He needed luck, masses of it, if he was to make a blue rose for Aldona Magna.

Sniffing the musky fragrance of the flower, Deon remembered the Lady Aldona, tall in pleated sapphire silk, her straight dark brows beneath the crown of braided hair, serene eyes regarding the newly-qualified Fabricators in the Academy's assembly hall. Her voice rang out like the noon chime of the Hour-Bell. Her eyes, whose colour matched precisely the blue of her gown, rested on each of them in turn. "In my task of maintaining the life of our City, I may ask great things of you. I may demand of you an iron horse, a harp of crystal, a cloak of wind, or a ship of air. And from one of you"— here her glance fell on Deon where he stood at the end of the rearmost row—"from one of you I may require a blue rose."

She smiled then, making a bow of her lips, from which flew an invisible arrow into the heart of Deon. "My Lady," he murmured, so softly that she could not possibly hear, "I will make for you a blue rose, and I will do it by the day of the Sun's Exaltation."

The memory lightened his feet, and he was at the top the Fourth Stair before the reality struck him like a bag full of grindstones—scarcely a month left before the Exaltation, and the rose he had injected with his latest elixir was a black and ugly mess.

Deon sank onto a stone bench under an ancient cypress whose lower limbs were supported by crutches fashioned by generations of tree-healers. The tiny red birds that lived in the cliffs made swooping arcs of scarlet through the air, uttering their high-pitched cries. From this height (only halfway to the Ninth Terrace where Sylvius lived), he looked across the river plain to where the green fields of grain and vegetables gave way to forests and scrub, and beyond them to misty, unguessed distances.

Sylvius knows. He was one of the Master Fabricators, who made colours and flavours, scents and textures. Always when Deon asked him questions, he gave answers. Almost always.

You must open your heart.

Three weeks ago, Sylvius had taken him to a euphorium on the Second level, behind the brick houses of the district, its door half-hidden under a swag of ivy. In the dimly-lit interior, crowded with a motley assortment of folk, they drank a fiery red spirit from small crystal glasses, and Sylvius talked. Talked in a way most unlike himself, quick and nervous.

"As a Fabricator, you know that Making merely rearranges the energies that flow through the world. But if you want—or need—to do something extraordinary, you must throw yourself into the work. Literally—mind, heart and body. You must open your heart and let your life-blood flow upon the dead stones. I see you don't understand. But you will, when you experience a great need, a great desire."

"A great desire..." Deon murmured.

He leaned over the parapet and removed the spectacles he wore for close work. A fat, bruise-coloured cloud lolled on the horizon, perhaps over the Blasted Lands. If the substance he needed didn't exist in the City, he would search elsewhere. He put the spectacles into a waistcoat pocket and continued on his way, rising stair by stair, as brick houses gave way to ones built of stone.

At the gate of the Ninth Terrace, Deon showed his copper token and muttered the password. The gate-guard admitted him with her usual silent stare and nod. A minute later he rang the bell of Sylvius's house.

There was no response for so long that Deon rang again, frowning. Where was Perrin? As if the second ring was the required element, the door opened, revealing Sylvius's butler, manservant and laboratory assistant, solid and familiar in his leather apron.

"Mr. Deon, Sir! I'm sorry, but Master Sylvius is not at home."

"Hello Perrin," he said. "When do you expect him back?"

"Not until late, I'm afraid, but Miss Luna is here. Oh, and Master Sylvius asked me to give you this." Perrin reached into his apron pocket and held out an envelope. 'Deon' was written on it in Sylvius's handwriting.

The envelope contained something lumpy, but before Deon could open it, a door opened at the end of the hallway, and a girl ran down the hall toward them. No longer a girl, he saw as she came closer, but a young woman. Luna, Sylvius's niece.

She was gawky, though past the age when gawkiness can be charming, and a bit plump. Her untidy long brown hair hung about her face, and she brushed it out of her eyes. "Deon! It's good to see you. It's been ages. Come along to the library."

She turned with such spirit that her skirts swirled about her legs. Still with the hem coming down, Deon noted with amusement. Some things never changed. He followed her because he could not think of anything better to do. Sylvius's study and library were the centre of his world. Deon had spent many hours there. Perhaps the familiar place would reassure him he'd made the right decision.

Luna closed the door and gestured toward the envelope in his hand. "Well, open it!" she said. "Perrin wouldn't let me, since it's addressed to you." She picked up a penknife from Sylvius's desk and handed it to him.

He didn't remember Luna being so bossy, but then he hadn't seen her in months. "Rightly so. Perrin's a great one for correctness. What are you up to these days? You're just out of your Academy, right? Are you apprenticed to the Council of Matriarchs or something?"

"I've been in the Guards for the past six months," said Luna. "Aren't you going to open that envelope?"

Deon slit it open and drew out a sheet of paper. Thrusting the envelope into a pocket, he unfolded the note and read.

It's now or never, and if you wait too long it will be never. Remember what I told you the last time we met? The enclosed should help. Sylvius.

"And you? Still wasting time in coffee salons with those aspiring poets?"

Deon was too elated to be annoyed. "My friends, you mean? I'm a Fabricator now. I have a laboratory."

"Really? Where?"

Deon hesitated. "On the Lower, actually. Near the canal, but it suits me."

"What do you make there? Singing flowers? Or flying ones? As if birds didn't do those things already."

Deon frowned. "Just because you're making yourself into one of the pillars of the City doesn't mean you can make fun of us Fabricators. Someone has to create beauty. Didn't you listen to the Lady's speech last week? Or were you too busy memorizing rules and marching in formation?"

Luna's face grew pink. She pressed her lips together. "Never mind. So what's in that envelope from Uncle Syl? It felt lumpy."

"Never *you* mind. Since you think I'm just a frivolous idler, you can't possibly be interested. I came to ask Sylvius a question, but since he's out, there's no point in my being here. And he did answer it, in a way." Deon held up the envelope. He went over to one of the bookshelves that lined the room, pausing by the collection of travellers' writings. "Luna, do you know—has Sylvius ever left the City?"

Luna hesitated. "I don't think so. Hardly anyone does that any more."

"Not now, maybe, but we used to. And Sylvius has nearly every book ever written by people who did." Deon pulled a heavy tome from one of the shelves. "*A Journey to the Southlands*. Griffon Descar. Everyone knows Descar's *Journey*. And then there's Alluna Pesca."

"Oh, Pesca! Everyone knows she made up all that stuff! A world of noise and smoke? Infernal machines? No one else ever saw any of it."

"That was in ancient times. What I'd like to see is a decent account of the Blasted Lands."

"There isn't one," said Luna, staring at him. "If anyone's ever gone there, they haven't lived to write about it."

"A few got close," said Deon. "Take Valery Nigill, for example. The trouble is, she never got closer than the edges and spent all her time painting pictures of plants." No blue roses, though, he thought.

"Sensible woman!" said Luna. "But then, women are sensible. Someone has to be."

274

"Oh, never mind!" Deon shoved the book back into its place, releasing a puff of dust. "Look, I've got to go now. Things to do, you know."

"I can imagine. I'll show you out."

Remembering the envelope in his pocket, Deon pulled it out. Inside were a bead of blue glass and a brass token. Good old Sylvius! He slid the envelope back into his pocket, an involuntary smile forming on his lips.

Luna closed the door of the library and Deon ran down the hall, startling Perrin, who emerged from the kitchen stairs.

"Sorry, Perrin, I've got to run." And run he did, to the funicular, making a list along the way. Home first, to get the necessities together. No time to go to his mother's Ministry; he would send her a message. *Going away for a few days.* No, it would be longer, a few weeks at least.

~o0o~

A week passed before anyone realized Deon was missing. Everyone assumed he was somewhere else. When his friends realized none of them had seen him for several days, a disorganized search was conducted. Soon after that, the Guard was informed, and an organized one ensued.

In Sylvius's study, Luna flopped into a chair. She wore her Guards uniform, wet with rain. "No sign of him anywhere," she said. "Uncle, I have to ask you something."

Sylvius finished writing a note and closed the books he had been studying. He slid his spectacles down his nose and turned to Luna. "Ask away, my dear."

"Do you think Deon has left the City?"

"What gives you that idea?" Sylvius asked.

"The last time I saw him was here, just about a week ago. Perrin gave him an envelope. It was addressed to him, in your handwriting. He opened it right there and seemed pleased at what he saw."

Sylvius nodded but said nothing. He rested his elbows on the arms of his chair and pressed his fingertips together.

"He didn't tell me what was inside, but I saw something that looked like an exit token for the Outer Gates."

Sylvius nodded again, studying his fingers.

"Did you give him that token?"

Sylvius dropped his hands and raised his head, looking at Luna with his clear grey eyes. "I did."

Luna leaned forward. "*Why?*"

"Because he was ready."

"Ready for what? Deon was—*is*—the most unready person I've ever known. Why would he need, or even want, an exit token?"

"He needed to go on a voyage of discovery, what we Fabricators call 'making a journey,' and I thought he was ready. Mentally, anyway."

"But no one leaves the City. Not really."

"You know that's not true, my dear. Misfits and criminal elements often choose to leave. Exiles have scraped a living beyond the walls for thousands of years. They fish and hunt and grow crops. A few scavenge the Blasted Lands."

"What for?"

"Materials unobtainable here that are of interest to Fabricators. There's a kind of inn about a day's travel from the City, where transactions are carried out."

"Have you been there?"

Sylvius nodded. "Several times."

Luna rested her chin on a hand. "Why would Deon need such things?"

"For a grand and rather impractical project, to turn a red rose blue. That was his stated reason. But the true reason is to discover himself and his abilities, and thereby inspire others."

Luna shook her head and slapped her palms on her thighs. "But going to the Blasted Lands! How could you sit here comfortably and encourage him to do something so stupid? He's probably dead."

"Oh, he has no reason to go to the Blasted Lands himself. I referred him to one of the more reliable groups of Exile scavengers. They'll keep him safe."

"Scavengers! They're unreliable and corrupt."

Sylvius raised an eyebrow. "The voice of experience? Unlike you, I've had dealings with Exiles. Just like us, they aren't all the same."

Luna drew a breath to protest, but Sylvius raised a hand. "Hear me out. You and I both know the history of our City, island of order and beauty in a chaotic world. We know that is because of the rules laid down by our Foremothers. You live by those rules every day. But beauty…"

Sylvius took off his spectacles and laid them on the desk. "Those who study birds know that in most species, it is the males that are brightly coloured and ornamented. You might also say that of us. Women, from the High Lady to the army of Cultivators, and all the grades and degrees in between, keep the City alive and orderly. We men, to counter our inherently destructive impulses, have been called upon to create things of beauty. Our combined talents have maintained civilization here for thousands of years. But those who seek the ineffable are privileged to engage in what some regard as frivolities. And some choose to seek out chaos."

Sylvius picked up the spectacles and toyed with them. "True beauty is born of chaos. Actions such as Deon's journey, which he decided to undertake with my help and encouragement, may benefit all Citizens by inspiring a few."

For a long moment, Luna sat looking at her tightly clasped hands. Finally, she spoke. "I can't see what benefit to anyone can come of sending a soft, untrained boy anywhere near the Blasted Lands."

"We will see, when Deon comes back."

"*If* he comes back."

~o0o~

Summer came and the City dreamed in warm air and sunlight. Birds nested and Climbers climbed to find eggs for those who could afford the exorbitant prices of these strictly regulated delicacies. Fabricators tinkered with their creations. Bee-gardeners tended their plots on the edges of the vine-terraces. The Cultivators cultivated and in due course, harvested.

Luna found herself drawn to a small garden on the Seventh Level, near the Temple of Music. Overgrown and unfrequented, it looked toward the empty country beyond the City's fields, and beyond that to the Blasted Lands.

The standard protocols regarding missing persons had been observed. Searchers had returned without result and there was deemed to be no reason to persist. Deon was of age and had left the City with the proper token. To travel with groups of Exiles, or for that matter, alone, was a choice available to any Citizen, although frowned upon and rarely made.

Through the winter, with its rains, frosts, icy winds and occasional snows, Luna continued to watch, fitting her vigils in the abandoned garden into her busy round of duties and responsibilities. She told no one about them, not even Sylvius. Every week or two, though, she spent an evening in his study, sitting on the rug before the fire, nursing a cup of steaming fruit brew and poring over travellers' tales. All her thoughts and speculations led to the same hard truths: Deon was gone into the wide world. Maybe he would return, and maybe not.

~oOo~

Small owls spent the winters in grottoes warmed by the steam escaping from the ductwork conveying volcanic heat to warm the City. Their presence was welcome because they fed upon rats that threatened stored foodstuffs. In spring the owls flew away to the forests to build their nests of sticks and the beardlike lichens that draped the northern sides of ancient trees.

One morning, Luna saw long strings of geese and ducks flying inland, to the rumoured lakes and marshes on the edges of the Blasted Lands. As their honks and cries died away with distance, she made up her mind.

That afternoon, she requested leave from her Captain and assembled equipment and foodstuffs. The evening before her departure, she knocked once more on Sylvius's door.

"I wasn't going to tell you," she began.

"But you thought you should give me a chance to argue with you," he said, smiling.

"Yes. Are you going to?"

"No," said Sylvius. "I know you're more than capable and ready. But I'll give you this." He went to a cabinet and returned with an object some two feet long, contained in a leather case.

"What is it?" Luna unfastened the clasps on the case.

"A firestick. An invention of mine. Perhaps you could test its effectiveness, should you find yourself in a tight spot."

He showed her how to use the device and gave her a supply of iron projectiles and explosive propellants. "Thank you, Uncle Syl," said Luna. "I can see why you didn't bring this to the attention of the Governing Council. But actually, I hope I won't need to use it."

Sylvius nodded. "It may be that what made the Blasted Lands began with something like this," he said, on his face a mixture of slyness and regret. "The Foremothers knew what they were doing when they wrote the laws. That's why I'm giving it to you."

~o0o~

It took three days for the City to vanish below the horizon. Luna let her mind drift, disengaging from the lifelong routines of the City while her body jogged along at the steady pace set by the Exiles. Sometimes she thought about her last conversation with Sylvius, feeling the weight of the firestick strapped to her knapsack. She thought how bleak the land seemed, flat and featureless compared to the heights and depths, the hollows and pinnacles of the City. She listened to the talk of the Exiles who were her guides and companions, noting the similarities and differences in speech and manner between them and the people of home. Otherwise, her mind traced the twenty years of her life, hovering over nameless summer days when two children played in sunlit gardens or pursued intricate games in the cobbled streets and alleys of their ancient home.

Only once did anything occur that might have been described as a "tight spot." They met another group of travellers. Greetings and exchanges of news developed into an argument, which became a fight. Fists flew and knives were drawn. Standing apart from the fray, Luna readied the firestick for action as Sylvius had shown her.

Which of the struggling shapes deserved to be impaled by an iron projectile? How would that improve the situation? Luna shrugged and aimed the firestick at a large stone several yards away. The loud bang and shower of sparks ended the fight. Luna ran to stamp out a small fire that had started. The grass was damp and it didn't take long.

"I haven't seen such a thing before," said the caravan's leader, eyeing the firestick as Luna returned it to its case.

"Something one of our Fabricators gave me," she said.

"Well, it gave our folk something to think about besides fighting."

A week on the road, they entered low hills. The road dipped and rose, twisting this way and that, showing bits of itself and then hiding. On one of the still distant segments, a number of moving figures appeared. Humans and an unfamiliar animal, the sight of which produced muttered remarks among Luna's companions. The next time the group appeared, she saw the humped beast clearly. Though she still did not recognize it, the sight stirred a memory of things she had read not long before her journey.

The third glimpse was a telling one. "Blasters," said a man walking at Luna's left.

"I know 'em," said another. "Barka's lot. They're not as bad as some. Rigged up some sort of outfits for protection, and don't go too far in."

"These people go into the Blasted Lands?" asked Luna.

"Said so, didn't I? Blasters. No one else has those humpalops. Capture them in the Lands, they do. Take a good look at those folk, young Citizen. I've heard they kill their worst cases soon's they're born."

The approaching group had vanished behind another hillock, but soon emerged over its top. Beside the humpalops walked seven people. The one in front was a woman; it was hard to tell about the others. Luna didn't pay them much attention once she realized there was an eighth person, riding on the beast's back.

There was a protocol, it seemed, for greeting Blasters. "Stay back a ways until I find out what's what," said Luna's caravan leader. "Looks like they've got someone sick there."

The two leaders approached one another and stopped several paces apart. Barka, the woman who led the Blasters, was a tall, robust type, like many in the Guard, except she had six fingers on one hand and three on the other. Her companions, who had looked normal at a distance, displayed more obvious signs of strangeness. Facial features oddly proportioned and distributed. A man with three legs, a woman with a tail. Hunched backs, rather like that of the humpalops. All had wrapped their heads with brightly-coloured cloths, except the one riding the beast. That figure's head was swathed in white, and so was most of its face.

The two leaders finished their palaver and approached Luna's group. "He wants to go back to the City," said Barka, pointing at the mounted figure. "We did what we could with him all winter, but..." She shook her head. "Ran off into the heart of the Zone, going after the Blue Shine, and we didn't see him again 'til the turn of the moon. Couple of my folk took the risk and fetched him. We know better than to touch the Blue Shine."

He. Him. The person being described did nothing, only sat placidly on the back of the humpalops, eyes closed. Luna stepped forward. The humpalops looked down at her disdainfully. Luna reached up to touch the bandaged hands that lay on the animal's back. "Deon," she said, and the veiled head turned toward her.

~oOo~

Another cycle of the Sun, another year. On the day of the Sun's Exaltation, the Lady Aldona Magna, Matriarch of the City, climbed to the Pinnacle to greet its first rays. Later, in the plaza before the Temple of the Twelve, she received the gifts of the Fabricators. Clad in black robes trimmed in the colours peculiar to his craft, each one stepped up in turn to present his creation. Articles of beauty and ingenuity shone in the new sunlight.

Last came Sylvius, with two of his students bearing a vessel of the sort used to contain plants in courtyard gardens. A white cloth shrouded the occupant of the pot. The students placed the pot among the other offerings, and Sylvius whisked away the cloth.

The small shrub's twisted stems bore pointed buds of a dark, vivid blue. A single open flower, recognizable as a rose, glowed indigo and sapphire, with golden anthers.

Luna stood with the other Guards who had escorted the Fabricators to the Peak. She was glad the rose had opened its first flower on this day. The other plant, the one on Deon's grave, was already in full bloom.

A crowd of young Fabricators talked and laughed as they waited to follow their elders from the City's heights. Luna wondered how many of them had read a slender book with the title *A Fabricator's Travels in the Blasted Lands*. A one-eyed man can write nearly as well as any other, and when Deon's strength failed near the end, his friends took turns writing down what he dictated. One of them printed a dozen copies and another bound three of them in blue leather. Of these three, one reposed in Sylvius's library. Deon's mother had the second, and the third had been presented to Aldona Magna, but not as an official gift. The other copies circulated in modest paper bindings.

Luna didn't need to read the book. Deon had told her his tale as she sat holding his hand or applied salves to comfort his ravaged skin. He had told her about finding the Blue Shine, a garbled account whose details didn't quite match from one evening to the next.

"The rocks sweated a blue ichor. It dried to a kind of crystal. The colours shifted, you know? From darkest indigo to purest sky blue. So beautiful." Deon closed his remaining eye and lay back on the pillows, smiling.

Deon had brought back a vial of the substance, and Sylvius had used a minute quantity of it to change an ordinary pink rose into the miracle of blueness he had unveiled today. But the two plants, grown from cuttings, were stunted and strange. Only their blue flowers gave them beauty. The remaining blue crystals were secured in a lead-lined vault, along with the ashes of the parent rose.

How many other young men would Deon's book inspire, Luna wondered. How many would be moved to make a journey, not merely to the inn where Citizens did business with Exiles, not only to the edges of the Blasted Lands, but into the Zone of Peril itself, seeking the Blue Shine.

Luna broke ranks as Sylvius passed the Guards, his face pale and eyes downcast. She tugged at his robe. "Will you be home tonight, Uncle Syl? I have a proposal for you."

AFTERWORD

I was inspired to start writing seriously by H.P. Lovecraft's serialized story "Herbert West, Reanimator." That led to a series of four novels. The first seven stories in this collection are by-products of that series and its sequel, *She Who Comes Forth*. Readers who find themselves curious about Herbert/Francis, Charles, or Alma may find out more about the series at the end of this book.

Once I was done with Herbert West, I thought I would take on Walter Gilman and HPL's "The Dreams in the Witch House." I imagined the first meeting between Gilman and his fellow lodger Frank Elwood. I gave them personalities and backgrounds and placed them in the setting where much of the action was to take place. At that point, I realized I had no desire to embroider on Lovecraft's plot. Poor Walter's deterioration and ultimate doom had been dealt with quite thoroughly by HPL and I had nothing further to add. I was sufficiently pleased with the scenes I had written, though, to include them here under the title **"Welcome to the Witch House."**

Something similar happened with Robert W. Chambers' story "The Repairer of Reputations," from his book *The King in Yellow*. That story's main character, the unfortunate Hildred Castaigne, is one of the all-time greats in the unreliable narrator department. I decided to supply a more reliable one in the form of Hildred's sister, Miranda, to investigate his death and what led up to it. I called the story **"The Deliverer of Delusions."** I owe a nod of thanks also to the graphic novel adaptation of *The King in Yellow* by I.N.J. Culbard.

The most mundane events may lead to thoughts that eventually shape themselves into stories. That was the case with **"The Ice Cream Truck from Hell"** and **"The Colour of Magic."** The title of the first popped into my head when I heard an ice cream truck playing a frenetic, unmodulated rendition of the Brahms Lullaby near my house on a late September evening. Of course I had to think up and write a story to go with it.

I've always been fascinated by colours and have accumulated dozens of paint colour samples over the years. Pale shades of purple, lavender, and violet seem to have a magical quality, suggesting the idea that a room painted in a specific magical tint could become a portal to another world.

Two of the stories were suggested by real-world events reported in the media. In 2016, a boy in Japan was left in a forest by his father, who was annoyed by the kid's misbehaviour during a mushroom picking expedition. He turned up safe several days later, having sheltered in a hut used by the military. The father apologized for overreacting, but I kept wondering what might have happened to that boy in the forest. What might he have encountered and how had it changed him? Then a couple of years ago I heard about a recording of weird sounds made by a family in the northern Ontario bush. The sound was creepy and disturbing enough to be the missing piece for **"A Howling in the Woods."**

What kid doesn't go through a phase of thinking they were switched at birth? In 2019, two men in the Canadian province of Newfoundland and Labrador discovered they had been sent home from hospital with the wrong sets of parents. They grew up ignorant of the situation until DNA tests revealed the truth decades later, unfortunately after all four parents had died. Here was another perfect setup for a story. I added a small Lovecraftian twist to **"The Glamour"** to spice it up.

"The Blue Rose" was to be part of a novel set in a fictional world in a distant post-apocalyptic future, incorporating elements from some of my favourite things—gardening, alchemy, and the colour blue. Alchemy appears in a symbolic way in the Herbert West Series. The blue rose is an unattainable, magical thing. Gardening is what I do when I'm not writing. The novel has not materialized as yet, but Rachael Ritchey's prompt photo for the 2018 Adventure Sci-Fi & Fantasy Short Story Contest pretty much matched my vision of its setting. I turned that abandoned beginning into "The Blue Rose," the story that concludes this collection. (It won third prize in the contest, by the way.)

A few years ago, I began messing around with cover images, using a free graphic design tool called Canva. I designed the images for the four Herbert West Series stories I published in 2016, which are included in this collection. I also designed the covers for my novel *She Who Comes Forth* and for this book. I've created images for stories that didn't even need covers, just for fun. Sometimes when I run out of imaginative power while writing, I make an image to represent whatever I'm working on. It's a distraction, but at least a creative one. All the images for stories in this book may be seen on my blog: audreydriscoll.com.

Other Books by Audrey Driscoll

The Herbert West Series

Book 1. The Friendship of Mortals
Herbert West can revivify the dead – after a fashion. Librarian Charles Milburn agrees to help him, compromising his principles and his romance with Alma Halsey, daughter of the Dean of Medicine. West's experiments become increasingly dangerous, but when he prepares to cross the ultimate border, only Charles can save his life – if his conscience lets him.

Book 2. Islands of the Gulf Volume 1, The Journey
Once, he was Herbert West, superlative surgeon and revivifier of the dead. Now he's lost his reputation, his country and his name. Rebuilding his life as a country doctor on Bellefleur Island, he struggles with doubts, emotional entanglements and terrible memories of the Great War. Above all, he must forge a new relationship with his old adversary—death—and negotiate with a new one—love.

Book 3. Islands of the Gulf Volume 2, The Treasure
Abandoned and abused, young Herbert West resorts to drastic measures to survive. At Miskatonic University, he becomes a scientist who commits crimes and creates monstrosities. Decades later, haunted by his past, he finds safety as Dr. Francis Dexter of Bellefleur Island, but his divided nature threatens

those he loves and forces him to face the truth about his healing powers.

Book 4. Hunting the Phoenix
Journalist Alma Halsey chases the story of a lifetime to Providence, Rhode Island and finds more than she expected — an old lover, Charles Milburn, and an old adversary, renegade physician Herbert West, living under the name Francis Dexter. Fire throws her into proximity with them both, rekindling romance and completing a great transformation.

She Who Comes Forth
Recently turned 21, France Leighton travels to Luxor, Egypt, taking with her two legacies — an antique cello and an emerald ring. Instead of the archaeological adventure she expects, she gets a lecherous dig director, hidden agendas, a risky balloon ride, and an enigmatic nuclear physicist. In the mysteries of the ancient tombs, France realizes she and her gifts may imperil the world — or save it.

About the Author

Three quarters of the way through a career as a cataloguing librarian, Audrey Driscoll discovered she was actually a writer. Since the turn of the millennium, she has written and published several novels and a short story collection. She gardens, juggles words, and communes with fictitious characters in Victoria, British Columbia. Her opinions on gardening, writing, and things that bug or delight her, along with information about her books, may be found on her blog at https://audreydriscoll.com